More Than One Night
Sarah Mayberry

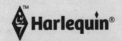

TORONTO NEW YORK LONDON
AMSTERDAM PARIS SYDNEY HAMBURG
STOCKHOLM ATHENS TOKYO MILAN MADRID
PRAGUE WARSAW BUDAPEST AUCKLAND

Recycling programs
for this product may
not exist in your area.

ISBN-13: 978-0-373-60689-4

MORE THAN ONE NIGHT

This edition published by arrangement with Harlequin Books S.A.

For questions and comments about the quality of this book please contact us at Customer_eCare@Harlequin.ca.

® and TM are trademarks of the publisher. Trademarks indicated with ® are registered in the United States Patent and Trademark Office, the Canadian Trade Marks Office and in other countries.

www.Harlequin.com

Printed in U.S.A.

"I had a great night."

Rhys spoke, then pressed a kiss to her lips. He lifted his head slightly and looked into her eyes. Charlie stared at him, stunned, her heart thudding against her breastbone. He palmed the nape of her neck, and then he was kissing her again, his tongue sweeping into her mouth this time, turning her legs to jelly.

After a long moment, he drew back. "Come home with me?" he asked very quietly, his voice husky.

Dear God, I thought you'd never ask.

"Yes."

He smiled and moved closer, wrapping his arms around her as she leaned into him. She wanted him. She'd indulged herself precious few times in her life, but she wanted this man, wanted the experience he promised with his dark eyes and hard body, and she was damn well going to have him.

"You keep that up, we're not even going to make it home," Rhys murmured against her mouth.

"What are we waiting for, then?"

Dear Reader,

My inspiration for this book was a common jumping-off point for romance novels—two people spend the night together and inadvertently make a baby. Sometimes in romance stories the baby then becomes a secret, but in this case, I wanted the baby to be a catalyst for Charlie, my heroine, and Rhys, my hero, to move beyond one night and into a relationship that neither of them think they are ready for.

I wanted to play out the reality of such a difficult situation, step-by-step. What would it be like to discover you're pregnant with the child of a virtual stranger? And how would you feel if a woman turned up on your doorstep and told you that you were going to become a father? At a certain point in the book, I realized that I'd put poor Charlie and Rhys in very complex, loaded circumstances. I felt so sorry for them! And I desperately wanted them to find their happy-ever-after—particularly Charlie, who hasn't had nearly enough love in her life.

By the time I had finished, I was satisfied that Rhys understood that Charlie coming into his world was the best thing that had ever happened to him—the reason he'd been searching for through all his striving to succeed, succeed, succeed—and that Charlie had at last found a place to call home. I hope you enjoy reading their story—I got so much out of writing it.

Until next time,

Sarah Mayberry

PS—I love to hear from readers! Contact me through my website, www.sarahmayberryauthor.com.

ABOUT THE AUTHOR

Sarah Mayberry lives on the bay in Melbourne, Australia, with her partner (now husband!) of nearly twenty years. When she's not writing, she tries to keep the jungle that is her garden under control with the help of her tireless green-thumbed mother. She also enjoys cooking, reading, going to the movies, shopping for shoes and hanging out with her friends and family.

Books by Sarah Mayberry

HARLEQUIN SUPERROMANCE

1551—A NATURAL FATHER
1599—HOME FOR THE HOLIDAYS
1626—HER BEST FRIEND
1669—THE BEST LAID PLANS
1686—THE LAST GOODBYE
1724—ONE GOOD REASON
1742—ALL THEY NEED

HARLEQUIN BLAZE

380—BURNING UP
404—BELOW THE BELT
425—AMOROUS LIAISONS
464—SHE'S GOT IT BAD
517—HER SECRET FLING
566—HOT ISLAND NIGHTS

All backlist available in ebook. Don't miss any of our special offers. Write to us at the following address for information on our newest releases.

Harlequin Reader Service
U.S.: 3010 Walden Ave., P.O. Box 1325, Buffalo, NY 14269
Canadian: P.O. Box 609, Fort Erie, Ont. L2A 5X3

As always, the two people who have kept me sane while writing this book are Chris and Wanda. If I was Bette Midler, I would say you were "The wind beneath my wings." Since I'm me, I'll settle for saying you both make me a better person and a better writer (not as poetic, but lighter on the fromage factor, hopefully).

Big thanks also to Lisa, the bestest neighbor ever, and to Joan for being my lovely sane writer friend who understands the joy and pain of being in the trenches wrestling with plot, character and grammar.

Last, but not least, I want to send a shout-out to the online romance writing and reading community. It's so awesome to know there are so many of us who live to read and dream and write about love and human relationships. Your collective generosity and smarts continually impresses me.

CHAPTER ONE

THE SOUND OF a champagne cork popping echoed in the small kitchen.

"Woohoo! We are going to have so much fun, former Warrant Officer Long. It's going to be just like old times."

Charlie Long smiled at her friend Gina's exuberant prediction.

"Save some of that perkiness for later. You don't want to peak too soon," Charlie warned as she passed a long-stemmed flute for filling. "We have a big night ahead."

A night that included lots of French champagne and some fine dining, if Charlie had any say in it.

"Don't worry, I'm pacing myself. I have lots of perkiness in reserve." Gina's grin was infectious, a perfect match for her cherubic face and blond corkscrew curls.

Charlie raised her glass. "To good friends with spare rooms and big hearts."

Gina lifted hers in turn. "To the rest of your life. To having a home that's all yours. To meeting a guy who doesn't know how to field strip a Steyr F88 rifle and who isn't going to ship out when things start getting good. And to never, ever having to wear khaki again."

Charlie laughed and clinked glasses with her friend. "Amen to that."

She felt a little disloyal as she threw back the first mouthful of champagne. The army had been good to her. It had been her family, of sorts, for almost half her life. Even though she was ready to move on, she didn't regret the years she'd given in service to her country. They'd made her who she was—defined her, really—for good or bad.

She felt the now-familiar lurch of nervousness as she contemplated life without the framework of the army.

So many possibilities to reinvent herself and her life. So much change. So much opportunity.

"How long do you think it'll take the airline to find your luggage?" Gina asked as she took a jar of olives from the fridge. After her own discharge two years ago she'd taken a job as manager of a busy catering company and her fridge was full to the brim with gourmet goodies and leftovers.

Charlie shook her head. "Who knows?"

As omens went, losing the bulk of her worldly goods on the first day of civilian life wasn't a great one. When Gina had collected her from the airport this afternoon, they'd stood and watched the luggage carousel snake round and round for a good half hour before admitting defeat and reporting the two suitcases lost.

"Damn it," she said as a new thought occurred. "What will I wear tonight?"

They had stopped by a mall to allow Charlie to pick up a few bare essentials to cover her for the "twenty-four hours" the airline had predicted she'd be without her baggage, but she hadn't even thought of buying something for tonight. She glanced down at her worn jeans, dark gray T-shirt and hiking boots. Not by any stretch of the imagination could they be considered suitable attire for the fancy-pants restaurant they had booked for dinner.

"Relax. You can borrow something of mine."

Charlie surveyed her shorter, slighter friend doubtfully. "I'm not sure that's going to work."

Size apart, there was also the small but important fact that she and Gina had very different taste in clothes. Charlie preferred tailored and neat and nondescript. Gina liked sparkly things that left the world in no doubt that she was a woman.

"We'll find something, C, don't worry," Gina said confidently.

The look in her friend's eyes made Charlie a little nervous. "Nothing crazy, okay?"

"Would I do that to you?"

Half a dozen incidents from their shared past flashed across Charlie's mind. "Yes."

Gina laughed and twisted open the jar. "Have an olive and stop stressing."

They stood at the counter drinking champagne and picking at the olives for almost an hour. Then Gina caught sight of the time and put down her glass with a decisive clink.

"Time to go make ourselves gorgeous. You shower first while I have a rummage and see what I can dig up for you to wear."

"At the risk of appearing ungrateful, could it not be a dress? I hate dresses."

"I have something in mind already, don't worry," Gina said mysteriously, shooing Charlie away.

Charlie padded obediently up the hallway of Gina's small Victorian-era cottage to her room. It had been three years since they had shared quarters near the Townsville barracks in Far North Queensland. When Charlie had first raised the notion of seeking a discharge, Gina hadn't hesitated in offering her spare room. It had taken Charlie only a moment's thought to say yes. For a woman with no ties to anyone or anything, a friendly face and a temporary place to stay had been as good a reason as any to pick Sydney as the site to start the next phase of her life.

She shut the bedroom door behind her. The

room was small but bright, with a vase of flowers on the bedside table, a snowy-white quilt and a colorful rag rug on the floor. Her overnight bag and the mall purchases lay on the end of the bed, but instead of unpacking her meager belongings, she closed her eyes and took a deep breath, absorbing the reality of the situation, allowing herself to catch up with everything that had happened.

She was in Sydney. For the next little while she would be living with Gina. And soon she would have a home of her own.

Home.

She tried the word out in her mind. It sounded...odd. Surreal, almost. For the past fourteen years, home had been wherever the powers that be chose to send her. She'd moved six times while enlisted, but not once had she allowed herself to call anywhere home. It was pointless to get too attached to anything or anyone when you knew you'd soon be moving on to the next posting.

Not anymore, though. Now she was in charge of her own destiny.

There was a tight feeling in her chest as she crossed to the window to inspect the courtyard garden outside. She'd die before she admitted it to anyone, but rather than being excited by all the choices and possibilities that lay ahead of her, she was feeling more than a little overwhelmed.

Everything was so open. So unpredictable. So possible. Which was great—in theory. In practice, it was a bit like standing on the high diving board, staring down, down, down at a pool that seemed far too small. She knew she had to take the plunge—but that didn't stop her from feeling pretty damn intimidated by what lay ahead.

Embarrassing when she considered some of the situations she'd dealt with during her time with her country's defense force. As a highly trained communications engineer with the Royal Australia Corps of Sigs, or R.A. Sigs, as it was more commonly known, she'd served as the vault custodian in Iraq, handling all the cryptographic material for the Australian forces, and she'd been deployed to East Timor as part of Operation Astute in 2006, helping to preserve peace and stability in the region. Over her years of service, she'd gained a reputation for being cool under pressure, a force to be reckoned with.

She wasn't sure where that coolness was right now. Maybe it was with her luggage, winging its way to an unknown destination. Or maybe she'd forgotten to pack it altogether. Maybe she'd left it behind, along with her khakis and a way of life that had constituted the entirety of her adulthood.

Stop freaking out. You can do this. How hard

can it be? You find an apartment. You buy some furniture. You start a life. It's not rocket science.

It only felt like it.

Clearly, more champagne was called for. But first she would shower, in accordance with Gina's instructions. All part of being a good guest.

Her thoughts fixed firmly on the here and now, Charlie made her way to the bathroom.

"OKAY, MR. WALKER. You've got twenty minutes and then I'm due on a plane. Make them count," Dieter Hanson said as he strode into the room.

Rhys Walker tried not to let the smile slip from his face as he shook hands with the tall, balding CEO. Rhys and his business partner, Greg, had been waiting for Hanson for nearly an hour past their appointed meeting time, cooling their heels in the hotel chain's vast boardroom. The CEO's assistant had popped her head in twice to assure them Mr. Hanson was "only five minutes away," and both times Rhys had suggested they reschedule. But the woman had been adamant that Mr. Hanson wouldn't be much longer.

Now Rhys eyed the man who had the power to change his life, irritation and adrenaline waging war in his bloodstream. He didn't like having his time wasted, but he and Greg had been wooing various executives at the Gainsborough Hotel Group for over two months, and they finally had been bumped to the top. Like it or not, Dieter Hanson had the power to say yay or nay to the contract Rhys had negotiated with the man's underlings. Which meant it was time to put his tap-dancing shoes on and sing for his supper.

"We'll keep this short and sweet, then," Rhys said. He glanced at Greg, who gave him the smallest of nods. It was enough to confirm that Greg was handing the presentation over to Rhys, no questions asked.

Rhys refocused his attention on the man at the head of the table. "I won't go over the details of what we're offering again. It's a pretty standard I.T. outsourcing contract. What I'd like to do is tell you a bit about myself and Greg and why we started Falcon, so you understand where we're coming from."

Rhys outlined their background in the I.T. and hospitality industries. He talked about the ethos behind Falcon and their goals, both short-term and long-term. Once he'd established their bona fides, he nailed the other man with a look.

"I'm going out on a limb and guessing that over the past twelve months, Gainsborough has experienced more than thirty software or hardware failures that have forced you to rely on manual systems to keep the doors open." Rhys listed ten of the most common issues with accommodation-booking software before hitting Hanson with an estimate of the amount of revenue his hotels had lost due to those same faults.

Hanson's interest sharpened when Rhys started to talk figures, and he knew he had him in the palm of his hand when Hanson began to ask questions about particulars in the contract. Rhys and Greg played tag team on the responses, and seventeen minutes after he'd entered the room, Hanson sat back in his chair and eyed first Rhys, then Greg.

"My team told me you guys were going to be hard to beat. I have to agree with them." Hanson pulled a pen from his breast pocket. "I assume you have the contract with you?"

Every muscle in Rhys's body tensed as he resisted the almost overwhelming urge to punch the air and whoop with triumph.

They'd done it. They'd freaking done it.

He extracted the contract from his briefcase and slid it forward. If Hanson noticed that Rhys's hands were trembling, he was pro enough not to comment on it. He signed the page with a flourish before returning the pen to his pocket and standing.

"Nice to meet you both. If you deliver on your promises, it will be even nicer."

"You can count on it," Rhys said.

They shook hands and left the room together. Hanson headed toward the elevators, while Rhys set his sights on the door to the men's washroom at the end of the hall. He knew without checking that Greg followed him, but neither of them said a word until they were on the other side of the polished wood door. Then they both dropped their briefcases to the floor and burst into relieved, triumphant laughter.

"Can you believe it? Can you freaking believe it?" Rhys said over and over.

Greg slapped him on the back so many times it started to hurt, but Rhys didn't give a damn.

"That's it. We're off and running. This is really going to happen," Greg said.

"Yeah, it is." Rhys felt dazed. They'd been working toward this moment for so long. And now they were here, it didn't feel quite real. With Gainsborough on board, it would only be a matter of time before they scored the next hotel chain. All it took was one big player to give them credibility, and they had that now. In spades.

Soon, they would be the go-to guys for hospitality I.T. in Australia. After that... Well, after that they were reaching into territory far beyond even Rhys's current ambitions.

Greg held his hands out in front of him. "Check it out," he said as his fingers trembled in midair.

Rhys offered up his own shaking hands and they started laughing all over again.

"Man, I'm wrecked," Rhys said. "I feel like I ran a marathon."

He pulled his tie loose and shrugged out of his jacket. Half moons of sweat radiated from beneath his armpits from all the nervous energy he'd expended.

"Let's go out, man," Greg said. "Let's grab this town by the scruff of the neck and not let go until it shakes us off."

"For sure. I'll call the office and tell the guys to meet up with us."

"And I'll tell Jess to hire a babysitter."

They were both grinning as they exited the washroom. They'd come in separate cars and they parted ways in the garage beneath the building.

"Café Sydney, ASAP. Be there or be square," Greg called over his shoulder.

"Bring your accessory liver, my friend. Because tonight is the night," Rhys said.

Greg's laughter echoed at him, bouncing off the concrete and the rows of parked cars. Rhys walked toward his ten-year-old BMW, aware that his cheeks were starting to ache with all his smiling.

So many people had raised their eyebrows when he'd quit his lucrative management role with a rival I.T. firm eight months ago. Friends, family members had all thought he was nuts to walk away from a cushy job when the global economy was still so shaky. But Rhys had always planned to start his own consulting company from the moment he'd earned his computer engineering degree. He'd saved every spare cent he'd ever earned, denying himself the luxury car and fancy apartment his salary could have commanded because he was determined to be his own master, to guide his own destiny. To make his mark on the world.

He pulled out his phone and dialed a number by heart rather than use his contact list, only registering that he was still underground when the phone beeped to let him know he had no signal. Shaking his head at his own woolly-headedness—apparently euphoria did that to a person, who knew?—he started his car and drove out into the dying light of a warm Sydney day. He tried his parents again and listened to the phone ring until finally the machine picked up.

"Hey. It's me," he said. "Just wanted you guys to know I got Gainsborough. Like I said I would. I want to take you out for dinner to celebrate, so let me know when you're available and I'll book someplace nice, okay?"

He ended the call as he braked at a stoplight. He drummed his fingers on the steering wheel, trying to think who else he should phone. The gang back in the office, obviously, but he felt as though there was someone else he was missing.

His thoughts ranged over his brothers and sisters, but he dismissed them after a moment's consideration. They were all so absorbed in their own things that they wouldn't really care. They would be happy for him, sure, but they'd never really understood what he and Greg were trying to achieve with the business and at some point in the conversation he would feel as though he was bragging—the younger brother trying to impress his siblings with his achievements. They would hear his news via their parents or at the next family function.

He frowned. For the life of him, he couldn't think of a single other person who would understand what today meant and share his excitement. The realization left him feeling vaguely dissatisfied. Shrugging off the sensation, he called the office, laughing as he heard the guys hollering in the background.

"Go home, put on your party clothes and meet us at Café Sydney," he instructed when they'd calmed enough to be coherent. "It's going to be a big one."

He followed his own advice, cutting across town to his apartment in Potts Point. He spared a glance for the Finger Wharf as he drove through Woolloomooloo. The sun glinted off the white rooftops of the luxurious apartments that had been built on top of the ancient timber wharf.

Home to Russell Crowe and a number of other high-profile Australians, the wharf was considered one of the best places to live in Sydney.

Not long now, baby.

He'd been eyeing an apartment in the wharf development for years now. The smaller apartments with the lesser views started at around half a million dollars, but Rhys didn't want a small apartment. He wanted space, he wanted views. If things went smoothly with Gainsborough, there was no reason why he couldn't start talking to real estate agents in earnest.

No reason at all.

A second rush of euphoria hit him as he considered what today meant. He wound down the window and let out a triumphant yahoo. A few people turned to stare. He felt a little stupid, but what the hell.

Today was the day his life had finally come together. All the planning. All the sacrifices. All the hours and hours of hard graft.

Life didn't hand out many moments like this, and he planned to enjoy every second of it. And then some.

"STOP FIDGETING." Gina slapped Charlie's hand away from the neckline of her top.

"I can't believe I let you talk me into this. Everyone in this restaurant knows I'm not wearing a bra. You know that, right?"

Despite her friend's admonition, Charlie once again tweaked the neckline of the metallic mesh halter she was wearing. No matter what she did, there was no hiding the fact that there was a lot of cleavage on show. Like the skintight black stretch-satin trousers she was wearing, Gina's top was not built for subtlety.

She glanced around the dark, woody interior of Café Sydney, hugely self-conscious in her borrowed clothes.

"No one knows you're not wearing a bra except you. And maybe the people at the next table now since we're talking so loudly. You need to relax. Here, have some more champagne."

Gina leaned over and plucked the champagne bottle from the ice bucket where their waiter had left it and poured them both another glass. "You look great, C. You look amazing."

"I look like I charge by the hour." Charlie shifted in her seat, wondering if it was possible for pants to be so tight they cut off circulation to vital organs.

"You know what your problem is? You're too used to trying to be one of the guys. Don't get me wrong, I understand why that's a good thing in the army, but you're not enlisted anymore. At the risk of sounding like a feminine-hygiene commercial, you need to embrace your womanhood."

Stung, Charlie paused with her glass halfway to her mouth. "I never tried to be one of the guys. I tried to be a good soldier." She could hear the defensiveness in her voice and she sat a little straighter. "Just because I'm not into pink and because I don't put everything out there on display doesn't make me butch or one of the guys."

Gina reached out and touched her arm. "I'm sorry. That came out the wrong way. I wasn't saying you were butch. That's not what I meant."

"What *did* you mean, then?"

Like it or not, Gina had hit a raw nerve and for some reason Charlie felt unable to let it go. There was so much else up in the air at the moment, having her sense of herself undermined felt like a step too far.

Gina studied her for a beat. "Do you honestly think you look bad tonight?"

"I don't look like me."

"That's not answering my question. Do you think you look good or not?"

Charlie glanced at herself. The black mesh of her top reflected the candlelight on the table and clung to her breasts in what she could only describe as an outrageously sexy way. The satin of her pants glowed with a more subtle luster, somehow lending her usually gangly legs a new voluptuousness.

"I look okay," she finally conceded.

Gina shook her head. "You're hopeless. You're the hottest woman in this room and you don't even know it. What a waste."

Charlie made a disbelieving noise.

"You don't believe me?" Gina asked.

"You don't need to blow smoke up my skirt. I know exactly where I fit in the man-woman food chain." From the moment she hit puberty she'd known. She wasn't blonde, she wasn't perky, and she didn't have that unknowable "something" that made men want to howl at the moon. A painful realization at the time, but now simply a fact of life. She'd long ago accepted that straight, mousy-brown hair, plain brown eyes and nondescript features were not going to set the world on fire.

"So where do you fit, then?" Gina asked.

"On a scale of one to ten? Five. Maybe six on a good day."

"You're nuts."

"Why are we even having this conversation? Let's talk about something else. Tell me more about this Spencer guy you're seeing."

Gina frowned. "Is this why you never went for it with Hamish in Townsville?"

"Good God. You have a memory like an elephant." Charlie took a gulp of champagne, hoping the action would hide the fact that she was blushing.

Her crush on Hamish Flint had not been her proudest moment. She'd mooned over the sexy, handsome warrant officer from afar for more than a year and never gotten the courage to do more than talk work with him.

Gina rested both forearms on the table and leaned toward Charlie. "I want you to indulge me in a little experiment. I want you to do a lap of the restaurant. All the way around the perimeter. And I want you to pay attention to how many men look at you."

Charlie rolled her eyes. "I'm not going to do that."

"Why not? Afraid I'm right?"

"I know you're wrong."

"Off you go, then. One lap, and pay attention. And no crossing your arms over your chest or sneaking around."

"Get off the grass."

Gina made a chicken sound.

Charlie rolled her eyes. "How old are you?"

"How scared are you?"

"I'm not *scared.*"

"Then put your moneymaker where your mouth is, lady," Gina said.

A surge of annoyance brought Charlie to her

feet. "Fine. I'll do it. But be ready to eat your words."

Gina gave her a finger wave. "I want an accurate tally. No fudging."

Charlie snorted as she turned from the table. Gina was an idiot. Well intentioned, but an idiot nonetheless. Charlie had lived with this body and this face for thirty-two years. As she'd said, she knew her place in the dating food chain. And it certainly wasn't at the top.

A server was backing away from the next table and she waited until he'd passed before taking her first step. Immediately she felt the subtle sway of her breasts against the top and had to quell the urge to cross her arms over her chest.

She lifted her chin and walked toward the first table for four. It was full of men in suits who had clearly come straight from the office, and all four of them glanced at her as she walked past. Two of them fixated on her breasts, the other two on her legs. There was no mistaking their interest and Charlie felt an odd squirm of…something in the pit of her stomach.

Okay, clearly a fluke.

The next table boasted six couples. Two men and one of the women gave her a fully body scan. Out of the corner of her eye she saw one of the men turn his head to check out her ass as she passed.

She frowned, adding two more to her tally. Gina hadn't told her to count women, after all.

Next up was a family grouping—three generations, if she was any judge.

No takers here, I'm sure.

She was almost out of range when the gray-haired patriarch looked up from opening a gift to offer her a cheeky, spontaneous smile, while the two teenage boys turned and stared unashamedly at her breasts.

Seven, eight, nine. Bloody hell.

By the time she'd reached the bar area at the rear of the restaurant she'd racked up seventeen checkouts. She inspected her trousers to make sure her fly was done up. It was. There was no other explanation, then—it had to be the pants and top. Somehow, a bit of slinky fabric had convinced everyone she was a sexy siren. How... bizarre.

And, if she was being honest with herself, kind of exciting. She'd spent far too many nights talking shop with the boys while watching other servicewomen beat off admirers with a stick to be above enjoying the very flattering male interest. She was only human, after all.

And maybe more than a little bit tipsy.

Experimenting, she pulled back her shoulders and injected some sway into her hips as she wove her way through the bar.

More eyes turned her way.

Huh. Look at that. I'm really getting the hang of this thing. Who knew it was so easy?

The thought had barely registered when she stumbled down an unexpected step. Her hand flew out instinctively, grabbing the nearest object—which happened to be a very solid male arm holding a *very* full glass of wine.

CHAPTER TWO

RED WINE FLEW as her weight dragged the arm down. She let out a startled yelp as her hip crashed into her unsuspecting rescuer. For a second she teetered on the brink of losing her balance completely, but he moved incredibly quickly, twisting to face her while his free hand grabbed her other arm. She glanced up and found herself looking into a pair of dark-lashed chocolate-brown eyes that were half concerned, half annoyed.

"You all right there?" he asked.

"I'm so sorry," she said. "I didn't see the step."

"But you're okay now?"

"Absolutely."

They were standing very close, almost chest to chest. She could smell his aftershave—something woodsy, with leather and spice notes—and she could see the fine lines around his eyes and mouth.

She realized she was staring and took a hasty step backward. Which was when she noticed the huge red stain down the front of his steel-gray shirt. "I ruined your shirt."

He glanced at himself. "I guess you did."

"I'll pay for dry cleaning. Or a replacement. And I'll buy you another glass of wine. Whatever you want."

His gaze dipped below her face as he gave her body a slow appraisal. "How about I buy you a drink and we'll call it even?" There was a cheeky, charming glint in his eye. His behavior was so removed from her usual interactions with men that it took her a moment to understand he was flirting.

"I can't let you do that. It was my fault."

The smile in his eyes extended to his mouth. "It was an accident. No harm done."

"Except to your shirt."

He made a dismissive sound and flicked his fingers in the air, never taking his eyes off hers.

She found herself smiling in return. "You're really not mad?"

"It's a shirt. No big deal." He offered her his hand. "I'm Rhys, by the way."

"Charlie," she said, shaking his hand. His fingers were long and strong, the nails beautifully manicured.

"Short for Charlotte?"

She nodded. "But I've always been Charlie."

He was still holding her hand. She knew she

should pull it free, but she was too busy staring into his face.

"Why don't you join me and my friends."

She glanced over his shoulder and realized that their whole interaction was being witnessed by a group of eight people.

She threw them a self-conscious smile. "I can't. I'm having friend with my dinner," she said. Then she registered what she'd said. "I mean, I'm having dinner with my friend."

His eyes crinkled at the corners as his smile deepened. Normally she'd be embarrassed by her gaucheness, but there was something about the way he looked at her that short-circuited all her usual responses.

"Right. He's probably going to come after me with an elephant gun if I hold you up much longer, huh?"

"It's a she. And she's probably thinking I've twisted my ankle in these shoes. Which I almost did."

"Then I'll let you go," he said, his fingers sliding from hers. "But maybe I'll see you later. We're going to be here awhile."

She had no idea what to say to the blatant invitation in his eyes. She'd never had a man look at her like that in her life. Although she could definitely get used to it, especially if they all had intense dark eyes and olive skin and broad, strong chests.

"Um. Maybe." She took a step backward. "Sorry about your shirt. Again."

"Forget about it. I already have."

She nodded and smiled and finally forced herself to walk away from the magnetic pull of his regard.

"Wow," she whispered to herself as she wove through the crowd.

So that was what it was like to be the absolute focus of a handsome, devastating man's attention. Heady, a little overwhelming and a lot exciting.

She glanced over her shoulder as she stepped down into the reception area. Her eyes met his and she realized he'd been watching her walk away. As though he couldn't take his eyes off her.

She lifted her hand and gave him the smallest of finger waves. He nodded his head slightly in acknowledgment. The urge to walk back and take him up on his offer of a drink was almost impossible to ignore.

Um, hello? Remember Gina? Earth calling Charlie...

Charlie forced herself to keep moving. The more distance she put between herself and Rhys-the-superhot, the more sane she felt. For a moment there, she'd bought into Gina's fantasy of who she was. Which was plain crazy.

"There you are," Gina said as Charlie returned to the table. "I was about to send out a Saint Bernard with a little barrel of whiskey strapped to his neck. What happened to you?"

"I nearly broke my ankle in these shoes of yours, for starters," Charlie said. "Plus, I gave some poor guy a bath in his own wine."

"No way!"

"Way."

Gina pressed her fingers to her mouth to stop herself from laughing.

"Go ahead and laugh," Charlie said resignedly.

"Give me your tally first. How many men looked at you?"

Charlie turned her head and gazed along the length of the restaurant. She could see the bar from here, but not Rhys's dark head. "Um, I'm not sure. I lost count," she said distractedly.

"You lost count. I rest my case."

The waiter arrived with their meals before Charlie could respond. She used the interruption to change the subject.

The champagne kept flowing as they ate, although Charlie was old enough and wise enough not to drink too much. Still, there was no denying that she was feeling very *relaxed* by the time she and Gina had polished off a dessert platter.

"Okay. Where to next?" Gina said as she licked the last smear of chocolate sauce off her spoon.

Charlie let her gaze slide to the bar again. Was Rhys still there? And if he was, would he still want to buy her a drink? Or had he already met some other non-wine-spilling woman who knew how to respond when a handsome man looked at her with approval?

"What about a drink at the bar?" she heard herself say.

Gina shrugged. "Sure, babe. It's your night. Let's go."

What are you doing? *What do you think is going to happen if you go to the bar? Have you forgotten who you are?*

She hadn't. Not really. She'd always been a realist, pragmatic and practical to her bones. But thanks to copious quantities of good champagne and her borrowed clothes, she was buzzing with a sense of possibility tonight. As Gina had said earlier, this was the first day of the rest of her life.

Everything was in flux—including, maybe, her sense of who she was. Because hadn't Gina proven to her that maybe her sense of self was a little outdated or skewed? Hadn't Rhys-the-sexy looked at her as though she was a morsel he wanted to devour? Hadn't nearly two dozen men eyed her with masculine approval when she'd walked past?

You've been drinking. You should walk out of

here right now and go home and eat some crackers and drink a whole lot of water.

The voice was probably right. It had saved her from making a lot of bad decisions in her life, that voice. But she didn't want to listen tonight. She wanted more of the feeling she'd experienced when she'd caught Rhys tracking her every move with his dark, heated gaze. For that precious handful of seconds she had felt powerful and knowing and invincible and incredibly sexy.

It might be an illusion—maybe even a delusion—but she wanted more of it. Even if it meant she was setting herself up to fail spectacularly.

RHYS TOOK A PULL from his beer, an ear tuned to the debate Greg was having with Brett, one of their engineers, while his gaze roamed the crowded bar.

She hadn't come back. He'd been hoping she would, but it had been more than an hour since the mysterious and sexy Charlie had sashayed her way to her table. Which probably meant he should put her out of his mind.

Easier said than done. It had been a long time since he'd felt such an instant attraction to a woman. Certainly a woman he'd met in a bar. He'd done his fair share of hound-dogging in his early twenties, but it had been years since he'd prowled a bar in the hope of meeting someone.

Not that that was what he was doing tonight, of course—they were here to celebrate. But there was no denying the instinctive, primal pull he'd felt when staring into Charlie's cinnamon-brown eyes. An attraction that had only intensified when he checked out the rest of her.

He'd never had a "type" of woman he was attracted to—he preferred to think of himself as an equal-opportunity admirer of the opposite sex—but there was something about Charlie's lithe, willowy body that really worked for him. Especially in that clingy, sexy top and pants she was wearing.

Give it up, man. She's gone home.

He gave the bar one last scan before focusing fully on Greg and Brett. Something caught the very edge of his vision and he did a double take—and grinned.

She was standing at the bar with a short, blonde woman. He watched as they had an intense discussion that involved the other woman pushing Charlie's wallet into the small handbag she was carrying and turning to the barman. Charlie shrugged philosophically, apparently resigning herself to having her friend buy her a drink. Then she turned to scan the crowd. Rhys felt a thud of satisfaction when she paid particular attention to the spot where they'd enjoyed their first encounter. His group had moved in the past hour, commandeering a conversational grouping of couches and armchairs, but Charlie didn't know that and the disappointed expression on her face when she found no sign of him did great things for his ego.

Not that he usually needed a lot of help in that direction, as his two younger sisters were always happy to inform him.

She'd come looking for him. Pointless to deny that he was pretty damn happy about that.

His gaze locked on her, he put down his beer and stood. "I'll be back in a moment," he said to no one in particular.

He made his way through the crowd, never losing sight of her. She'd turned to face the bar by the time he reached her side and he took a moment to admire the long, slender lines of her body. Her halter top left most of her back exposed, revealing pale, creamy skin and finely honed muscles. His gaze slid to her butt, showcased in some kind of shiny, slippery-looking fabric that made him want to reach out and touch. She had a great ass—small and tight and perky as hell—and legs that went on forever.

He wanted her. Badly.

Her friend handed her what looked like a margarita and he waited until she'd taken a sip before speaking.

"I thought we had a deal."

She glanced over her shoulder and he knew he wasn't imagining the warmth in her eyes.

"You can buy my next drink," she said, then they both simply stood there and ate each other up with their eyes.

Her friend nudged her none too subtly in the ribs and Charlie blinked.

"Sorry. Rhys, this is Gina, my friend. Gina, Rhys."

Gina's gaze went immediately to the stain on the front of his shirt. "So you're wine guy. Nice to meet you."

"I guess I am. Nice to meet you, too." Rhys's gaze returned to Charlie. "Come join us."

Charlie looked at Gina, clearly gauging her reaction.

"Sure. Why not," Gina said.

"We managed to score a couple of couches," he explained before making his way through the crowd. At a certain point he sensed they weren't following him and he turned to find Charlie and Gina engaged in a quick, quiet discussion that involved lots of hand gestures from Gina and an embarrassed, self-conscious little smile from Charlie.

He liked that smile. It told him a lot about Charlie and what she wanted. She glanced up and realized he was waiting and offered him a broader, brighter smile before starting toward him.

"Sorry," she said when she reached his side.

He offered her his hand. "In case I lose you again."

After the tiniest of hesitations she slid her hand into his. He was close enough to see the way her pupils dilated at the small contact. His gaze dropped to her mouth and he eyed her plump bottom lip. He wondered what she'd do if he kissed her right now, the way his instincts were demanding. He wondered what she'd taste like, what she'd feel like. Whether she'd push him away or press her body against his.

Someone jostled him and he realized he was staring.

"Come on." Using their joined hands to tow her behind him, he led them to his friends. There was only one empty seat—his—and he gestured the two women toward it. It was a modern, square chair with wide, flat padded arms, and Gina dropped into the seat while Charlie perched on the arm.

He performed a quick round of introductions before perching on the arm of the chair nearest her. The move put them at the same level, creating a cozy sense of intimacy and connection between them.

"So," he said.

She smiled, looking a little nervous. "So."

She had fine features—a delicate nose, a neat,

pointed chin, a small but plump mouth. He liked the way she'd made up her eyes to seem smoky and mysterious, and he really liked her shiny red mouth.

"Tell me, Charlie, what do you do when you're not having dinner with your friend on a Friday night?"

She took a big gulp from her glass, almost as though she needed the liquid courage. "I just received my discharge from the army after fourteen years of service. I guess I'm officially unemployed. But I'm in the process of setting up a web-design business."

He was surprised, and suspected it probably showed in his face. She looked far too slight to be in the armed forces.

"This is going to get me in trouble with feminists, but you look way too nice to be running around with an AK–47."

"Actually, we carried Steyr F88s. And I worked in R.A. Sigs, which means I was in charge of making sure people could talk to each other, not shooting stuff up."

"So you're a comms expert, huh?"

"You could say that. How about you? What do you do when you're not walking around wearing my mistake down the front of your shirt?"

"Greg and I are partners in an I.T. consulting firm."

"So you're self-employed?"

"Yep." He could hear the satisfaction in his own voice and so, apparently, could she, because she smiled and cocked her head slightly.

"And loving it, I take it?"

"Today I am. We just landed a major contract."

"Ah. So this is a celebration?"

"Definitely. Tell me more about the army," he said. "I don't think I've ever met a woman in uniform before."

"Well, officially, I'm a woman out of uniform now." She blushed the moment she said it and he knew she hadn't intended the double entendre. His gaze slid down her body again.

She was an interesting contradiction. Her clothes and body screamed sexy vixen, but her attitude and expression told a different story. A more shy, less confident one.

"What made you join up?"

She appeared relieved that he hadn't capitalized on her faux pas. "My father was in the army. So I suppose I was following in his footsteps more than anything. Especially at the start."

"And now you're going to be a web designer?"

"That's the plan."

"Competitive business these days."

"I have a couple of clients lined up already," she said, shrugging modestly.

He liked her quiet confidence. She might be a

little skittish when it came to him, but she clearly felt on top of her career.

"So how are you finding civilian life?"

"Day one is shaping up okay so far."

"Are you telling me this is your first day of freedom?"

"Yep."

"Oh, well, that definitely calls for a celebration."

"You're already celebrating."

"True. Maybe we should add our celebrations together. See if the sum isn't greater than its parts."

Her gaze held his. "Maybe we should."

He smiled, and her mouth curved in response. Arousal and curiosity and the need to conquer buzzed through his veins, a heady cocktail of potential.

He reached for his beer and raised his glass in a casual toast. "To celebrations."

"To celebrations," she echoed.

IT WAS TWO IN THE MORNING when Charlie dragged her gaze from Rhys's face and registered that Gina was long past the wilting stage and close to dropping off to sleep.

"We should probably think about heading home," she said regretfully.

Rhys's mouth quirked as he took in the way

Gina's head was propped on her hand and her eyes closed. "Yeah. Probably a good idea."

Disappointment washed through her at his easy acquiescence. She'd never had a one-night stand in her life, but she didn't want this night to end. She wanted to keep talking to Rhys, wanted to keep listening to his deep, mellow voice, wanted to have the chance to touch the hard, hot body that had been so close to hers, driving her more than a little crazy.

But apparently the feeling was far from mutual. So much for her sense of herself being outdated.

He was always out of your league and you know it.

True, but it had been fun while it lasted. More fun, more exciting, than anything she'd experienced in a long time.

"I'll walk you down," Rhys said.

"Sure." She gave Gina's knee a little shake. "Hey, Sleeping Beauty. Time to go home."

Gina started. "What?"

Charlie laughed. "Come on. Let's get you into bed."

She stood and waited for Gina to gather her things together, then the three of them navigated the thinning crowd to the elevators. Charlie was very aware of Rhys standing by her side as the car dropped smoothly toward the ground. She shot him a quick glance. He was staring straight ahead, an unreadable expression on his face.

She gave a silent sigh as she registered for the millionth time how handsome he was. Not in a perfect, pretty-boy way, but in a real, rugged, masculine way. He had a strong jaw and a straight nose with a bump near the bridge. His lips were chiseled yet still soft looking. His dark hair and eyes made her wonder if he had Greek or Italian heritage. Then there was his body...

As though he felt her regard, he glanced her way. She felt herself blush.

Busted. *Good one, Long. Too subtle.*

"Is your background Italian?" she blurted, as though asking about his forebears would excuse the fact that she'd been ogling him.

"There's some Spanish blood in there some-where, I think. But my dad keeps telling me we're Black Irish. Whatever that means."

"Huh."

The doors opened and they entered the echoey foyer of Customs House. It was all but deserted at this time of night and even the bar at ground level had whittled its patrons down to hard-core players.

The night air was cool on her bare shoulders as they exited to the street. Customs House was situated smack-dab in the middle of Circular Quay, usually a busy hub for buses, trains and ferries, but at this time of night the last ferries had well and truly gone and bus service was reduced to bare bones. The taxi stand was located at the end of the street. A handful of cabs idled, waiting for passengers.

"It's like a ghost town," Charlie said as they made their way across the cobblestones toward the taxis.

"I'm sure there are still plenty of idiots raising hell in Kings Cross," Rhys said, referring to a part of the city that was infamous for its nightlife and girlie bars.

She stumbled on an uneven cobble and Rhys grabbed her shoulder to steady her.

"Thanks," she said ruefully. "Believe it or not, I *have* worn high heels before tonight."

"You're freezing," he said, his hand tightening on her shoulder.

"No, I'm fine." The words were barely out of her mouth before Rhys's arm wrapped around her shoulder. Heat unfurled in her belly at the feel of his strong arm around her body.

"Better?" he asked.

"Yes." She risked a glance toward his face. He was watching her closely. Almost as though he was trying to get a read on her.

Gina had walked ahead of them and was talking to the first driver through the open passenger window.

"He'll take us," she called.

Charlie's hip bumped against Rhys's as they walked the last few feet. Gina slid into the backseat, leaving the door open. Charlie turned to face Rhys, hoping that the regret she felt didn't show in her face.

"I had a good night." She held her breath, waiting for him to ask for her phone number or give some indication that his interest in her extended beyond casual flirtation.

"I had a great night," he said. Then he reached out and tucked a strand of hair behind her ear.

She forced a smile. "Well—"

He leaned closer and she swallowed the rest of her words as he pressed a kiss to her lips. He lifted his head slightly and looked into her eyes. She stared back at him, stunned, her heart thudding against her breastbone. He palmed the nape of her neck, and then he was kissing her again, his tongue sweeping into her mouth this time, turning her legs to jelly.

She pressed her body against his, her skin on fire, desire beating a tattoo through her veins. His tongue stroked hers gently, provocatively, and she reached out and gripped his shoulders with both hands.

After a long, long moment he drew back. "Come home with me?" he asked very quietly, his voice a low husk.

Dear God, I thought you'd never ask.

"Yes."

He smiled. There was so much hot promise in his eyes that she squeezed her thighs together.

"Hold that thought." She slipped from his arms to approach the taxi and ducked her head inside.

"Let me guess, I'm on my own," Gina said.

"Yeah." Charlie laughed. She sounded like a giddy schoolgirl, but she didn't care. She wanted this. Wanted the way Rhys made her feel.

"When was your last drink?" Gina asked.

"Sorry?"

"I want to know how drunk you are so I can decide if I'm being a good friend letting you go home with this guy."

"I'm not drunk. I'm not sober, but I know what I'm doing."

"Okay. You're a big girl. Have a good time, C. Be safe."

"I'll see you tomorrow."

Charlie straightened, shutting the door. The taxi took off immediately and the reality of what she'd agreed to hit her like a bucket of cold water. She didn't know this man, after all. He could be anyone. And she'd agreed to get naked with him and share the most intimate of acts with him.

A warm hand landed on the small of her back and a second later she felt Rhys brush the hair away from her nape before pressing a kiss there.

Everything inside her tensed with delight as his whiskers rasped against her skin.

He moved closer, wrapping his arms around her from behind. She felt his erection against her backside, and every sane thought flew out her head like so much dandelion fluff.

She wanted him. She'd indulged herself precious few times in her life, but she wanted this man, wanted the experience he promised with his eyes and hard body, and she was damn well going to have him.

She rested her hands over his and pressed into his hips. He opened his mouth against her neck and she felt the hot press of his tongue. A shiver of need raced down her spine and her nipples hardened.

"Where do you live?" she whispered.

She hoped it was somewhere close because she was so turned on it almost hurt.

"Potts Point. About five minutes."

She twisted in his arms and kissed him, her hands sliding to his hips and then, boldly, to his backside. She made a small approving sound in her throat as her hands felt hard muscle.

"You keep that up, we're not going to make it home," Rhys murmured against her mouth.

"What are we waiting for, then?"

CHAPTER THREE

RHYS SLIPPED HIS hand into hers and led her toward the next cab.

"Potts Point," he said as he climbed into the backseat, pulling her behind him.

She wanted him to kiss her again very badly. Instead, he slid his arm around her and tugged her against his side.

"You smell good," he said as the cab drove away from the curb.

"So do you." She put her hand on his thigh, her belly tightening as she felt the firm muscle beneath her fingers. He had a beautiful body. She couldn't wait to see it.

Rhys leaned close and started to kiss her neck, small, delicate caresses that made her limp with need. She let her head drop to the side and tried not to moan out loud.

She was aware that they'd arrived at their destination only when the taxi jerked to a halt. Rhys gave a surprised grunt and removed his arm from around her shoulders to pull his wallet from his back pocket.

"Keep the change," he said as he handed the driver two twenties.

They slid out of the car.

"You realize you gave that guy an eighty percent tip, right?" she said.

"It was worth it." He took her hand and led her toward the entrance of a modern apartment block. She felt light-headed with lust, all her thoughts concentrated on what was about to happen upstairs. In his bedroom.

His thumb brushed gentle circles inside her wrist as they rode to the sixth floor.

"This is me," he said as he led her toward a nondescript gray door. He unlocked the door, flicking on a light as he led her inside.

"I've got beer or wine—"

Charlie pushed him against the wall and pressed her body to his. "I don't want beer or wine."

She kissed him, channeling years of frustrated desire into the meeting of their mouths and tongues. He responded with equal hunger, his hands sliding up her rib cage and onto her breasts. His thumbs found her nipples with unerring accuracy and she jerked her hips against his as he squeezed them gently.

"Man," he muttered against her mouth.

She slid her hands onto his backside and urged his hips closer to hers, rubbing herself against his erection. He responded by pushing his hands beneath her top and cupping her bare breasts. He teased her mercilessly, to the point where she started to pant.

"Charlie, you are so damn hot," he said, breaking their kiss to look into her face.

"I need to be naked." She had no idea where the demand came from. She'd never been this sexually aggressive in her life, but there was something about this man...

"The feeling is totally mutual."

He held her gaze as he slid a hand over the front of her trousers. She gave a small, needy whimper as he cupped her sex, his fingers pressing against the spot where she needed him the most.

"Are you ready for me, Charlie?" he asked, his voice very low.

She answered with her body, pressing herself forward, into his hand. She reached for the stud on his jeans at the same time, her fingers fumbling for the warm metal of his zipper. It gave readily and she felt him tense as she slid her hand into the opening she'd created. Her fingers found warm cotton over hard flesh. She gripped him firmly, stroking her hand along his length. He shuddered and closed his eyes for the briefest of seconds. When he opened them again his eyes blazed into hers.

"Let's go."

She removed her hand from his jeans as he pushed them both away from the wall. He led her into a darkened living room and up another hallway. She was too intent on the man walking ahead of her to pay much attention to her surroundings. As he entered what she assumed was the bedroom, she reached for the hem of her top and dragged it over her head. It hit the floor with a metallic hiss and Rhys turned to face her, his gaze dropping immediately to her naked breasts.

He mouthed a four-letter word, the appreciation in his eyes lifting her desire higher still.

"You're going to have to help me with these stupid pants," she said a she reached for the snap on her trousers.

"Those pants are not stupid. They're a modern miracle," he said as she lowered the zipper, revealing the plain black cotton panties she wore beneath.

She pushed her trousers down her legs and he helped her slide them past her knees.

"That's better," she said.

His gaze roamed her almost naked body. "It certainly is."

Charlie had never had an easy relationship with her own body, but the way he looked at her made her feel like a goddess.

"Take your clothes off," she said.

She moved to the bed, crawling onto the mattress before rolling onto her back and hooking her thumbs into the waistband of her underwear. Her gaze locked with his, she slipped her panties down her legs.

"Man, you are killing me here, Charlie." He fumbled with his shirt buttons, then simply grabbed either side and ripped before shrugging the shirt off to reveal a broad, well-muscled chest. She eyed him avidly as he pushed his jeans down, toeing off his shoes at the same time. His belly muscles rippled as he shucked his own underwear and her gaze gravitated to his erection. Hard and proud, the sight of it made her want to purr like a cat.

He smiled, obviously enjoying her unashamed inspection. He strode toward the bed. The mattress dipped, then the hard, hot weight of his body was pressing against hers and pure instinct took over.

He lowered his head, sucking one of her breasts into his mouth. She hooked a leg around his hips, sliding a hand onto his erection at the same time. She stroked him confidently, greedily, while he sucked and kissed and gently bit her breasts. Within minutes she was panting, losing her own rhythm, aware only of the need to have him inside her. Now.

"Rhys," she breathed.

He lifted his head from her breasts and grinned. "Don't tell me you can't wait."

"Rhys." She tightened her grip on his shaft.

He leaned across to the nightstand and yanked open the drawer. She closed her eyes, barely holding it together as she heard the rustle of a foil package being opened. She opened them again as she felt him pressing against her entrance.

She held her breath, waiting for him to push inside her. Instead, Rhys looked deep into her eyes while one hand traveled down her belly to between her thighs. She lifted her hips reflexively as his fingers delved into her intimate folds. She knew he could feel how wet she was, how ready for him she was. His gaze grew hooded and a muscle in his jaw ticked. He stroked her, monitoring the small catches in her breathing and the way she moved her head on the bed and the way her body trembled beneath his.

Just when she was about to scream with frustration he flexed his hips and slid inside her. Her body welcomed him as he buried himself to the hilt. She let out a broken little sob, almost tearful over how good it felt to be filled by him, how hard and thick and hot he felt inside her.

He started to move, and within seconds she'd found his rhythm. Every clumsy sexual encounter she'd ever had, every second of self-consciousness over her body or her own needs, every doubt she'd ever experienced went out the window as she gave herself over to the moment.

There was only him and her and the place where their bodies were joined and the suck of his mouth at her breasts and the feel of his back and shoulders and chest beneath her hands and the steady, deep thrusting of his body inside hers. All too soon her body tightened toward release and she curled her fingers into his backside and shuddered beneath him. He pressed kisses to her forehead and cheeks and mouth and then slowed his pace and inserted a hand between them. She gave a little gasp of surprise when his thumb found her and he began to coax her toward a second climax. She was shuddering, legs wrapped around his hips, his name on her lips by the time she peaked again, and this time he went with her, his body tensing as he rode out his moment of release.

He collapsed onto the bed beside her, his face buried in the pillow. They were both breathing hard and she could feel her heart banging away like a trapped bird inside her chest.

She blinked at the darkened ceiling as she slowly came back to awareness. She could feel the coolness of sweat behind her knees and beneath her arms, could smell the musky, earthy scent of sex. Her legs felt shaky, and when she lifted a hand to push her hair from her face it was trembling.

Beside her, Rhys stirred. He lifted his face from the pillow. She was gratified to see he looked as blown away as she felt. For a long moment they simply stared at each other. Then his mouth curled into a smile, and before she knew it he was grinning and she was grinning back at him.

"I'm going to give that a nine," he said.

"Only a nine?" she asked, one eyebrow raised.

"I think we can do better."

"Really?" She could hear the incredulity in her own voice.

"Yeah. Really."

He trailed a finger down her chest and onto her left breast. Her nipple beaded to hardness long before his finger arrived there. This man turned her on so much that the mere thought of him touching her was enough to make her crazy.

He stroked her nipple gently, drawing small circles around it before pinching it lightly between thumb and forefinger. Charlie shifted restlessly as she felt the pull of desire between her thighs again.

She frowned. How was it possible to want a man again so quickly, especially when she'd come twice?

"Sixty seconds," he said, rolling away from her.

He disappeared into the bathroom to dispose of the condom and returned well within his own deadline. He settled beside her, resting on his side. His gaze ran over her body.

"You were right. You're definitely a woman out of uniform," he said.

He surprised her into laughter. He glided a hand over her breasts and down her belly to her thighs. His fingers delved into her warm, slick heat and again she moved restlessly.

"Too soon?" he asked, even as he stroked her.

"N-no," she breathed.

"Good."

He took his time making love to her, caressing her until she was quivering and begging for him. When he did finally slide inside her, he worked her slowly and deeply and thoroughly, building her to a climax that had her arching off the bed, her fingers digging into his shoulders. He came not long afterward, and they lay panting, hearts racing. After a few minutes he went to the bathroom then came back to the bed and flicked off the bedside lamp.

"Give me an hour," he murmured as he rolled onto his side and pulled her against his chest, her bottom tucked against his hips.

She was already mostly asleep. The last thought she had before she drifted off was that if the first day of the rest of her life was like this, then she was in for one hell of a ride.

CHARLIE WOKE with a start. For a long moment she had no idea where she was. Then it all came back to her—Café Sydney, lots of champagne, meeting Rhys, talking to Rhys, kissing Rhys. Finally, coming home with Rhys. Making love with Rhys. Again and again and again.

A headache accompanied her return to reality. She worked her tongue around her mouth. She needed water. In large quantities. And painkillers. And a trip to the bathroom wouldn't be out of order, either.

A heavy arm lay across her belly. She lifted it gingerly, rolling from beneath it. She slid to the edge of the bed, glancing over her shoulder to ensure Rhys was still asleep.

He was, his dark lashes twin fans against his cheeks, his hair tousled.

It seemed impossible, but he was even more beautiful in the early-morning light than he'd appeared last night. His coloring, his bone structure, the rugged handsomeness of his face… And his body. She didn't even know where to start with his body. She'd had two boyfriends who had been in the service, both of whom had done physical labor day in, day out. Neither of them had looked like Rhys. Through some accident of genetics and fate, he had the sort of body that exactly fit her notion of the masculine ideal. Broad shoulders. Defined chest, but not so much that he was in danger of having cleavage. Flat belly. Muscular thighs. Even his feet were perfect, long and sleek and strong.

She stood, putting a hand to her forehead as a wave of dizziness hit her. Moving slowly and quietly, she entered the en suite bathroom and eased the sliding door shut inch by silent inch. Once it was closed she made a beeline for the toilet. It was only when she'd taken care of business and was washing her hands at the vanity that she caught sight of her reflection in the bathroom mirror.

And gasped with horror.

Her hair was matted to her head on one side, while the rest stuck up in a crazy haystack. All the makeup that Gina had so artistically applied last night had migrated down her face, leaving twin panda circles of kohl and shadow smeared around her eyes and on her cheeks. Her mouth looked red and puffy, the skin surrounding it red and irritated.

Her face pinched with dismay, she rubbed at the redness but only succeeded in making it appear even more irritated. It took her a moment to realize it must be whisker rash.

She had a similar rash on her breasts, as well as a small suck mark on the inner curve of her left breast. She ran the tap and used her fingers to try to comb her hair into submission. The only thing that seemed to work was weighing it down with water, so she kept patting her wet hands on her hair until it clung to her scalp in a sodden cap. She pumped liquid soap from the dispenser on the vanity into her hands and scrubbed her face clean, wincing when it stung her eyes.

When she'd finished, the woman in the mirror had been transformed from the slutty walking dead into a red-eyed, pale-faced drowned rat, about as far from the sultry vixen of last night as it was possible to get.

She mouthed a four-letter word. She looked terrible. Really, really terrible. Without Gina's clever makeup and saucy clothes, she was reduced to plain old Charlie—emphasis on the plain—and any minute now, the perfect god sprawled across the bed in the next room was going to wake up and she was going to have to watch the disappointment register on his face as he figured out who he'd really come home with last night.

She couldn't do it.

Didn't *want* to do it.

Last night had been one of the headiest experiences of her life. She'd felt sexy and confident and desired and bold. She didn't want that memory tainted with the cold reality of today.

And she definitely didn't want to hang around while Rhys said all the right things while ushering her toward the exit. The very thought made her stomach roll with nausea.

She moved to the door and opened it a crack. Rhys was still sleeping.

Thank. God.

She pushed the door open only enough to slip into the bedroom. Then she crouched down and started collecting her clothes.

She found her panties all rolled up in the corner, a darker shadow on the graphite-gray carpet. The mesh top was near the door, her satin pants at the foot of the bed, her purse next to the nightstand. For the life of her, she couldn't find Gina's stilettos, and she scurried around the bedroom on tiptoe, the bundle of clothes pressed to her chest as she searched for them. She was about to admit defeat when Rhys stirred. She froze in a half crouch, naked and utterly exposed, eyes riveted to his prone form.

Please, please, please, please, don't wake up. Don't wake up. Don't wake up. Don't wake up.

He frowned, his mouth working. Then he pushed at the pillow before rolling onto his other side, his back to her.

She remained frozen for long seconds after he'd stopped moving, keen to ensure he really was still asleep. When his breathing evened out, her shoulders dropped with relief.

She turned toward the door and nearly stumbled over Gina's shoes. Scooping them up, she stepped into the hallway and pulled the bedroom door shut behind her. She walked briskly into the living room and dropped her clothes onto a seen-better-days leather couch. Grabbing her panties from amongst the pile, she pulled them on, then reached for the trousers. Predictably, they fought her every inch of the way as she dragged them up her legs. She was almost sobbing with frustration by the time she'd yanked them over her hips, and she had to lie on the floor to get the fly zipped. She tugged the mesh halter over her head, grabbed her handbag and the shoes, and headed for the door.

She had her hand on the knob, ready to make her escape, when she remembered Rhys's ruined shirt. Grinding her teeth at her own stupid con-science, she went back into the living room. A quick scan of the messy space located a memo pad by the phone. By some miracle a pen rested beside it and she scribbled a quick note.

Thanks for last night. I had a great time. Sorry about your shirt, and good luck with everything.
Charlie

She reread it, displeased with the overly effu-sive tone. She tore the note free and crumbled it

into a ball, stuffing it into her purse. She tried
again but stalled halfway.

*For God's sake, what is wrong with you?
You're never going to see this man again. Write
the note and get the hell out of here.*

She scrawled a quick note. Then she pulled two
fifty-dollar bills from her purse and left them and
her missive on the coffee table. She had no idea
how much a shirt cost these days, but if she gave
him any more she wouldn't have the taxi fare to
get home. It would have to do.

Mission completed, she bolted for the door.
Only when she was on the street, walking away
from his building, did she allow herself to breathe
easily.

It was cool this early in the morning and her
wet hair didn't help any. She leaned against a tree
for balance while she tugged on her shoes, then
wrapped her arms around herself as she walked
slowly up the hill toward what looked like a
coffee shop.

A woman walking her dog gave her a disdain-
ful head to toe as they crossed paths. Charlie
ducked her head and reached into her handbag
for her phone. She dialed for a cab, only then
realizing that she had no idea where she was. She
asked the operator to wait while she walked to the
nearest corner and found a street sign. Twenty
minutes later she was in the back of a taxi that

smelled of stale vomit and cigarette smoke, heading for Gina's house in Balmain.

She felt as though she'd scaled Mount Everest by the time she paid the driver and climbed the two steps to Gina's front door. Last night she'd had the good sense to take the key Gina had given her and she let herself in. Slipping her shoes off, she made her way to her room.

"Hey."

She glanced over her shoulder to see Gina standing in her bedroom doorway wearing a pair of shorty pajamas, knuckling her eyes blearily.

"Sorry. Did I wake you? I tried to be quiet," Charlie said.

"No worries. You okay?"

"Yeah. Of course."

"Okay. Good. See you in the morning, then."

"I hate to break it to you, but it's morning already," Charlie said, amused despite herself by her friend's muzzy-headedness.

"See you in the afternoon, then. I plan on sleeping through my hangover so I don't have to actually live through it."

Waving goodbye, Gina shuffled into her room. Charlie shed her clothes and grabbed her towel, then went straight to the bathroom. Stepping beneath the shower, she leaned against the tiled wall and bowed her head, simply letting the water roll over her. After long minutes she stirred and soaped herself down. She felt infinitely better by the time she toweled herself dry.

Returning to her room, she dressed in the pajamas she'd purchased yesterday and pulled her laptop from her carry-on. Her eyes felt gritty from lack of sleep but her head was whirling and she knew herself well enough to know sleep was out of the question. She opened up the folder for her first client, a boutique stationery business that had been set up by a former comrade in arms, and spent the next three hours refining her design concepts and building a template for the landing page.

She heard Gina stir at a certain point, and at midday there was a tap at her door.

"You awake?" Gina asked quietly.

"Yep."

"Good."

The door swung open to reveal Gina with a tray bearing two tall glasses of orange juice and a big pile of buttered toast with Vegemite. Her friend had wet hair from the shower and was wearing a pair of cotton pants and a tank top.

"Oh, hey, thanks," Charlie said, touched by the thoughtfulness. She put her laptop to one side.

Gina set the tray in the middle of the bed, sitting cross-legged on the other side. "So?" she asked as she reached for the first piece of toast.

"So what?"

"So, did you have a good time? Is he going to call? Are you going to call him?"

Charlie shifted uncomfortably. This being her first one-night stand and therefore her first morning-after debrief, she wasn't sure what the protocol was. She didn't want to offend Gina by telling her to butt out, but she wasn't about to spill the intimate details of what she'd shared with Rhys, either. It may have been a one-off, it may mean nothing in the larger scheme of her life, but right now it felt far too immediate and fresh for her to share with anyone else.

"It's okay, I don't want gory details," Gina said, apparently reading her reluctance. "Just tell me if he passed the I-want-to-see-him-again test."

"I'm not seeing him again," Charlie said firmly.

Gina pulled a face. "Really? That bad, huh? And he looked so promising. Don't tell me he was one of those good-looking guys who figures that all he has to do is lie there and be gorgeous and he's done his bit?"

The need to correct Gina's misinterpretation overrode Charlie's natural modesty. "He didn't just lie there. That part was…fine. But I realized this morning that there was no future in it, so I left."

Gina paused, a piece of toast halfway to her mouth. "The bastard. What did he say?"

"He didn't say anything. He was sleeping and

I figured that I should probably get out of there before he woke up. So I did." She shrugged as nonchalantly as she could as she reached for a piece of toast.

"Wha-huh? You left before he woke up? Am I getting this straight?"

Charlie chomped into her toast, eyeing her friend stubbornly. Gina's eyebrows rose toward her hairline.

"Why would you do that if last night was *fine?* Don't you want to see him again, see if it goes anywhere? You seemed really into him last night."

"Last night was last night. This morning is this morning."

"I don't really know what that means."

No way was Charlie about to give a blow-by-blow accounting of the reasoning behind her decision to flee. She knew Gina well enough to know that if she pointed out the fundamental disparity between godlike, perfect Rhys and plain-Jane her, her friend would spend the next hour trying to convince Charlie that she was beautiful and desirable and Rhys's equal in every way. Last night, with the aid of good lighting, great makeup, a sexy wardrobe and generous quantities of alcohol, she'd allowed herself to be sucked into the same illusion. This morning, in the brutal light of a new day, she knew better.

"It's really not a big deal. I had a nice time, it was what it was, and now it's over," she said firmly.

"So he'll simply wake up and find you gone?"

"He's going to wake up and heave a huge sigh of relief that I saved him an awkward morning-after conversation."

"You don't know that, Charlie."

Charlie smiled grimly. She knew that, absolutely. She'd seen herself in the bathroom mirror. She knew how the world worked. She'd known how the world worked ever since Billy Hendricks had refused to go into the closet with her during a game of Spin the Bottle when she was thirteen years old.

"I was thinking that we could go car shopping today, if you're up to it," Charlie said. "Is there some area around here with lots of car yards?"

"I take it that's your way of saying you don't want to talk about it anymore."

"Bingo."

"Okay. All right. If you want to drop it, we'll drop it. But I'd like it on the record that I think it's a damn shame. He seemed like a decent guy and he was really into you."

"Duly noted. So, tell me, who did you buy your car from? Should I go private or dealer? What do you think?"

This time Gina followed her lead, and by the

time the plate of toast had been cleared, they'd formulated a plan of attack. Gina took the tray to the kitchen, while Charlie dressed. She spotted her borrowed clothes scrunched in the corner as she was about to exit the room and took the time to rescue them, smoothing the cool mesh of the top with her hand before folding the satin trousers neatly.

She felt an odd sense of...not quite regret, but something similar to it as she remembered those few heady hours when she'd felt amazing and invincible and glamorous.

It may have ended with a whimper, not a bang, but seeing how the other half lived had been fun while it lasted. But as she'd said to Gina, last night was last night, and today was today.

She set the clothes on the end of the bed, collected her handbag and headed for the door. She would get the outfit dry-cleaned on Monday, then she would hand back her borrowed plumage and get on with carving out a new life for herself. After all, she was a grown-up and a realist. She knew the score.

RHYS WOKE with the mother and father of all hangovers beating down a door in his brain. Rolling over in bed, he pressed his hands against his aching skull for long minutes before making his way to the en suite to stick his mouth beneath the tap. He gulped enough water to fill a wading pool then sluiced a couple of big handfuls over his face. It was only when he lifted his head to inspect his bleary-eyed reflection that he remembered he hadn't come home alone last night.

"Charlie."

He stepped into the bedroom. The bed was empty. Frowning, he grabbed a towel and slung it around his waist.

"Charlie?" he called, walking into the living area.

It was empty. Which meant she really had gone without waking him up to say goodbye or leave her number or anything. Unless she'd left him a note…

It only took him a few seconds to spot the piece of paper and the two fifties sitting on his coffee table. He crossed the room and collected the paper.

I had a nice time. I hope this covers a new shirt.
Thanks, Charlie

He read the note three times, but each time he reached the same conclusion: *she'd blown him off.*

After one of the hottest nights of his life, she'd sneaked away in the early hours and left him a hundred bucks to cover his shirt. As though he was some down-on-his-luck gigolo who needed a handout.

Wow.

He screwed the note into a tight little ball. He'd thought they'd had a good time last night. A *great* time. He'd thought they'd really connected.

Sure, he'd been a little worse for wear, but not so drunk that he was making things up. He could remember it all.

The interested, engaged light in her eyes.

The way she'd stroked the stem of her glass unconsciously as she talked to him.

The way she'd tasted.

The smooth, warm satin of her skin.

The needful, heated rush of making love to her.

Yet she'd simply rolled out of bed and out of his life without so much as a backward glance. And no, the money for the shirt didn't count.

I had a nice time.

That was what she'd said. *Nice.* Was there a more lukewarm, halfhearted word in the English language? She might as well have patted him on the head and given him an elephant stamp for effort.

He strode into the kitchen and hit the button on his coffee machine. It would take at least forty minutes to warm up—the price he paid for his addiction to café-quality coffee—so he killed some time banging cupboards and drawers as he emptied the dishwasher. Then he stomped around a little more until his sense of humor reasserted itself.

Can you see yourself? You're acting like an outraged virgin. What's the big deal, anyway? You had sex and she left without turning it into a big production. You should be thanking her, buddy.

It was true. Except he didn't feel grateful. He felt disappointed. As though he'd been promised something spectacular and special, and instead had been given a big fat raspberry. And it wasn't just about the hot sex, either. Not entirely.

He liked her.

Yeah, well, get over it. You had a great time, she had a nice *time. She's gone, and life goes on.*

Another undeniable truth. He was on a roll, apparently.

He stood in the middle of his living room, mulling it over. Then he shrugged. Charlie had made her decision when she'd left his apartment without leaving him some way of contacting her. Whether he liked it or not, messages didn't come any clearer.

He scrubbed his face with his hands. Then he went to check on the coffee.

CHAPTER FOUR

THE NEXT EIGHT weeks flew by. Charlie's luggage arrived two days later than the airline had promised, but by that time she was so relieved to have her things that she could barely muster the energy to complain. After a week of deliberation and research, she bought a car, a small white SUV that was easy to park and maneuver. It took her longer to find somewhere to live, but she finally found a one-bedroom apartment two streets from Gina's house. She planned to buy eventually, but she needed to build up her business before a bank would consider her for a loan, and the twelve-month lease she'd secured gave her plenty of time to get to know the city better.

Her second-floor apartment was one of just six and featured high ceilings with decorative plasterwork, a mint-green-and-black bathroom that dated back to the thirties and a small but recently renovated kitchen. Most important, it boasted a neat study area off the bedroom that had become her new home office, a bonus that had sealed the deal for her even though the rent was slightly more than she'd hoped to pay.

With transportation and accommodation settled, she committed herself to the handful of start-up clients she'd generated before leaving the service, while also trying to drum up future business. Thanks to her background, she had in-depth knowledge in certain highly specialized areas and, as she'd hoped, her credentials opened a lot of doors amongst suppliers either already dealing with the military or hoping to.

By the time April rolled into May, she had work booked for the next two months, with prospects for more in the pipeline. She'd made friends with the woman across the hall and Gina's circle of friends had embraced her. Her initial qualms about civilian life faded as she found her feet and her days took on a rhythm of their own.

She was surviving. No, not simply surviving— she was thriving. She had a home all her own, she had a business that was on the uptick, she was putting down roots and forming new friendships. It was all good.

The only off note, if it could be called that, was the fact that every now and then, when her guard was down, a rogue, rebellious part of her brain wondered what might have happened if she'd hung around and waited for Rhys to wake up all those weeks ago.

Every time she caught her thoughts drifting in that direction she gave herself a mental slap and reminded herself that she was a realist and that she'd played it smart, leaving the way she had— even if it meant there might be a part of her that wondered "what if."

She was giving herself the Rhys Lecture, as she'd come to think of it, late one Friday afternoon in early May when a knock sounded. She was preparing dinner for herself and Gina and she put down the knife she'd been using before heading for the door.

"I come bearing gifts," Gina said. She was carrying a bottle of red wine and a white bakery box and looked as though she'd come straight from work.

Charlie made a show of checking her watch. "You're about two hours early for dinner. You know that, right?"

Gina shrugged. "I got off early. Plus, they'd just finished making these mini quiches for a function tonight—feel the box, they're still warm from the oven—and I knew you'd be up for some early piggery."

Charlie smiled wryly as she waved her friend inside. "You know me so well."

"I know your appetite, that's for sure." Gina dumped the bottle of wine on the counter and glanced at the chopping board. "So, what are we having?"

"Potatoes dauphinoise, green beans with garlic and coq au vin."

"God, I wish you were a man. I would so marry you."

"What say we hold off on the proposal until after we've eaten? This is all a bold experiment at this stage."

Cooking had never been one of Charlie's strong suits, but she was determined to improve now that she was personally responsible for all her own meals. The days of making excuses for living off canned and frozen meals were over.

"You want to eat these little puppies now or later?" Gina asked, nudging the bakery box suggestively.

"What do you think?"

"This is why we're friends," Gina said with a happy sigh.

Charlie grabbed two wineglasses and the bottle and followed Gina into the living room.

"You make me feel like such a slattern every time I come here." Gina dropped onto the white couch.

"Why?" Charlie asked, startled.

"Because your place is always so organized and clean and perfect," Gina said, one hand making a sweeping gesture.

Charlie glanced around at her black leather Eames chair and ottoman, white wool Florence Knoll sofa and midcentury glass-and-wood coffee table. Art books sat in a neat stack beside the open fireplace, arranged so their spines formed blocks of color, and a cluster of thick, creamy pillar candles sat in the empty grate. Apart from a handful of red-and-black throw cushions on the couch and a single white vase on the mantel, the room was bare.

"Is it too sterile?" She loved it like this—calm and clean—but she knew that her minimalist bent gave some people the heebie-jeebies.

"No. It's soothing, actually. I just don't know how you maintain it."

"Magical elves. With tiny hoovers and feather dusters."

"I knew you'd been holding out on me, bitch," Gina said amicably. "You need to send some of that elf magic my way."

Charlie smiled as she opened the wine and poured. "I'll see what I can do. But even elves have their standards, you know."

"Careful, or I won't share," Gina said, flipping off the lid. The smell of cream and cheese and bacon filled the room.

"Oh, boy, this is going to be good," Charlie said.

"Word," Gina agreed.

They dived into the box. They both made appreciative noises as they scoffed their first quiche before going back for seconds.

"So good," Charlie said around a mouthful of food.

"Tell me about it," Gina mumbled.

The phone rang, catching Charlie in the act of reaching for her third quiche. Rolling her eyes at Gina over the bad timing, she wiped her buttery fingers on a napkin and went to grab the phone.

A softly spoken woman identified herself as a nurse at the hospice where her father had spent his final days, and Charlie listened in bemusement as she explained that they'd discovered a previously overlooked box of personal belongings with her father's name on it in their storage room.

"I was under the impression my father had either given everything away or thrown it out," Charlie said.

"Well, there's a box that didn't go either way. What would you like us to do with it?"

Charlie gave the woman her address and credit card details to cover shipping the stuff from Melbourne, then ended the call and returned to Gina.

"What was that all about?" Gina asked as she sipped her wine.

Charlie explained briefly before changing the subject. There wasn't much to discuss, after all—

her father was dead, and the odds were good that the box contained a bunch of meaningless bits and pieces. Keith Anderson Long had been too organized and orderly a man for it to be any other way.

They continued to slurp their wine and made each other laugh with anecdotes from their respective days as they consumed the pastries. Finally the box was empty and Gina pushed herself to her feet.

"Fantastic. I'm now going to loll on your couch and complain about how full I am and how I couldn't possibly fit another thing in while you finish making dinner," she said as she headed for the bathroom.

"Or I could put you to work, stringing the beans and whatnot."

"Hard-hearted wench," Gina said, her voice echoing down the short hallway.

Charlie smiled as she sat back in her chair, sipping her wine.

"Hey, Charlie—my stupid period has come early. Can I borrow a tampon?" Gina called, her voice muffled by the closed door.

"Sure. In the cupboard behind the mirror."

There was a short pause then Gina called out again. "There's nothing here."

Charlie set down her glass and stood. "Did you

have a boy look or a girl look?" she asked as she headed for the bathroom.

"I had a girl look. A really good one. Smarty-pants."

Charlie paused outside the bathroom. "You decent?"

"Give me five secs. Okay, come in."

Charlie entered. Gina was standing in front of the open bathroom cabinet, a frown on her face.

"I dare you to find a tampon in there."

"Watch." Charlie stepped toward the cabinet, one hand already raised in anticipation of finding what she was looking for. She frowned as her gaze scanned over toiletry and medicinal products and failed to find the familiar pink-and-white box.

"That's weird," she said. "They should be in here. I always make sure I restock after my period."

"Guess you must have forgotten last month, then," Gina said lightly. "No worries. I've probably got one lurking in the bottom of my handbag."

She slipped past Charlie, who remained staring at the bathroom cabinet, her frown intensifying as she tried to remember when she'd had her last period...and couldn't.

"Don't be stupid," she muttered to herself.

She must be getting mixed up somehow. She

could remember having her period in Perth because the cramps had come at exactly the wrong time. Two weeks later, she'd cleared out the flat she'd been sharing with another female officer, packed her bags and flown to Sydney.

And she hadn't had her period since.

And in the interim, she'd had sex with Rhys-the-unforgettable. *Three times in the one night.*

Adrenaline fired in her belly, sending a shock wave through her body. She took a step backward, appalled by the thought that had snaked its way into her brain.

"Told you I'd have one," Gina said as she returned. "Hey. What's wrong? You're pale."

Charlie took another step backward and sank onto the edge of the tub.

"What's the failure rate for condoms?" Her voice sounded as though it was coming from a long way away. Cleveland, perhaps. Or maybe Moscow.

"I don't know. Not high. One or two percent, maybe?" Gina was still frowning, but suddenly her eyes rounded and her eyebrows headed for her hairline. "Oh, my God. Tell me you're not thinking what I think you're thinking."

Charlie looked at her friend, her mind busy doing the math and getting the same answer over and over.

"I've missed two periods. I've been so busy

getting everything sorted that I didn't even notice. That's why there are no tampons in the cupboard."

Gina swore and sank onto the bathtub beside her. There was a moment of profound silence as they both processed their own thoughts.

"Okay. First things first—before we hit the panic button, we need to know what we're panicking about." Gina looked at her watch. "It's only four-thirty. The pharmacy around the corner should still be open."

"Good idea," Charlie said. She pushed herself to her feet. A wave of anxious dizziness hit her and she sat again.

"I'll go," Gina said instantly. "You stay here. Don't start freaking yet, okay? I'll run all the way."

"Okay," Charlie said meekly.

Gina's hand dropped onto her shoulder, warm and reassuring. "It could just be stress. Changing your life is a big deal."

Charlie nodded. Gina gave her a quick squeeze before she slipped past. Charlie stared at a cracked floor tile, her mind ricocheting from one thought to the next.

If she was pregnant…

But she couldn't be. They'd used condoms. A new one each time…

But condoms failed. That's why they weren't

one hundred percent foolproof. Still, what were the odds of one of them failing and it being the exact right point in her cycle…?

Big. Too big. Way too big. Huge. She couldn't even calculate the probability it was so large. She probably had a better chance of winning the lottery.

And yet she'd missed two periods.

"Oh, God," she said, bracing her elbows on her knees, her head dropping into her hands.

She couldn't be pregnant. She simply couldn't. She'd just started her own business. She'd barely unpacked from the move. She was single, in a new city, essentially unemployed if anything went wrong with her business.

She moaned, digging her fingers into her skull. *Please let it be stress. Please let it be stress. Please let it be stress.*

The front door slammed and when she looked up Gina was standing before her, a bag in hand. "Okay. I have no idea how these things work, but I'm sure we can figure it out."

She handed over the bag and Charlie pulled out a slickly branded box. Her hands were shaking so much that she couldn't pull the flap from the slot and Gina took it from her.

"Whatever happens, we'll work it out, okay, Charlie?"

Charlie nodded, enormously grateful for her

friend's use of the plural even though she knew in her heart of hearts that if she really was pregnant, the responsibility would land squarely on her shoulders, no matter what she decided to do.

"Okay. We have instructions," Gina said as she pulled a folded sheet from the box.

They pored over the instructions for a few minutes, then Gina handed Charlie a cellophane-wrapped stick.

"Do your thing," she said.

Charlie managed a small smile, only letting it drop when her friend left the room. Her stomach knotted with dread, she pulled down her jeans and sat on the loo. For a moment she thought she was going to have to try later, but her body finally came to the party. She followed the instructions and then set the stick on the edge of the vanity while she flushed, pulled up her jeans and washed her hands.

"Okay," she called.

Gina opened the door and passed Charlie her glass, now brimming with red wine. "For courage."

Charlie stared at it. "I don't know if I should. If it's positive…"

She couldn't quite bring herself to say the word *pregnant* yet. But if she was, then alcohol was on the no-go list. Especially in bucket-like quantities.

"Shit. You're right. Sorry."

Gina set down the glass on the vanity and they both sat on the edge of the tub.

"I take it that means you wouldn't consider a termination, then?" Gina asked.

Charlie frowned. Her brain hadn't gotten that far yet.

Or maybe it had, since she'd been so quick to reject the wine.

"If it seemed like the best thing to do, I would."

"But…?"

"I don't know. When I was younger, I wouldn't have thought twice about it. There was no way I would have been able to cope then. But now… it might not be convenient. It might not be easy or wise or planned or anything. But I could do it now." She spoke slowly, thinking out loud. "I think I could be an okay mum. And I've always imagined that one day I'd have kids."

Although the image of herself with a child had always been part of some nebulous future-vision of her life that incorporated a man she loved, the whole notion was so far off and distant in her mind that it was barely in focus.

"I think you'd be a great mum. But it's hard yards doing it all on your own."

"I know." Charlie studied the back of her hands, mulling things over.

"You don't have to make any decisions right

now," Gina said. "Let's take this one step at a time."

Charlie glanced at the white stick on the vanity. "Do you think it's been five minutes yet?"

Gina checked her watch. "Right on the knocker."

Charlie continued to stare at the stick without moving. She could feel her heart pounding inside her chest and her palms were suddenly sweaty. Funny that she'd felt almost exactly the same way when she'd been flirting with Rhys all those weeks ago, hoping he felt the same way she did.

Not funny ha-ha, obviously. Funny weird.

Funny scary.

"Want me to…?" Gina offered.

"I'll do it." Charlie roused herself and reached for the test. Her fingers closed around the thumb grip and she lifted it. For a moment the light hit the stick so directly that she couldn't see anything. Then she blinked and she was staring at two pink lines.

All the air left her lungs in a rush.

She was pregnant.

Oh, wow.

She was pregnant.

An elbow dug into her ribs.

"Don't forget to breathe, okay?" Gina said.

Charlie realized she hadn't inhaled for a while and she sucked in a big lungful of air.

"You want a glass of water?"

"No. I'm okay. I just… This is surreal. God. Maybe you should pinch me."

Gina's arm slid around her shoulders, warm and reassuring. A human anchor tethering her to reality.

"This is the last thing I ever imagined happening to me," Charlie said. She couldn't take her eyes off the two lines. "I mean, I could hardly get a guy to look at me in high school. Then I meet Rhys and we have one night together—one measly night—and now I'm pregnant? We had sex *three times*. We used protection. It just doesn't seem possible."

"I know, but the stick says it is." Gina's arm tightened around her shoulders. "Come on. Let's go into the living room. Sitting on the tub like this is making my bum numb."

Charlie allowed her friend to usher her onto the couch. Charlie tried to pummel her shocked brain into action. She needed to think. She needed to strategize.

"We have a few options before us, Ms. Long," Gina said as she sat beside Charlie. "We can talk this to death. I can distract you with fripperies and foolishness. Or I can go home and come back tomorrow and we can talk this to death."

Charlie looked at her friend. She honestly had no idea what to do or say next.

Gina smiled sympathetically. "I'm going to go with option C, because you look as though you've been hit by a truck. I'll go home, but I want you to call me, no matter what time it is, if you need to talk, okay? No matter what. There is no such thing as convention or common courtesy in a crisis."

"Thank you," Charlie said simply, because suddenly being alone felt exactly like what she needed.

Gina gave her a big hug. "I'm warning you, if I don't get a phone call at one in the morning I am going to be so disappointed."

"I'll do my best."

Charlie saw her friend out and found herself in the kitchen looking at the half-prepared meal she'd planned. Without really thinking about it, she picked up the knife and started to slice the tops and tails off the remaining green beans. When she'd finished with the beans she moved on to the garlic and shallots and potatoes. And all the while her brain was whirling away.

The idea that there was a child growing inside her right now made her feel almost giddy with disbelief and anxiety—but underneath the shock and fear, buried deep, there was also the tiniest tickle of something else.

All her life she'd essentially been alone. Her mother had died giving birth to Charlie, and her father had been an undemonstrative man, gruff and withdrawn at the best of times. He'd demanded a lot of her and given little back in terms of affection or approval, a dynamic she'd managed to repeat in the two serious relationships she'd had in her life so far.

But a baby didn't have its own agenda. All a baby wanted was love and warmth and food and security, and she had all that to give and more. As she'd said to Gina, she thought she had it in her to be a good mother.

But that didn't stop her from being terrified by the prospect. In a perfect world, the test would have confirmed Gina's stress diagnosis and she would have been drinking a toast to a close call with her friend.

Charlie stared at the potato peelings and bean ends strewn across the counter. Since when had the world—her world, at least—ever been perfect?

She cleared off the counter and put the prepared vegetables in the fridge. Maybe Gina would be free for dinner tomorrow night.

A single question spun around her mind as she worked.

What do I want? What do I want?

She wasn't naive enough to assume that a termination would be the easy option. She knew herself well enough to know that the decision would be one that stayed with her for some time, should she choose that route. She didn't believe it was a decision that any woman made with blithe, carefree indifference. But definitely her dilemma would end with a visit to a family planning clinic. If she chose to keep the baby, the challenges would only become more and more profound.

What do I want? I want for this not to have happened. For me not to be in this horrible situation, between a rock and a hard place. I want to hit the reverse button and go back in time and erase the moment when being pregnant was even a possibility.

She ate toast for dinner, sitting on the couch staring at the TV. She had no idea what she watched. Afterward she went to bed and stared at the ceiling. Finally she fell asleep.

She woke in the small hours, her heart pounding. She sat up in bed and reached blindly for the phone. Gina had said to call. She was going to take her friend at her word.

"Charlie. You okay?" Gina asked the second she answered the phone.

Charlie didn't need to ask how Gina knew it was her.

"I'm going to keep the baby."

The decision had been there in her mind the

moment she'd surfaced from sleep. Maybe it had always been there, she simply hadn't been ready to acknowledge it.

"Okay. Good. Congratulations, C. You want me to come over?"

Charlie looked at the clock. It was five in the morning. Her natural inclination was to lie and deny herself, as she always did, but she needed her friend right now.

"Would you mind?"

"Be there in five."

Gina arrived in her pajamas, a sweater and running shoes, her hair pulled into two fluffy pigtails. Charlie handed her a cup of coffee and a plate of toast and they made themselves comfortable on the couch.

"It took me a while, but I realized that deep down inside, there was a part of me that didn't think this was the worst thing that could happen. Not perfect, you know, but not the worst. I think I can do this."

"Of course you can. You can do anything you set your mind to," Gina said.

"Thanks for the vote of confidence."

"I'm not pumping you up, C. You're one of the smartest, most resourceful and determined people I know. I know you can do this. If you want to."

"I do. It's not what I would have planned, but..."

Gina nodded, taking a big bite of toast. "So…
what about Rhys?" she asked around her mouthful.

Charlie blinked, dragging her mind away from
thoughts of child care and medical bills. "Sorry?"

"Rhys. What about him?"

Charlie stared at her friend, the meaning
behind her words slowly sinking in. Because she
hadn't made this baby on her own. It was Rhys's
child, as well as her own.

"Oh, God," she said. Bizarre as it seemed, she
hadn't thought about him once.

"Are you going to tell him?" Gina asked.

Charlie's response was utterly instinctive and
out her mouth before she could even think it over.
"Yes. Absolutely."

She said it fiercely, almost angrily, and Gina
held up a hand.

"Just asking the question," she said soothingly.

"Sorry." Charlie rubbed her forehead. "My
mum died when I was born. If it's at all possible, I want this baby to have two parents." There
was a lump in her throat merely saying it out
loud. Ridiculous after all these years, but in many
ways, her mother's absence had defined her life.
Certainly it had defined her childhood. It wasn't
something she talked about a lot, and it wasn't
something she'd ever shared with Gina before.

"I didn't know that. You never talk about her."

"I didn't know her."

Gina hesitated a beat. "Look, I hate to be the voice of doom here, but you realize that Rhys might not be thrilled to hear from you, right? Setting aside the fact that we have to work out how to find the guy in the first place, this is going to be a huge bolt from the blue for him."

"It's not something I was expecting myself, you know."

"Sure. I'm simply flagging it in case he's an asshole about it, so you can be prepared. Legally, he has to support the baby, of course. But that doesn't mean he can't be sneaky."

"He didn't seem like an asshole."

Charlie shook her head as soon as she heard her own words. She didn't know anything about Rhys, not really. She knew he worked in I.T. and that he had a low, mellow voice and that when he looked at her he made her feel as though she was the center of the universe. But she didn't know his last name, and she didn't know what his childhood had been like, if he had siblings, what his politics were, if he was religious, if he was good or bad with money, if he was loyal or kind or generous...

She felt sick as the full import of her own thoughts struck home. She'd made a baby with a stranger. For the rest of her life, her world and his were going to be inextricably entwined. And she knew nothing about him.

"I need to work out how to contact him," she said, forcing herself to focus on the practicalities of the situation.

"Do you remember his address?"

Charlie thought for a moment, but her mind was blank. She'd been so focused on getting inside Rhys's apartment that night that she hadn't paid much attention to anything else.

"No. But I think if I went over there and walked around I could probably find the apartment block again."

"Okay. Then I guess it's a matter of hanging around till he comes home," Gina suggested.

The idea of lurking in the street to confront the father of her child felt incredibly sordid and sad to Charlie, but she was well aware that she didn't have the luxury of being proud at this point. Not if she wanted her child to know his or her father.

And she did.

"I don't suppose you remember the name of his company at all?" Gina asked.

Charlie frowned. "It was something to do with an animal. Right?"

Gina shrugged apologetically. "Sorry. I remember him mentioning it once or twice, but the details didn't stick."

Charlie's frown deepened as a memory tickled

at the back of her mind. It was something to do with his apartment. Something she'd seen there. A business card? Something to do with a logo or writing or something…

She shot to her feet suddenly. "My bag. I need my bag." She glanced left and right but couldn't see it.

"Where do you usually leave it, creature of habit?" Gina asked.

Charlie turned on her heel and almost ran into the bedroom. Her bag hung by its strap from the inside door handle. She grabbed it and returned to the living room. Without looking at Gina, she emptied the contents onto the coffee table. A handful of spare change rattled onto the glass, a couple of sticks of chewing gum, three pens, a small memo pad, her wallet, a pair of sunglasses, a couple of hair ties…and a small, crumpled ball of paper.

She snatched it up.

"Share, please. What is it you're looking so excited about?" Gina asked.

"I wrote him a note before I left. But the first one was no good, so I threw it into my bag and wrote another."

"Only you could write two drafts of a morning-after note," Gina said fondly.

Charlie found an opening in the ball and used her thumb to tease it wider. Gina leaned forward as Charlie smoothed the piece of paper flat on the table.

Charlie closed her eyes with relief when she saw the graphic in the top right corner—a soaring falcon, with the name Falcon I.T. and two phone numbers printed beneath it, as well as a street address.

"That's the easy part sorted, then. Now you just have to ring him and tell him the big news."

Charlie's stomach tensed. Whether she liked it or not—whether Rhys liked it or not—they'd made a baby that night eight weeks ago. He needed to know he was going to be a father, and she needed to know what kind of man he was.

"Couple more hours and he should be at his desk," Gina said.

"I don't think it's the kind of conversation you have over the phone. I can't call out of the blue and tell him something this big."

"What are you going to do, then? Go over to his office and tell him in person?"

Charlie thought about it for a few seconds. "Well, yeah. I guess I am."

"Man. You have balls of steel, my friend. I would totally make a phone call. Better yet, I'd send an email."

"I want to start things on the right foot. If there *is* a right foot in this situation."

"I'm not sure there is. But I'll come with you if you like."

Charlie felt a rush of affection for her friend. From the moment they'd met in recruit training, Gina had been a rock, funny and loyal and always on Charlie's side.

"Thank you," she said, her chest tight with emotion. "You're the best."

"So are you. And we'll get through this, don't worry. I'm a pretty good auntie, if I do say so myself. I bet my sister's got a bunch of old baby stuff you could have, too. And there are heaps of parent groups around here."

Charlie nodded, unable to speak past the lump in her throat. She was having a baby. Unplanned, unexpected—but not unwanted, surprising as that was to realize.

How…extraordinary.

RHYS WALKED to the terrace railing and looked out over the bright blue waters of Sydney Harbour. Behind him, the Finger Wharf stretched toward the shore. He could hear the real estate agent talking on his phone on the other side of the terrace, but he tuned out the man's voice as he gazed across the water. It was a clear day and the wind was brisk, the force of it making his suit jacket billow behind him. He focused on a luxury yacht cutting its way across the harbor, the Manly ferry laboring in the distance behind it.

This was a great view. One of the best in Sydney. It had a price tag to match, too—but Rhys's gut told him there was a deal to be done here. The agent had called him this morning with the news that an apartment had come up in the Finger Wharf complex. The vendor wanted a quick sale—something to do with a divorce settlement—and Rhys had shuffled his appointments in order to make time for a viewing.

He'd known from the moment he walked in the door that this was exactly the kind of place he'd been looking for, but he'd kept his poker face on as he toured the three bedrooms and open-plan living area. Now he did some rapid mental calculations. He'd need to talk to the bank to confirm their willingness to extend his credit, but he was pretty sure he could stretch to within ninety percent of the price tag on this place. And if he couldn't negotiate the agent down ten percent, he had no business being in business, full stop.

"So, what do you think?" the agent asked.

Rhys turned to face him. "Yeah, it's nice." He deliberately kept his voice uninflected, his face expressionless.

"Pretty amazing view."

"Sure." Rhys turned and gazed at the neighboring properties. Then he shrugged, doing his damnedest to appear nonchalant. "What's the vendor looking for again?"

The real estate agent named a figure in the high one millions.

Rhys nodded. "Let me think about it and I'll get back to you."

"Don't want to leave it too long—this one's going to go fast," the agent said with a toothy smile.

Rhys didn't bother responding. He wasn't about to be pressured into anything, certainly not a decision as big as this one.

"Thanks for the heads-up," he said as he walked to the door. "I'll talk to you later."

The agent hurried to catch up with him. "So we'll speak tonight, yeah? What time would you prefer?"

"I'll call you," Rhys said.

He stepped out of the apartment and onto the plush carpet of the suspended walkway that led to the elevators. He waited until he was safely in the elevator car before allowing himself to grin.

With a bit of luck, he could be calling this place home in a few weeks' time. If the bank was willing to play ball.

He was pretty sure they would be. The Gainsborough contract was about to kick in, and Greg was in the process of wooing another big hotel chain. Their existing clients were all ticking over…

It was all coming together. Which meant he was perfectly positioned to swoop down on this place, after years of making do in a too-small apartment full of hand-me-down furniture. The elevator chimed to announce his arrival on the ground floor. Hands in his pockets, he walked slowly toward the shoreline, past bobbing yachts and wheeling seagulls and glinting water. His phone chirruped as he reached the commercial portion of the complex where restaurants and cafés spilled out on to the wharf. He pulled his phone from his pocket. The text was from Greg, checking a figure with him. He punched in the numbers his partner was seeking, then increased his pace to a brisk walk. Time to get back to work.

It took him fifteen minutes to make his way to Falcon's offices at Bondi Junction. He made a call to the bank as he drove, leaving a message for his business banker, Peter. Sometime between now and this evening he needed to decide whether he was going to put an offer in for the wharf apartment, and he couldn't do that without Peter's imprimatur.

He parked in the garage beneath the building and made his way up to the fourth floor. He could see their receptionist, Julie, talking on her headset as he approached the double glass doors to reception. There were a couple of people in the waiting area and he checked his watch. He didn't have any appointments until midday and it was only ten-thirty, so they were probably for Greg.

"Yo, Julie," he said as he pushed through the glass doors.

"Rhys. You're back." Julie shot a glance toward the waiting area, her brow furrowed.

"I am. Like I said I would be." He reached for the handful of phone messages with his name scrawled across the top.

"I'm expecting some people at midday, okay?" He headed for his office.

"Wait," Julie said, stopping him in his tracks. She lowered her voice. "There's someone here to see you. I told her that you were busy and to leave her name so you could set up an appointment, but she insisted on waiting."

He was aware of movement in the waiting area. He glanced over and saw a tall, slender woman rising to her feet. She was dressed conservatively in tailored navy trousers and a navy dress shirt, her hair pulled into a neat ponytail. Her features were small and nondescript and his gaze slid off her face and back to Julie's.

"I'm sorry," the receptionist said anxiously.

"It's fine," Rhys reassured her.

The woman walked toward him and he put

on his best professional smile and turned to deal with what was almost certainly an unsolicited pitch for the business's telephone contract or office supplies.

He went very still as he found himself staring into warm, cinnamon-brown eyes.

"Charlie."

CHAPTER FIVE

SHE WAS VERY PALE. His gaze raked her from head to toe, taking in her businesslike—almost uniformlike—clothes, the sensible shoes, the no-nonsense hairdo.

She looked completely different from the woman he'd spent the night with two months ago. That woman was sultry and lithe and sexy. This woman looked as though she'd be great at doing his taxes.

His gaze returned to her face. She was watching him closely, her expression guarded.

"Rhys," she said. Her voice caught on the single word and she cleared her throat. "I'm sorry to drop in on you like this, but do you have a moment to talk?"

He was still trying to catch up with the idea that she was here. That after dashing off a note then leaving his apartment in the early hours, she was suddenly at his place of business, wanting to talk.

"I was pretty sure I would never see you again."

It sounded like an accusation and it was his turn to clear his throat.

Her hands were clutched together at her waist. "Is there somewhere we can talk?" she asked.

He glanced over his shoulder. Julie was watching them with avid eyes. She was young, as were a lot of his team. He didn't particularly want the entire staff knowing about his personal life. Especially since most of them had been at Café Sydney the night he met Charlie.

"There's a coffee shop across the road."

He automatically took Charlie's elbow to guide her to the door, but after a few steps she slipped free. He eyed her as he hit the button for the elevator.

"What's going on, Charlie?"

She glanced up the hallway toward the stairwell, almost as though she was looking for an escape route.

"Maybe we should wait until we're across the street."

The elevator arrived. She stepped inside and he followed. He was getting over the shock of seeing her so unexpectedly, his brain starting to work again.

It had been two months. And since she was the one who had walked out on him, he guessed she must have a powerful reason for suddenly making contact with him. A number of options sprang to mind and he didn't like any of them.

Her head was bowed, and his gaze gravitated to the delicate hollow at the nape of her neck. He'd kissed her there, pushing her hair to one side. She'd shivered and pressed her body against his...

He shoved his hands into his suit pockets and focused on the floor indicator. Now was not the time for a trip down memory lane.

She stepped into the foyer when they arrived at the ground floor, shooting him an uncertain look over her shoulder. He took the lead, directing her outside and diagonally across the road to the no-frills coffee shop where he usually grabbed lunch.

Jenna and Carl both looked up from behind the counter as he entered, Carl lifting a hand in greeting. Rhys gave them a tight smile before heading for the corner table. Charlie pulled out her own chair before he could do it for her. Her hands were shaking, a fact she tried to disguise by hiding them beneath the table. The edgy feeling that had been creeping up on him intensified as he looked at her.

Charlie shifted in her chair. "Um, how have you been?"

"What's going on, Charlie?"

She closed her eyes for a long moment. Then she opened them and looked him dead in the eye. "I'm pregnant."

"What?" He sat back in his chair as though he'd been pushed. "That's not possible. We used condoms. Lots of them."

"I know. I'm still pregnant. Eight weeks and two days, to be exact."

He stared at her. His brain was an empty echoing space. He couldn't think.

"I've done two tests, and I've got a doctor's appointment tomorrow afternoon to confirm it. But I haven't had my period for two months so I don't think there's much doubt." She offered a weak smile.

"But we used condoms," he said, leaning forward, as though he could drive home the truth of his words with the force of his body language.

"Condoms are only ninety-five to ninety-eight percent effective," she said. "I looked it up."

Rhys shook his head. "No. This can't be right. No one has sex three times and gets pregnant."

She sat a little straighter. The tendons showed in her neck and, when she swallowed, the sound was audible. He studied her small, neat features, some distant part of him surprised anew by how different the reality of Charlie was from his memory of her. But maybe he shouldn't be surprised. It had been a long time, after all. And they'd known each other only a few hours. In effect, the woman sitting across the table was a complete stranger, despite the fact that he'd been incredibly intimate with her.

Despite the fact that, according to her, she was pregnant with his child.

He couldn't process it, it was so huge. So life changing.

"Are you sure?" he asked, thinking out loud. "I mean, are you sure it's mine?"

She blinked a couple of times. "Yes. I'm sure." She was blushing, the rush of blood turning her pale skin an unattractive red.

"I take it you're planning on keeping it?" he asked.

Because she wouldn't be here otherwise, would she? There was no point telling him if she'd already made the decision to terminate.

"Yes. It's not something I was exactly planning for... But there it is."

"And what do you want from me? I mean apart from money, obviously. I assume you have it all worked out."

This was not part of his plan. Not even close. A baby with a woman whose last name he didn't even know. A child who would be a part of him forever.

"I don't want your money." Her expression remained neutral—polite—but there was a steely edge to her voice. "I thought you deserved the courtesy of knowing you were going to be a father. I thought it might be something you'd be interested in."

"Right. Because it's something I've thought about a lot."

She gave him a long, steady look. "I understand that you're shocked. But this is not my fault. It's not yours, either. It's an accident."

"It's a freaking nightmare, that's what it is. I signed up for one night of fun, not a baby."

She flinched. Her movements jerky, she reached for her handbag and pulled a business card from the inside pocket.

"If you need to contact me for anything, you can reach me on either of those numbers. I'll let you know when I'm due once I have confirmation from the doctor."

She was standing before she'd finished speaking, sliding her handbag over her shoulder.

"Charlie. Wait." He shot to his feet.

She paused, her posture stiff as she waited for him to say more. He knew he'd been rude, that he hadn't said any of the things a better man would have said under the circumstances—that he'd be there for her, that they would work this out, that she'd be okay. He knew that he was being graceless and immature and small.

"This isn't what I was expecting," he said.

That didn't come close to explaining the confused cocktail of anger, outrage, guilt, frustration and shock that had taken up residence in his gut.

She didn't say a word, simply turned on her heel and headed for the door.

This time he let her go. Once she'd disappeared from sight, he slumped onto the chair and closed his eyes for a long, heavy moment.

This was not how he'd imagined becoming a father. Not that he'd put a lot of energy into imagining parenthood and all its accoutrements—a wife, a family, a mortgage on a place in the suburbs and a white picket fence. He'd been too focused on the business, on achieving the goals he'd set for himself. He'd worked hard, and if he had any plan at all for his personal life, it had been to enjoy the fruits of his labors before tying himself down with a family. An apartment on the wharf, a sleek European performance car, travel to interesting, sophisticated places… All of it a million miles removed from the cramped three-bedroom home he'd grown up in, the hand-me-down clothes, the pretend holidays camping in the backyard because his parents' salaries as teachers hadn't covered real holidays for two adults and five kids.

Barely an hour ago, he'd been standing on the wharf at Woolloomooloo, the first part of his dream almost within reach. Now, if Charlie was to be believed, he was going to be a father.

His thoughts flashed to the moment when he'd questioned her certainty that he was the father of her child. He remembered the way she'd colored, clearly deeply embarrassed. But she hadn't broken eye contact as she'd confirmed her certainty.

He pressed the heels of his hands to his eyes.

He believed her. He didn't know why—he didn't know her from a bar of soap—but he believed she was speaking the truth.

Which meant everything he knew about his life was out the window. Just like that.

Shit. Shit, shit, shit.

"You want a coffee? Something to eat?" a voice asked beside him.

Rhys dropped his hands and glanced at Carl. "No. Thanks. I need to get to the office." He stood and pulled his wallet from his back pocket.

Carl laughed. "What are you doing? You didn't have anything."

Somehow, Rhys mustered a smile. "Right. Of course. I'll see you later."

He headed for the door. He had clients due in an hour's time. He needed to clear his head, put on his game face.

And somehow, he had to make sense of this bombshell. Find a way to learn to live with it. Because he was going to be a father.

Bloody hell.

CHARLIE MADE IT as far as the parking lot before she threw up. Hands gripping her thighs above her knees, she bent over and lost what little she'd managed to eat for breakfast beneath a straggly-looking gum tree. She remained hunched over for a few seconds afterward, in case there was more to come, but her stomach had apparently had its say. She spat a couple of times to clear her mouth, then walked to her car. She'd left a bottle of water on the passenger seat and she rinsed her mouth out several times before returning to the tree to wash away the mess she'd made.

She hadn't experienced any morning sickness so far, but she suspected her nausea had more to do with anxiety and anger than with the pregnancy.

I signed up for one night of fun, not a baby.

Her lip curled. What an ass. What a selfish, immature, thoughtless ass. It had taken her the whole weekend to psych herself up to approach him and she'd had such high hopes as she'd waited in his reception area. Nothing ridiculous or overblown—she wasn't an idiot—but she'd hoped that he'd be reasonable, after the initial shock of her bombshell had passed. She'd hoped that he'd express some interest in the baby. That the warm, funny, clever man she remembered from that night hadn't been a figment of her imagination and that somehow, like her, he'd see the good in this situation.

But he hadn't been warm or funny. He'd been shocked. Or maybe horrified was the better description. And he'd been angry, so angry. As though she'd deliberately set out to dupe him into becoming a father. As though she'd tried to trap him.

"They were your condoms, buddy. I'm the one who ought to be angry with you, not the other way round," she told her windshield as she made her way home to Balmain.

She tried to hang on to her anger, but slowly it seeped away and only disappointment remained.

She wanted her baby to have both parents. She wanted him or her to feel loved and secure and safe. But apparently the baby would have to look elsewhere for that. Apparently, Charlie was going to have to dig deep and provide her child with everything all on her own.

Her hands tightened on the steering wheel as nerves fluttered in her belly.

It wasn't that she didn't think she was capable. She wouldn't have decided to keep the baby if she thought otherwise. But she wanted to give this baby so much. She wanted his or her life to be full to overflowing with all the things Charlie had missed out on as a child—unconditional love and patience and support and approval. She wanted to be worthy of the tiny life growing inside her, and it would have been so much easier to be and do all those things knowing she had someone else backing her up.

The moment she felt herself slumping in her seat, she straightened her spine and lifted her chin. If the army had taught her anything, it was that mental toughness was as important as physical fitness. She had always been disciplined, and she wasn't about to give up the habits of a lifetime now that she needed mental toughness and discipline more than ever.

So what if Rhys Walker was a dick? She could do this without him. She *would* do this without him.

She parked her car and walked up the two flights to her door. The first thing she did when she entered her apartment was head for the bathroom. She brushed her teeth and rinsed with mouthwash, then glanced at herself in the bathroom mirror.

She hadn't allowed herself to think about that moment when she'd first set eyes on Rhys again, but as she looked at herself in the bathroom mirror it was impossible not to remember those few humiliating seconds when he'd turned toward the waiting area and his gaze had skimmed over her indifferently, clearly finding nothing to hold his interest. She'd understood immediately that he hadn't recognized her without Gina's clothes and clever makeup—and that without all the above she held little appeal for him. It was only when she'd practically been in his face that he'd made the connection between her and that night eight weeks ago. She'd briefly thought she would have to introduce herself. An added humiliation she'd been grateful to avoid.

In the mirror, her lips formed a straight, uncompromising line.

For weeks she'd been torturing herself by wondering what might have happened if she'd girded her loins and stayed that morning instead of making a strategic retreat. Now she knew. And for the rest of her life she would be everlastingly grateful that she'd had the smarts to get out before Rhys had woken up.

Yeah, what a save. Now you're bound to him for life because you've made a baby with him. That's so much better. Congratulations.

Charlie turned away from the mirror and walked to the study. She'd been working on an illustration for a client's logo this morning and she dived into the file, grateful for the fact that her work was so absorbing. She'd spent far too much time in her own head recently and she needed a break from the constant cycle of worry, wonder and yet more worry.

As she'd told herself hundreds of times over

the past seventy-two hours, the world was full of single parents, most of whom coped just fine. There was no reason she should be any different.

She was so successful at distracting herself that it wasn't until the courier arrived with her father's belongings that she registered she'd missed lunch. She was in no mood to open the box and deal with its contents now, so she pushed it into the corner beside her desk and promised herself she'd look at it first thing tomorrow.

She walked into the kitchen to make herself something to eat. Her stomach had settled since the incident in the parking lot and she decided on poached eggs with whole-grain toast and a side of spinach for some iron. She was dishing up when the phone rang. She leaned across to snag the phone with one hand while pulling open the drawer and extracting cutlery with the other.

"Charlie speaking," she said, tucking the phone between her ear and shoulder so she could reach for the plate.

"Charlie, it's Rhys. Can you talk?"

The cutlery slipped from her suddenly nerveless fingers and hit the counter with a clatter. It took her a moment to get her voice to work.

"Yes. I can talk." She hadn't expected to hear from him again. Not so soon, anyway.

"I wanted to apologize for this morning. I said some things I hadn't really thought through…"

His voice sounded very low and she pressed the receiver against her ear to catch everything he said.

"Can we start again? Or try again, at least?"

She frowned. "Try again?"

"Can we talk? This is a huge thing, and we need to sort a bunch of stuff out."

She stared at the worn wooden floor. A part of her wanted to say no, to tell him that he'd had his chance. But she knew that was her pride—and her hurt feelings—speaking. He was the father of her child. She needed to do everything in her power to give him the opportunity to be a part of her child's life.

"When?"

"What are you doing now?"

She glanced at her rapidly cooling lunch. "Nothing that can't wait."

"Where would you like to meet?"

She thought about giving him her address, but she didn't want him in her personal space, for a variety of reasons. Then she caught herself. If they were going to have any kind of relationship, they needed to understand one another.

"Why don't you come to my place," she said before she could talk herself out of it.

"What's the address?"

She gave it to him along with instructions about where to park.

"I should be about twenty minutes or so," he said.

"Sure."

"And, Charlie? Thanks for this."

She put down the phone. For a long moment, she simply stared blankly into space. Then she gave herself a mental shake. Her food was luke-warm at best, but she sat at the small table she'd squeezed into the corner of the kitchen and ate every bite, slowly and methodically. She was eating for two now, after all, and she didn't have the luxury of being lazy about meals anymore. Just as she didn't have the luxury of protecting herself or her pride, either.

Once she was finished, she rinsed her plate and set it on the drainer to dry. The urge to head to the bathroom to check her appearance was almost overwhelming, but she resisted. Rhys was not coming to see her. Besides, she already knew how she looked—the same as she always did: plain. Fussing over her hair wasn't going to change that.

A knock sounded at the door. She paused briefly in the hallway to compose herself. Then she reached for the lock and opened the door.

"Hi." Rhys offered Charlie a small, nervous smile.

She didn't smile in return. Instead, she took a

step backward and gestured for him to enter her apartment. Given the tenor of their last meeting, her attitude wasn't exactly surprising.

He'd finally broken down after lunch and told Greg what was going on. His business partner had been suitably gobsmacked and outraged by the shitty hand life had dealt Rhys, and Rhys had been grateful for Greg's quick and easy understanding of exactly how he was feeling. But a strange thing had happened as Greg paced, expanding on how unlucky Rhys was and suggesting that he demand a paternity test before he hand over a cent and mourning the loss of his previously carefree bachelor existence.

Rhys had felt ashamed.

Hearing his friend say all the things that had been circling his head for the past few hours had thrown them into stark relief. Every thought he'd had, every word that had come out of his mouth had been about him. About *his* life. About what *he* wanted. If he'd thought about Charlie, it had only been to lay the blame at her feet for the tectonic shift that had occurred. He hadn't thought about her circumstances. About what this meant for her. About how she might be feeling.

And he certainly hadn't thought about the baby they'd made between them.

The realization had sent a flush of self-conscious heat up his chest and into his face.

He'd sat behind his desk, burning with shame as he'd reviewed his knee-jerk reaction and found it lacking on every single front. He'd spent a half hour after Greg had left his office thinking things through before calling Charlie to try to make things right.

If she'd let him.

Now he eyed her straight back as she led him into a bright living room. Usually he wasn't the type of man who paid a lot of attention to furniture and decor, but he stopped on the threshold, a little taken aback by the stylish scene before him—the designer armchair and ottoman, the sleek sofa, the single vase on the mantel.

"This is nice," he said.

She shot him a look and he knew she'd detected the surprise in his tone. Although why he should be surprised he didn't know. He didn't know Charlie, certainly not enough to have formed an opinion about how she might live. Yet she'd surprised him with the lean, stark lines of this room.

"Grab a seat," she said.

She took the armchair, which left him with the couch. He sat on the edge of the cushion and leaned forward, elbows resting on his knees, marshaling his thoughts before he opened his mouth and stuck his foot in it for the tenth time that day.

Charlie didn't say anything. She simply waited him out, her expression perfectly composed.

"I'm sorry," he finally said. "There's a bunch of stuff I could say that would only sound like excuses, so I'm going to stick to that. I acted like an asshole this morning."

"You were shocked."

"That doesn't mean it was cool to blame you. Hell, they were my condoms, and we both laid down on that bed."

She shifted as embarrassed color washed into her cheeks. "It was an accident. That's all."

She had long, slender fingers. He watched as they brushed the leg of her trousers nervously. For the first time he became aware that her feet were bare, the high, elegant arches visible beneath her cuffs.

As though she was aware of his scrutiny, her toes curled into the floor and she shifted so that her feet were sitting neatly side by side.

"How are you feeling?" he asked, his gaze returning to her face. "Both my sisters had killer morning sickness when they were pregnant."

"I've been fine."

"You said you've got a doctor's appointment tomorrow?"

"That's right."

The tension in the room was palpable and he reached up to loosen his tie.

"Look, Charlie, I'm not really sure what the etiquette is in situations like this. I mean, this isn't exactly something I've had to deal with before."

For the first time emotion showed on her face as her eyebrows rose incredulously. "And I have?"

"No! That's not what I meant." He leaned forward, hands extended in a pacifying gesture. God, he was such an idiot. Why did he keep saying the wrong thing? "I just meant that we're in the dark here. Floundering around. Both of us."

She looked at him for a long moment. Then the corner of her mouth lifted a fraction of an inch. "I prefer flailing to floundering, if you don't mind."

His shoulders dropped a notch. "There's a difference?"

"I have no idea, but I hate seafood, so the flounder reference kind of creeps me out."

"Noted. From now on, it's flailing all the way."

Her eyes were warmer now. Less wary. "Would you like something to drink?"

"That would be great, thanks."

She rose, the movement unconsciously graceful. "Coffee? Tea?"

"Don't suppose you have brandy?" he joked.

"I have wine."

Even though he would kill for a soothing shot of something, he shook his head. Alcohol was not going to make this situation any better.

"Coffee would be great, thanks."

She left the room, her bare feet silent on the

polished boards. He pulled his tie free, removing it, and opened the top button on his shirt. He could hear her moving around in the kitchen and he stood and walked to the window. There was no view to speak of, only a corner of the neighbor's roof and a bunch of treetops. He turned back to the room, his gaze once again skimming the clean, modern lines of Charlie's furniture. This was nothing like his own place, with its mishmash of hand-me-down furniture and haphazard housecleaning. Charlie's apartment looked and felt as though she'd put a lot of effort into making it just so, as opposed to his place, which was essentially a crash pad and a glorified walkin wardrobe.

Charlie returned, carrying a small wooden tray with a single cup of coffee and a matching milk-and-sugar set.

"I wasn't sure if you took milk," she said as she put the tray on the coffee table.

"You're not having one?"

"I've already had one today." She made a gesture toward her stomach and he realized she was abstaining for the sake of the baby.

"I didn't realize you can't have coffee."

"It's one of those things the jury is still out on."

They both sat again. He cast about for something to say. "How is work going? You were starting to set things up when we last, um, spoke," he said.

"Work is good. I've signed up some more clients. Between new site designs and ongoing maintenance work I'm doing okay."

"Yeah? That's great. Really great." He could feel himself sweating, his armpits clammy with nervousness. "This place is nice. I like your furniture. I need to get some new stuff, but I've been holding out till I move into a new apartment."

Charlie frowned suddenly. "This is stupid."

"Sorry?"

"You don't know me. We're not friends." She waved a hand in the air to indicate how disconnected they were. "But we're sitting here having this stupid polite conversation like two old ladies over tea and scones. There must be things you want to ask me. I know there are things I want to ask you." Her expression was very earnest as she waited for his response.

"I have questions."

"Good. Fire away. Anything you need to know." She made an encouraging gesture with her hand, inviting him to speak.

"You go first. I'm happy to tell you anything you need to know."

"Okay. Are your parents still alive?"

"Yes. Both of them. Still married, too. How about yours?"

"My mother died when I was born, my father last year."

"Hey, I'm sorry." Rhys's parents sometimes drove him crazy, but he couldn't imagine his life without their warm, steady presence.

She made a dismissive gesture and he was smart enough not to pursue the issue. They might be strangers, but he was starting to get a read on Charlie's body language.

"What about brothers and sisters?" she asked.

"Two brothers, both older, and two younger sisters, who also happen to be twins."

"Wow. I guess your house must have been pretty crowded when you were kids, huh?"

"Ah, yeah. I shared a room with Tim until he left home when I was sixteen, and there was only one bathroom between all us kids, so you can imagine the pileups in the morning. Especially when Kim and Becky discovered makeup. Any bathroom-hogging siblings on your side?"

"Nope. Just me. Are there any family illnesses I should know about?"

He thought about it for a moment. "Does being a smart-ass count? Because there's a high degree of smart-assery in my family."

She smiled, her first real one since she'd opened the door. Suddenly he saw a resemblance to the woman who'd captivated him so much that night at Café Sydney.

"As long as it's not chronic or fatal, I don't think so. I don't think there's anything on my side, either. So that's good."

They both fell silent. Rhys studied his coffee for a few seconds before asking the question that had been bugging him for weeks now.

"Why didn't you wake me before you left? Or at least leave your number?" He glanced up in time to see her body stiffen.

"I thought I'd save us both an awkward morning-after conversation."

"It might not have been awkward."

She shrugged, her face shuttered. "I guess we'll never know, will we?"

"No. I guess not."

They talked for another half hour, exchanging personal information, filling in the blanks. Slowly but surely, Rhys began to build a picture of Charlie Long, former army officer and present-day web designer, a picture informed as much by what she didn't say as what she offered up to him. It didn't take him long to work out that she was an introvert, and if the apartment was anything to go by, a bit of a perfectionist. She was smart, observant, honest and a little prickly when pushed into corners she didn't want to explore. He suspected she'd been a good soldier—that she'd be good at anything she put her mind to—and that she probably worked many more hours than she ever billed her clients for. Slowly it dawned on him that given the circumstances of their meeting and the situation they were in, he'd lucked out big-time.

She was a good person, a decent person. Early days to be making that kind of judgment call, perhaps, but he'd always trusted his gut when it came to people and it hadn't failed him yet.

"I want you to know that I'm up to this," he said as Charlie finished describing the site she'd completed for her newest client. He'd caught her by surprise and her gaze was unguarded as it met his.

"I know I wigged out this morning, but I want you to know that whatever you want, whatever you need, we'll work it out," he said.

"I want my child to know he or she is loved. I don't want him or her to suffer because of our mistakes," Charlie said, her voice low and intense and very serious.

"Okay."

She eyed him steadily for a moment. Then she nodded. "Okay."

He checked his watch. "I have to go. It's my nephew's birthday and Mum is doing a roast."

"How old is he?"

"Five, going on forty. Mum keeps telling me I was way more precocious than he is when I was a kid, but I don't think it's possible." He stood, automatically collecting the tray.

"I'll do that," Charlie said, extending a hand.

"Sorry, no can do. My mother trained us with an iron fist. The Walker men always clean up after themselves." He thought about his messy apartment. "When we're in someone else's domain, anyway."

"Your mum sounds like a rare and insightful woman."

"She has her moments."

Rhys set the tray on the counter in Charlie's small, neat kitchen. A cookbook lay there, the pages open to a recipe for tarte tatin. Charlie closed the book, a hint of color in her cheeks.

"Trying to teach myself how to cook," she said with a self-deprecating shrug.

"More power to you. I pretty much live on takeout and toast. Greg keeps telling me I'm going to turn into a fat bastard one of these days now that I'm over thirty." He patted his belly.

Charlie's gaze dipped to his waist before lifting to his chest for the briefest of moments. She frowned slightly, then turned away. "I don't want to hold you up."

He followed her to the door and stepped into the hall. The neutral expression was back, her eyes giving nothing away as she faced him.

He wondered where all that self-control came

from, if it came naturally or if it was a result of her years in the army.

"How would you feel about having dinner sometime next week?" he asked.

She blinked. "I'm not sure…"

"The more we know about each other, the better. This is a pretty full-on situation we're in, you have to admit."

Her frown deepened, but she didn't object again. He decided to take that as a yes.

"I'll call tomorrow to work out a time and check in after your appointment, okay?"

"Okay."

He offered her a small smile and started down the hall. He'd reached the top of the stairs when Charlie called out to him.

"Rhys."

He glanced over his shoulder. She'd stepped into the hall and was fiddling with the top button of her shirt.

"Thanks for calling. And for coming over. I appreciate it."

He nodded, then, because it seemed that they'd said everything they needed to say in the short term, he started down the stairs. He only registered how exhausted he was when he exited to the street.

It had been a big day. A huge day. This morning he'd been standing on the wharf in Woolloomooloo contemplating the purchase of a million-dollar-plus apartment. And now he was going to be a father.

It didn't seem possible, or even probable. Even now, after talking to Charlie for close to an hour, a part of him was still waiting for the other shoe to drop—for something to happen that would allow him to keep living his life in the way that he'd envisaged it. For the second time that day a wave of pure, unadulterated anger washed over him as he contemplated the future.

From a very early age he'd always looked ahead, and he'd always had a plan to achieve the goals he spied on the horizon. As a ten-year-old he'd set his sights on occupying the bottom, rather than top, bunk bed in the room he shared with his brother, and he hadn't stopped badgering Tim until he caved and accepted Rhys's new bike in exchange for the lower berth.

When he was thirteen, Rhys had fallen hard for Sophie Goodwood and spent more than six months wooing her to the point where she finally allowed him to kiss her.

At eighteen, he'd looked around the world, decided that I.T. was an area where a determined person could still make his mark and set about gaining the education and expertise that would allow him to one day be master of his own destiny.

Maybe he'd been fortunate, but there had been

precious few instances in his life when his ambitions and plans had been thwarted. He'd always found his way around roadblocks, and he'd never taken no for an answer.

But there was no way around a baby—apart from the obvious, and Charlie had already made that decision for both of them. There was no way he could negotiate with biology. This was one roadblock that could not be charmed, wined and dined, bulldozed or outmaneuvered.

He was stuck, whether he liked it or not, and—determination to do the right thing aside—it didn't sit well with him. Not at all.

He unlocked his car and slid behind the wheel. In a perfect world, he'd head straight home and dig out a large bottle of scotch to drown his sorrows and quench his frustrated anger. In the real world, he was due at his parents' place at six-thirty. For a few seconds he toyed with the idea of canceling, but he already had his nephew's present in the car. Just because he'd screwed up didn't mean Garth should miss out.

Rhys scrubbed his face with his hands, then reached to start the car. It wasn't until he was pulling on his seat belt that he registered his missing tie and remembered that he'd left it on Charlie's couch. He was tempted to leave it, but then he remembered the spartan neatness of her apartment.

He turned off the engine and got out of the car. As he climbed the stairs to the first floor, it hit him that this was probably the first of many times that he'd have to put Charlie's sensibilities and preferences ahead of his own.

Something else he needed to get used to. Somehow.

CHAPTER SIX

CHARLIE tidied the kitchen, washing Rhys's mug and the milk jug before drying everything and putting it away. She wiped down the counter, even though it was already spotless, then went into the living room and straightened the pillows on the couch.

She was aware of an insistent burning sensation at the back of her eyes and a heavy, tight feeling in her chest and throat, but she staunchly kept working, willing the unwanted feelings to go away. She was plumping the last cushion when she discovered Rhys's tie crumpled between the arm and cushion of the couch. She picked up the striped length of silk and folded it neatly, placing it on the coffee table. The next thing she knew, tears were streaking down her face.

She used the sleeve of her shirt to wipe them away, but they kept coming. Her breathing became choppy, and she squeezed her eyes shut as she tried to get a grip on herself.

She'd never been a crier. Her father had trained that out of her at a very young age. "If you want my attention, you earn it," he'd said. And the army had reinforced the notion that tears were a form of weakness, a child's way of expressing herself. Soldiers didn't cry. Soldiers sucked it up and moved on.

And yet she couldn't get the tears to stop, and for the life of her, she didn't understand why. She'd had a perfectly agreeable conversation with Rhys. Things were looking far better than they had this morning. So why was there this desperate pressure pushing out from behind her breastbone? Why did she feel so fragile and frightened and forlorn?

A knock echoed through the apartment. She started, then used her sleeve to mop her face again as she walked to the door. She squinted through the spy hole, her whole body tensing when she saw Rhys, a small frown on his face as he checked his watch. It only took her a second to join the dots—he wanted his tie, of course. Which meant she needed to let him in.

She took a step backward. No way could she allow him see her like this. No. Way.

She raced to the bathroom, splashing her face with cold water before blotting it on a towel. Rhys knocked again as she exited the bathroom. She pinned a polite smile on her face as she unlocked the door and swung it open.

"Oh, hi," she said, feigning surprise.

"I forgot my tie."

She couldn't quite make herself look him in the eye, afraid he'd guess that barely thirty seconds ago she'd been blubbering like a big baby. She settled for focusing on his left earlobe.

"I found it. I'll grab it for you." She pivoted and walked briskly into the living room. She collected the tie and turned, only to find that Rhys had followed her and was studying her with slightly narrowed eyes.

"Is everything all right?"

"Yes. Of course," she said too quickly.

"Look, Charlie, if I said something to upset you before, I'm sorry." He sounded both confused and cautious.

"You didn't. I'm fine." She took a step toward him, expecting him to fall back and let her pass. He didn't move, however, and he didn't take his gaze from her face.

"If you're fine, then why have you been crying?"

Her first impulse was to deny it, but she wasn't in the habit of lying, not if she could help it. "I'm fine."

"No, you're not."

He said it gruffly, but there was an undercurrent of kindness in his tone that forced her to blink back a fresh bout of tears.

"Honestly, it's all good," she said, but she could feel her chin wobble.

"Charlie. What's going on?"

She felt a tear trickle down her cheek, closely followed by another. Humiliation joined the many other emotions choking her throat. "I'm sorry. I never cry. I don't know what's wrong with me..."

Rhys reached into his pocket and pulled out a handkerchief. "Here."

She took it and used it to wipe her face, but the tears were getting worse, not better. "I'm s-sorry." She half turned away from him.

She clenched her hands around the handkerchief, willing her stupid body and emotions to obey her, willing him to get the hint and leave her alone.

"Here," he said, and the next thing she knew he was pulling her close.

She stiffened and tried to pull away, but his arms were firm around her.

"You don't have to apologize for being upset," he said, his words vibrating from his chest through to hers.

She was about to push him away when she felt his palm smooth a circle on her back in an age-old gesture of comfort. Fresh tears welled as the fragile feeling washed through her all over again. She turned her face away from him and sobbed.

"It's okay, Charlie," he said, his hand moving in another one of those soothing, gentle circles.

"I don't even know why I'm upset," she hiccuped. "I mean, it's not as though I have to do this all on my own. You turned up. You said all the right things. I should be relieved."

He took a moment to respond. "Then maybe that's all this is. Relief."

She thought about it for a moment, remembering the dizzying sense of loneliness she'd felt this morning when she'd stared down the barrel of going through all this—pregnancy, childbirth, parenthood—on her own.

"Maybe."

But it still didn't explain why she'd suddenly turned into a watering pot. She pushed away and this time he let her go. She used his handkerchief to dry the worst of the tears, feeling more and more self-conscious with every passing second.

"I'm not usually like this, I promise," she said, risking a quick glance his way.

His dark eyes were very serious as they watched her. "I'm sorry I was such a dick this morning."

She shrugged. "It doesn't matter."

"Yeah, it does. I'm not proud of the way I reacted. Believe me, it's not great to learn that when the chips are down your first impulse is to be a selfish bastard."

"My first thoughts were selfish, too. How I'd cope, what I'd do about my business. The only difference was that I didn't say any of it out loud."

"Seems like a big difference from where I'm standing. I meant what I said before, Charlie. I'm up for this. You're not on your own, okay?"

She nodded. She realized that she was still holding his tie. "Better take this or you'll have to come back again and God knows what I'll be doing then."

He smiled faintly. "I'm almost tempted to find out."

"But then you'd be late for your nephew's party."

"True." He turned and she followed him to the front door.

"Have a good night," she said as he stepped into the hall.

"You too. And, Charlie? Call me if you need anything, okay? Even just to talk."

"Sure. Thanks."

She managed a small smile, but this time she shut the door rather than watch him walk away. She went into the study instead and jostled the mouse to wake her computer from hibernation mode. She reached for the keyboard and realized she was still clutching Rhys's handkerchief. Strange—he was the last person she would have pegged as a handkerchief kind of guy. He seemed too driven and forward thinking and dynamic to be bothered with putting a little square of cloth in his pocket every morning. Yet clearly he had—

this morning, at least—and he'd insisted on clearing his own dishes.

He'd also pulled her into his arms to comfort her.

She smoothed the wrinkled linen flat on her desktop as she remembered the way his arms had wrapped around her. Only now did she allow herself to think about how hard and warm and strong his body had felt against hers.

He'd been wearing the same aftershave he'd worn that night. Masculine and earthy and warm. There had been nothing sexual in his embrace, but the memory of it triggered other memories inside her. Hotter, more intense, more dangerous memories…

You have got to be kidding. Don't even go there. Don't even consider the possibility of it.

She crumpled the handkerchief into a ball and stuffed it into her pocket. Reaching for the mouse, she opened the file she'd been working on and very deliberately focused on her work.

Because she was not a fool, appearances to the contrary.

RHYS THOUGHT ABOUT Charlie for the entire sixty minutes of the rush-hour drive to his parents' place on the North Shore. He'd grown up with two younger sisters who had never been shy about using whatever means at their disposal to get their own way, so he was no stranger to tears. Charlie's tears, however…those had hit him in the gut.

Perhaps it was because she'd been so obviously reluctant to give in to her emotions, fighting the tears even as they slid down her face. Whatever the reason, it only made him more determined to get this right, to shoulder his share of the burden they'd inadvertently created.

The street outside his parents' place was already choked with his siblings' cars by the time he arrived. He managed to wedge his car behind his eldest brother's beaten-up van before collecting Garth's present and the bottle of wine he'd bought and heading for the house.

East Pymble was one of the most exclusive and established suburbs in Sydney, full of gracious homes on leafy streets. His parents lived in far less exclusive West Pymble, in the modest 1950s yellow brick home he'd grown up in, surrounded by other modest yellow brick homes. He stepped over the gaping crack in the concrete path—the same crack that had been there since he was twelve years old—and climbed the three steps to the concrete porch. A jumble of shoes sat there—a pair of his father's sneakers, his mother's gardening clogs, various mismatched pairs of flip-flops. He knocked briefly on the door to announce his arrival before trying the handle. It opened easily and he stepped into the hall, inhaling the scent of roasting chicken.

"We're in the kitchen, Rhys," his mother called.

Where else? The kitchen had always been the heart of the Walker home. He could hear the laughter and chatter as he approached and, for the second time that night, he felt the strong, visceral urge to bail on his family and go find a quiet corner and a bottle of whiskey to lose himself in.

Instead, he took a deep breath and plunged into the social chaos that was the Walker family en masse.

His mother was holding the fort at the stove, stirring something in a pot while chatting to his sister Rebecca. Holly Walker had been as dark as her children when she was younger, but now her short, curly hair was salt-and-pepper gray. The smile she sent his way was warm with affection and welcome. His father, Ken, stood to her right, dicing up something green and frondy-looking on the chopping board. His shirt was wrinkled around the collar and only half tucked in and he needed a haircut, his graying hair shaggy around his ears and nape.

He glanced up from his work to acknowledge Rhys. "Almost the last, but not quite. Good timing."

"I try," Rhys said.

"I'll take that," Rebecca said, slipping the bottle of wine from his hand and checking the label with interest. "Is this one of your fancy ones or something more suited to us plebs?"

"If you don't know, I'm not telling," Rhys said.

The rest of the family were gathered around the scarred kitchen table. Rhys's older brother, Tim, sat with his wife, Amber, on his knee, one arm around her waist, the other holding a very full glass of red wine. Next was Mark, his youngest daughter in his arms. The other twin, Kim, was at the opposite side of the table, her husband, Lee, sitting beside her. The eldest of his many nieces and nephews—there were eight in total—occupied the rest of the chairs, while the smallest members of the family had taken up residence beneath the table where they appeared to be playing "guess which feet belong to whom." Obviously they were still waiting on a few arrivals, since Rebecca's husband, Rod, was nowhere in evidence or his other sister-in-law, Meg.

"There he is, the captain of industry. Take over any businesses today, mate? Got any good stock tips for us?" Mark greeted him.

"If I did I wouldn't waste them on you," Rhys said easily.

Last time he'd tried to pass on a hot stock tip to his family, Mark had given him a lecture on the social evils brought about by free trade and the "myth of the global village."

Mark laughed good-naturedly.

"Here," Rebecca said at his elbow, and he saw she'd poured him a glass of wine.

"Thanks."

Conversation swirled around him as he took a big gulp. Tim and his father were discussing an education department directive that had caused some kind of controversy at the school they both taught at, while Kim and Amber were laughing over the antics of one of Kim's patients. Rhys let the noise wash over and around him as he took a second big pull from his wine.

"Hard one, sweetheart?" his mother asked.

He realized she was watching him, a frown pleating her forehead.

"Just the usual." Apart from the small matter of learning he'd made a baby with a woman he hardly knew. But there was no point burdening his mother with that particular piece of bad luck.

His hand tightened on the glass as it hit him for the first time that his mistake—his monumental, life-changing mistake—wouldn't remain a private matter for long. Charlie was going to have a child, and that child would be cousin to all these noisy children. It was going to be a part of the Walker family, whether he'd planned for it or not. Whether he was ready for it or not. And he knew absolutely that his parents would want to be involved once they learned what had happened.

"Bloody hell," he muttered under his breath.

Just when he thought he had a grip on how big this thing was, it grew an extra set of arms and legs and another head.

"Is that for me, Uncle Rhys?"

Rhys focused on the slight figure in front of him. Garth's hopeful gaze was fixed on the brightly wrapped parcel Rhys had left on the table when he came in.

"Garth Michael Walker, what do you think you're doing?" Amber said, rising from her perch on her husband's knee. "Did we or did we not have a conversation about being gracious on your birthday and that spending time with loved ones is more important than anything someone might buy for you?"

Garth frowned. "I waited a whole five minutes. What more do you want from me?"

Rhys made a solid attempt to hide his smile at his nephew's cheekiness, but Amber shot him a reproving look nonetheless.

"Thanks for the backup there, Uncle Rhys."

He shrugged. "Doesn't hurt to know what you want in life and not be afraid to go for it."

"Why do I always have a picture of Alex P.

Keaton in my head when you say things like that?" Kim said.

Rhys gave his sister a dry look. Comparisons to the success-oriented character Michael J. Fox had played on *Family Ties* had grown old a long time ago. "That's the best you can do? Really?"

Kim grinned at him, utterly unrepentant. "I thought it was pretty good, actually."

"You have low standards," Rhys said.

"Now, now, children. No squabbling until dessert," his mother said.

"Good luck with that one, Mum," Rebecca said with an inelegant snort of amusement.

"I'm with your mother. Let's pretend to be civilized for a few more minutes," his father chimed in.

"I'm confused. Does this mean I get my present or not?" Garth asked plaintively.

Everyone burst into laughter, including Amber.

"You're incorrigible, you know that?" she said, reaching out to give her son an affectionate shove on the shoulder.

"Happy birthday, Garth," Rhys said, handing the gift over. "May it annoy your parents for many hours."

Tim's eyes narrowed. "If this takes lots of batteries and means I have to wear my noise-canceling headphones when I'm marking, you're in big trouble."

Rhys smiled mysteriously as Garth tore the paper off a set of state-of-the-art walkie-talkies.

"Oh, man. These are so cool," Garth said, eyes wide with awe.

"Don't forget to spy on your parents, okay?" Rhys said.

"Again, thank you, Uncle Rhys," Amber said dryly.

"My pleasure."

Garth stepped close and flung an arm around Rhys, his head burrowing into Rhys's stomach. "Thanks heaps, Uncle Rhys."

Looking at his nephew's dark head, feeling his skinny arm around his waist, Rhys felt something odd and unfamiliar shift in his chest.

Bending at the knees, he crouched to his nephew's height and gave him a proper hug, what was left in his glass slopping dangerously close to the rim. Garth seemed surprised for a second, Rhys being more of a wrestling-on-the-rug kind of uncle than a demonstrative one, but after a second he returned the embrace and pressed a kiss to Rhys's cheek.

Again, there was that unfamiliar feeling in his chest.

I could have a boy like this. Or a girl like Alison or Sami. Dark hair, dark eyes. A little person to love and protect.

Out of nowhere, his throat got tight. He released his nephew and stood, using the excuse of straightening his jacket to cover the unexpected rush of emotion. Amber was watching him with a faint smile when he finally glanced up.

"You big softy," she said.

He shrugged off the comment, but only relaxed when Mark started talking about a new supplier he'd found for his organic-produce store.

Meg and Rod arrived within ten minutes of each other and his parents set about serving dinner to the gathered hordes. Rhys sat between Meg and Sami, his eldest niece, and did his best to keep up his end of the conversation. Twice he caught his mother giving him a searching look and he made a point of picking a fight with Mark over the merits of food miles, since it was the sort of thing he would normally do at a family gathering.

In that way the Alex P. Keaton reference wasn't a mile off—he was the only one who had chosen to enter the world of commerce and chase the almighty dollar, while the rest of them all held community-based jobs that focused more on social good than personal wealth. While he admired them a great deal, he didn't see anything wrong with being ambitious and having big dreams, and he definitely didn't believe that being successful and being a good human being were mutually exclusive concepts. His siblings—and, he suspected to a certain extent, his parents—begged to differ, and it usually resulted in some kind of standoff when they were together.

In fine family tradition, the debate carried them into dessert and only ceased when the lights were dimmed and the candles lit for Garth's cake.

Rhys cheered and hooted with everyone else when Garth failed to blow out all five candles at once, but he sneaked a quick glance at his watch as Amber and Kim took the cake to cut it. It was nearly eight-thirty, which meant things would start to wind up pretty soon, since the younger kids would need to be in bed. He decided he'd leave after the first of his siblings had made their exit and applied himself to the cake he'd been served. Afterward he helped clear the table and rinse the dishes for the dishwasher alongside Mark and Tim.

"It's getting late. We'd better head off," Meg said as the men finished with the pans and baking trays.

Her youngest, Helen, was asleep in her arms, her head resting on Meg's shoulder.

Rhys heaved a silent sigh of relief as Mark started gathering their baby paraphernalia and their other two children together in preparation for departure. Rhys finished rinsing out the sink and was about to announce his own intention to exit when his mother appeared at his side.

"Could you help me take the garbage out?" she asked, indicating the dual bins beneath the sink.

"Sure." He grabbed the garbage while she tackled the recyclables and they made their way out to the patio. The bins were stationed on the side of the house nearest the driveway and Rhys dumped his load before lifting the lid on the second bin for his mother.

"Right. That's that sorted," she said, dusting her hands together. She fixed him with a steady eye. "Now, you want to tell me what's going on with you?"

Rhys did his best to look surprised by her question. Despite having five children to spread her attention amongst, his mother had an uncanny knack for sniffing out anything out of the ordinary in her children's lives.

"Nothing's going on."

"Rubbish. You've been quiet all night."

"No, I haven't."

"You have. You're not your normal self. Is there something wrong with work? Has that big deal fallen through?"

"No. Of course not."

"I know you were excited about it, but I don't want you thinking that anyone is going to judge you or feel sorry for you if things have gone pear shaped."

Rhys smiled faintly at her concern. When he'd

told his parents about landing the Gainsborough contract they'd been almost disbelieving when he'd explained what it would mean for the business and what his growth projections were over the next few years.

"Nothing's wrong at work, Mum."

"Then what's going on?"

He looked at her concerned face. He could hear his family in the kitchen, the ebb and flow of their laughter and conversation. This was hardly the time to tell his mother what had happened.

And yet, somehow, he found himself taking a deep breath and saying the words. "I'm going to be a father."

"But—but you're not even seeing anyone at the moment. Are you?"

For a moment he considered fudging the truth a little, but then he remembered his mother's sixth sense, the same sixth sense that had led to this conversation in the first place. She would know if he was snowballing her.

"I met Charlie when we were out celebrating the Gainsborough account. She tracked me down this morning to tell me she's pregnant and that she's keeping the baby."

"Oh, Rhys." Two words, but they contained a world of understanding and disappointment.

He fought the urge to shuffle his feet like a

naughty schoolboy. "Before you ask, we used condoms. I don't know what went wrong."

His mother's face was creased with worry. "When is she due?"

"She's seeing the doctor tomorrow, but based on the dates, I'd say in November sometime."

"And what do you know about this woman? You said she tracked you down—I assume that means what happened between you was a one-night-only sort of arrangement?"

"Her name is Charlie. Charlie Long. She recently left the army to set up her own web-design business."

"The army. Well, that's not what I was expecting. How old is she?"

"I'm not sure. Thirty, if I had to guess."

He could feel his face heating. He wasn't in the habit of discussing his love life with his mother and he had to swallow the impulse to explain to her that it wasn't his usual practice to take home unknown women for the night. But failed condom or not, there was no way to make what had happened between him and Charlie sound less stupid and irresponsible.

"And she wasn't on the pill? I hate to say this, Rhys, but can you be sure this baby is yours?"

"She says it is and I believe her."

"I see. When can we meet her?"

"I'm not sure. We need to sort a few things out first."

"Does she have family in Sydney?"

"No. She's an only child and both her parents are dead."

His mother gave a small, humorless laugh. "Of all my boys, you're the last one I would have imagined this happening to. Tim, maybe, before he met Meg. He was always so forgetful. But you're the organized one. The planner."

"Yeah, well."

She reached out to take his hand. "This is going to change your life, you know that, right? Having a baby is no small thing."

"Who's having a baby?"

Rhys's gut got tight as Mark exited the house.

The many, endless joys of having four siblings. His mother looked at him, leaving it up to him to respond to his brother's question. Mark followed their mother's gaze and the curious expression on his face morphed into amazement.

"No way," Mark said. "But you're not even seeing anyone at the moment."

"It was kind of an accident."

"An accident? Are you kidding me?" There was no mistaking the judgment in his brother's tone.

"A condom failed, okay?" Rhys said tightly.

Mark's expression became more neutral.

"Right. Well, I guess there's not much you can do about that."

"You think?" Rhys snapped.

His mother lay a calming hand on his forearm.

"So, who is she? And how come we haven't met her yet? And when is the baby due?" Mark asked.

Rhys ran a hand over his face. All he wanted to do was go home, but he knew his brother well enough to know that there was no way he was going to let this go with the minimum of fuss.

"Her name is Charlie..." he said.

CHAPTER SEVEN

CHARLIE SMILED AWKWARDLY as she exited the clinic bathroom and handed the specimen jar to the nurse.

"You can go in now," the woman said, gesturing for Charlie to reenter the treatment room.

The space was empty and Charlie resumed her seat next to the doctor's desk. Her hands were cold and she rubbed them together in an attempt to warm up. When the doctor didn't return immediately, Charlie guessed she must be attending another patient and settled in for an extended wait.

Various charts covered the walls—a cross section of an eye, a detailed diagram of the lymphatic system, a cross section of a heart and lungs. Above the examination table was a chart depicting the various stages of pregnancy. Charlie crossed to get a closer look.

Her gaze ran over the first few weeks until she found week eight. According to the chart, her baby was no bigger than a kidney bean inside her womb, a tiny constellation of cells that was even now dividing and multiplying, dividing and multiplying, building a new life one building block at a time.

Unless, of course, there's been some kind of mistake and you're not really pregnant.

The thought hung in Charlie's mind as she stared at the chart. That was what the urine sample had been for, of course—so the doctor could confirm what the home test had shown. Which must mean there was a chance she wasn't pregnant, otherwise they wouldn't bother checking her result…

For a moment she allowed herself to consider the possibility that it had been a big, messy, confusing mistake. That she wasn't really pregnant, and that she didn't really have to make things work with Rhys for the next fifty or so years.

She felt a little dizzy as she imagined being able to go back to her plans for her business and her future. There would be no huge unknown lying in wait in seven months' time. Life would be infinitely simpler.

She walked slowly to the chair. It was odd, because she'd never thought of herself as an instinctive or feeling-driven person before, but she *knew* she was pregnant. Knew it in her bones. Which was probably why she found it so hard to picture a future without this pregnancy. Somehow, without her being aware of it, she'd moved beyond shock and panic into acceptance that she was going to be a mother.

She looked up at as the door handle rattled. Dr. Phillips entered, a smile on her face.

"A positive result. Congratulations, Charlotte."

Charlie smiled. "Thanks."

Twenty minutes later, she left the clinic with a fistful of pamphlets and a number to call to arrange for her first ultrasound in three weeks' time. Dr. Phillips had been happy with her overall health but had encouraged her to keep on top of her calcium intake—plenty of dairy and leafy green vegetables—prescribed folic acid and had recommended a couple of good books on pregnancy. Charlie waited until she was in her car before pulling Rhys's business card out of her purse pocket.

She hesitated a moment, reminding herself that he'd said that he would call her. Then she gave herself a mental shake. They weren't dating, playing some kind of hard-to-get game. They were about to become parents together. She didn't need to wait for him to call her.

She dialed his number and tapped her fingernails on the dash while she waited for the call to connect.

"Rhys speaking, how can I help you?"

His voice sounded so clear and deep that she started. She'd assumed she'd have to talk to the receptionist first, but Rhys had clearly given her his direct number.

"Rhys. It's me. Charlie."

There was a short pause before he responded. "Charlie. How are you? I was going to call you later this afternoon."

"I know, but I wanted to let you know that I've been to the doctor and she's confirmed everything. So, I'm still pregnant. Sorry about that."

She felt a little pang of guilt as she heard herself apologizing for the kidney bean growing inside her. Her hand moved to her belly instinctively in wordless remorse.

"From what you said yesterday, there wasn't much doubt. Was the doctor happy otherwise?"

Charlie filled him in on the rest of what the doctor had said. He asked a few more questions, noting the date for the ultrasound.

"I'll call you afterward to let you know how it goes," she said.

"Right," Rhys said slowly. "I was thinking I might go with you. If that's not a problem."

She was surprised and it took her a moment to find her voice.

"Um, sure. If that's what you want. But I know you're busy."

"So are you. I told you, Charlie. We're in this together."

"Okay. Then I'll call you to let you know what time the appointment is."

"Good. Have you had a chance to check your calendar for the week? When are you free for dinner?"

Dinner. Right. She'd agreed to have dinner with him, hadn't she?

"I don't really have any plans yet, so any night is good."

"How does Wednesday sound?"

"Sure. Where do you want to meet?"

"How about I pick you up? It's tough enough finding one parking spot around town these days," Rhys said.

"You don't want to drive all the way across town to pick me up." Plus, she would prefer to have her car on hand, in case she needed or wanted to leave.

"It's no bother."

"You don't need to chauffeur me around."

It took him a second or two to respond. "Okay. If you'd rather drive."

He sounded a little put out and she guessed he was probably used to getting his own way where women were concerned.

"So where would you like to go?" she asked.

"Do you like Asian food? Chinta Ria in Darling Harbour does a little bit of everything, Malaysian, Indian, Chinese…"

"Sounds good."

Rhys gave her directions and they agreed on a time. Charlie fiddled with the phone for a few minutes after the call had ended.

There was so much she and Rhys didn't know about each other. She didn't know how to interpret the pauses in his speech or the inflections in his tone. She didn't know if he had a temper, and if so, what might set it off.

But that was what dinner on Wednesday night was all about, after all. Getting to know each other. Becoming comfortable with each other before they suddenly had to manage a baby between the two of them.

From this vantage point, it seemed like an impossible task. Insurmountable. But it had to happen, for the baby's sake.

Dropping the phone onto the passenger seat, she started the car and headed for home.

WEDNESDAY NIGHT found her standing in front of her meager wardrobe, flicking back and forth between a pair of black trousers and a pair of jeans. Smart casual or casual? She had no idea. Shaking her head at her own indecision, she pulled out the black pants and threw them on the bed. Better to be overdressed than under.

She dragged on a black turtleneck and hustled into the bathroom to tackle her hair. As usual, it hung in a straight blah-brown curtain around her face. She knew from experience that there was no point trying to do anything with it, so she put it in a neat ponytail and reached for her makeup bag.

She was about to swipe on some eye shadow when she looked into her eyes in the mirror and came down to earth with a thud.

This wasn't a date. Yet she was acting as though it was, running around like a chicken with its head cut off. Worrying about her clothes, her hair, her makeup. Tonight was about the baby she and Rhys had made together. Nothing else. He wasn't interested in her as a woman. He might be putting a good face on it, stepping up and doing and saying all the right things, but she'd seen the moment of absolute denial in his face when she'd first broken the news to him. This was the last thing he wanted, the last thing he'd had planned for his life. She and the baby were millstones around his neck.

She didn't hold it against him. But she wasn't going to let herself get sucked into a false reality. Her relationship with Rhys was founded on obligation and responsibility. No more, no less.

She set down her eye-shadow compact. She allowed herself lipstick and a spritz of perfume because she'd put both on no matter where she was going or who she was meeting, then she left the bathroom. She collected her coat, and made her way out to her car.

Thanks to heavy traffic, she was running ten minutes late when she approached the rustic, Asian-themed facade of Chinta Ria. A couple exited and she caught the studded wooden door before it closed behind them and slipped into the restaurant. The interior had high ceilings with exposed beams, polished concrete floors and groups of tables surrounded by chairs painted in bright tropical colors. Carved friezes decorated the roof supports and huge silk lanterns swayed gently overhead. The dining area was crowded, the noise level loud. Charlie hovered near the entrance, scanning the tables for Rhys's dark head. She couldn't see him anywhere.

Then her gaze slid over to the bar and got caught on a tall, broad-shouldered figure talking to one of the barmaids. Rhys was wearing a dark charcoal suit and one of his elbows rested on the bar as he chatted easily with the pretty blonde. He'd pulled his tie free and opened his collar and he looked handsome and successful and incredibly appealing. As she watched, the barmaid laughed at something he said and swatted his arm in a classic flirty move. Something tightened in the pit of Charlie's stomach as she watched Rhys laugh in response.

So none of your business.

She shrugged her bag higher on her shoulder and set out across the restaurant. She didn't take her eyes off him the whole way, but Rhys was so absorbed in his conversation that he didn't register her presence until she pulled out the stool next to him.

"Sorry I'm late," she said as she sat.

"Charlie. You made it."

His smile was warm and genuine and she had to force herself not to pull away when he leaned in to kiss her cheek.

"I've been getting some menu advice from Zara. She recommends the king prawns and the toh beef."

Charlie made eye contact with the barmaid. Up close, she was even prettier than she'd appeared at a distance. A little young, perhaps, for Rhys, but—again—really none of her business.

"Sounds good," she said with what she hoped was an easy smile.

"You want wine or something first?"

Charlie was about to decline when he shook his head.

"Sorry. You can't drink. Ignore me. Let's grab a table."

Charlie slid off the stool, watching out of the corner of her eye as Rhys thanked Zara for her expert advice. Then he led Charlie to the far corner of the dining room where a number of tables for two were still available.

"Any preferences?" he asked.

"Not really."

He took her at her word and chose the coziest table. She slid into her seat and faced him across the flickering amber light of a tea-light lantern.

"Sorry for keeping you waiting," she said. "I keep underestimating the travel time. Sydney's much busier than when I lived here last."

"When was that?"

"It was my first posting after recruit training. So, I guess it must have been nearly thirteen years ago now."

"You must have seen a bit of the country, one way or another. What was your favorite posting?"

Rhys propped his elbow on the table, his dark gaze scanning her face with warm interest. Despite everything—their situation, the stern talking-to she'd given herself, her own very well-developed common sense—a part of her couldn't help responding to the magnetic pull of his personality. She was only human, after all, and he was undeniably a handsome, charismatic man.

Obligation, remember? And in case you didn't notice, he looked exactly the same when he was talking to the blonde, down to the elbow on the bar.

She dragged her gaze from his face and reached for her napkin, spreading it across her lap.

"Townsville was good. Mostly because I roomed with my friend Gina and we had a good crew in Sigs up there. The people make more of a difference than the place, at the end of the day."

"I get that. It's the same in I.T. My last job, the money was great, but the owner of the firm was a narcissistic jerk and the corporate culture was poison. Greg and I both made a deal that we'd hang in there for two years to fund our start-up, and both of us wanted to bail at twelve months."

He smiled self-deprecatingly as he said it, his eyes crinkling at the corners attractively.

"Did you? Bail, I mean?"

"Nope. Even though it almost killed us both, we hung in. But man, did we bitch our asses off at lunchtime." His grin was irresistible, equal parts naughty boy and knowing, confident man. It was impossible to stop an answering smile from curving her own mouth.

"How long before they became strategy meetings?" she asked.

"Not long. Nothing like being miserable to spur a guy to change his situation."

"I believe that's the stick component of the carrot-and-stick theory."

He laughed. "Yeah. I guess it is."

She felt a warm sense of achievement over

having made him laugh. Which was dangerous and just plain dumb. She made a big deal out of examining the menu, which doubled as a place mat.

"Wow. There's a lot to choose from." She kept her gaze glued to the menu. It seemed safer that way.

"It's been a while since I've eaten here, but everything I've had is good."

"Great."

A silence fell as they both studied the menu. Charlie told herself it was companionable, but she knew it wasn't. This was too new, too forced, and there was so much riding on whatever relationship they were able to cobble together out of this mess. Under the table, she pulled back her sleeve and tilted her watch so she could see the face.

Barely ten minutes had passed. Dear God. This was going to be the longest night of her life. Ironic, given that the night they'd met she'd wanted it to last forever.

She made an effort to relax her shoulders and glanced across the table at Rhys. "So, what looks good?"

RHYS WATCHED CHARLIE as she gave her order to the waitress. She was smiling and she'd responded to everything he said and made her own comments and jokes, but he could see the tension in her body and her face. Under any other circumstances, he'd order them both a drink and wait for the lubricating effect of alcohol to chill them both out. Since that wasn't going to happen, he needed another strategy.

The waitress left and Charlie reached for her water glass.

"Look at it this way—it has to get easier from here on in, right?" he said.

Her eyes widened over the glass rim and she swallowed with an audible gulp.

"Beg pardon?"

"The weirdness. It can only be this bad at the start, right?"

She stared at him for a moment as though she couldn't quite believe he'd said what he had. Then a slow smile dawned across her face. She sat back in her chair, her shoulders visibly dropping a notch.

"It's not just me, then?"

"Oh, it's definitely you," he said, deadpan.

Her smile broadened. "Thanks for the confirmation."

He leaned forward, driven by an urge to cut through all the bull. "This is like speed dating, only with higher stakes. We need to take a crash course in each other."

"A crash course. Right. There isn't something a

little less violent we could do?" Despite her words there was an appreciative light in her eyes.

"Five questions. No holds barred. No formulating responses, just whatever comes into our heads. Okay?"

Her gaze grew sharper. "Who goes first?"

"We alternate."

"But someone still has to go first."

"We can toss for it. Unless you're volunteering?"

She raised her eyebrows. "One thing you learn fast in the army—never be the first to volunteer for *anything.*"

"I'm sensing a story there."

She tilted her head enigmatically, neither confirming nor denying. He reached into his pocket for a coin. "Heads or tails?"

"Heads."

He flipped the coin.

"Tails. You first," she said.

"Be kind."

She propped an elbow on the table and rested her chin on her hand. She studied him for a moment, a small frown between her eyebrows. She wasn't wearing any makeup, but she had naturally long lashes and her brown eyes were warm with interest and intelligence.

"Why aren't you married or living with someone?"

It wasn't what he was expecting and he blinked as his brain struggled to catch up.

"No formulating responses, remember?" she said.

"I haven't met anyone I like enough to spend the rest of my life with yet."

Her chin lifted as though he'd surprised her.

"What's the best thing that's ever happened to you?" he fired back.

"Being posted to Iraq."

That surprised him and he made a mental note to follow up on it later.

"What are you most afraid of?" Charlie asked.

"Failure. What about you?"

Her gaze dropped to the table.

"No thinking," he said.

"I have to think."

"Not too much. Go with your gut."

She lifted her gaze to his face. "Not being able to cut it as a civilian."

There was something in the way she held herself that made him think she wasn't giving him her first answer. Her real answer. He thought about pushing, then decided against it.

"What's your biggest regret?" she asked.

Getting a virtual stranger pregnant. But he knew better than to say that out loud. "Not starting Falcon sooner."

Something shifted behind Charlie's eyes and

he knew she'd guessed that he'd offered up his second answer, too.

"What about you? What's your biggest regret?" he asked.

"Never knowing my mother."

There was no doubting the sincerity behind her answer this time.

"What's your worst personal fault?" she asked.

"Selfishness. No—laziness."

She laughed. "How about indecision?"

He smiled. "That, too. What's your favorite food?"

"Chocolate. In any form. If you could have any superpower, what would it be?"

"Flying. Hands down. But I wouldn't mind X-ray vision, either."

He was down to his last question and he thought for a moment before he spoke again.

"What makes you happy?"

She stared at him for a long beat before glancing down at the table. "I don't think it's possible to give one answer to a question like that."

Her hand found the fork positioned beside her place mat, nudging it a fraction of an inch toward the middle of the table.

"You don't have to limit it to one answer."

She nudged the fork again. "Then I guess I'd have to say that my friends make me happy. And doing a good job for someone, making a site that's attractive and functional. Knowing I'm good at something, I guess. That I'm earning my place in the world. Apart from that, all the usual clichéd things. A sunny day, puppies, blah, blah."

"Those are all pretty good things," he said, although he wasn't sure that he'd ever hung his happiness on the knowledge that he'd *earned his place in the world.* But clearly Charlie had a much stronger sense of duty than he did—witness her fourteen years in the armed forces. Only someone with a desire to give back would sign away so much of her life.

"Tell me about Iraq," he said. "Why is it the best thing that's ever happened to you?"

"Because it was hard, but it was rewarding, too. I was in charge of the vault, which means I handled all the encrypted communications for the Australian contingent. It's one thing to train for stuff, but it's not until you're in the field that you know if you're any good or not."

"And you're good?"

She met his eyes. "Yeah. I am. Or maybe I should say I was. Not much call for encrypted comms in Balmain."

"And hallelujah for that."

She smiled. "Yeah."

Their meals arrived and an hour slipped by as they settled into easier, more relaxed conversation. They talked about her work and his business, and she asked about his family, and before he knew it, the waitress was back, asking if they wanted dessert.

"There's no way I could fit another thing in," Charlie said.

"Me neither. Just a coffee, thanks."

The waitress looked to Charlie and she shook her head to indicate she didn't want anything to drink, either. It wasn't until the waitress had left the table that he remembered Charlie was cutting back on caffeine.

"Sorry. I forgot you can't drink coffee."

"It's okay. I'm not going to lunge across the table and tear it from your hands in a frenzy. I can take it or leave it at the best of times."

"Lucky for me, then. Otherwise I'd be dealing with some of those black ops moves they teach you in the army."

"Oh, yeah, you'd be in big trouble."

A strand of her hair had come loose from her ponytail, framing her face and softening her features. A memory flashed into his mind: Charlie lying beneath him on his bed, naked and flushed, her hair a sexy tangle around her face.

He shifted in his chair and cleared his throat. "I told my parents about everything last night. They want to meet you."

Charlie's gaze flew to his. "Oh. That was fast."

"My mother has a nose for secrets. She cornered me."

She smiled faintly, but she looked worried.

"It's my twin sisters' birthday next week and they asked me to bring you along," he said.

"Does that mean everyone will be there? All your brothers and sisters?"

"And the kitchen sink."

She nodded, but she had her poker face on now and he had no idea whether she was pleased, intimidated, terrified or delighted at the prospect of meeting all his family in one fell swoop.

"What do you think?"

"You said you told your parents everything last night. Did you tell them how we met?"

He was smart enough to know he was on potentially dangerous ground.

"I didn't go into detail, but I figured I might as well be honest. I don't know about you, but I wasn't exactly keen on making up some story to tell everyone for the rest of our lives."

Charlie's lips formed a straight line. "So instead we tell them how we met in a bar and had one night together before going our separate ways?"

"They won't judge you, if that's what you're worried about," he said.

"You mean judge both of us."

"Believe it or not, that *is* what I meant," he

said. "My brother already thinks I'm an idiot for messing up with the condom."

Charlie closed her eyes for a pained second. "You discussed condoms with your family?"

She looked so appalled he had to suppress a smile. "I forgot. You don't have brothers and sisters."

"No."

"When you meet them, you'll understand. As a group, they're the human equivalent of a steamroller."

"Wow. You're really making this seem like an appealing prospect."

"I can tell Mum you're busy, if you like. We can arrange something later. When things are more settled."

Charlie shook her head, straightening in her seat. "No. Let's get it over and done with."

She sounded like a Christian anticipating a run-in with a Colosseum full of lions.

"If it gets really bad, I'll light a fire and you can make a run for it."

"I may take you up on that."

"I'll make sure to bring a box of matches."

His coffee arrived, along with the bill. He was reaching for the sugar when he noticed Charlie pulling out her wallet.

"It's on me," he said easily, waving her wallet away.

"I can't let you do that."

He watched as she pulled out a twenty and a ten and put them with the bill. He'd never gone Dutch on a date in his life and he was about to hand her money back when it occurred to him that this wasn't a date. He wasn't sure what it was, but it definitely wasn't a date.

A partnership, maybe. Hopefully the beginnings of a friendship. God knew, they were going to need some kind of connection to sort this mess out.

He swallowed his objection and plucked a few notes from his own wallet to add to hers.

He finished his coffee and they left the restaurant. The night air was cooler than it had been last night. Charlie crossed her arms over her chest and gave him a self-conscious smile.

"This was a good idea. Thanks."

"We should do it again."

"We should."

"Where are you parked?"

She pointed across the harbor. "Beneath the casino."

"I'm the other way." He pointed over his shoulder.

"Then I'll see you next week."

"I'll email you with the details for the party."

"Great." She lifted her hand in farewell and started to swivel on her heel. Then she seemed to catch herself. She turned toward him, took a step forward and surprised him by pressing a kiss to his cheek.

"I heard there's a really good Mexican restaurant in Surry Hills. Maybe we could try that next time," she said.

Then she was gone, her slim figure weaving efficiently through the crowded walkway.

He stood with his hands in his pockets and watched until she disappeared from view. For a moment, he wondered how things might have turned out if she hadn't left that morning two months ago. If she'd stayed and he'd taken her out for breakfast the way he'd planned to. If breakfast had led to a second date, and a third...

He shook his head, irritated by his own musings. The only thing that mattered was what *had* happened. She'd left, he'd gotten over it, and now they were going to be parents together.

More than enough to get his head around without him fooling around with what-ifs.

Hands still in his pockets, he headed for his car.

CHAPTER EIGHT

"So, HOW DID IT GO?" Gina asked as she settled on Charlie's sofa the next day.

Her friend had dropped in for lunch, obviously keen to get the lowdown on Charlie's dinner with Rhys. Since she'd brought delicious-looking sandwiches with her, Charlie was prepared to do a little horse trading—to a point.

"It was okay. A bit awkward at first, but not a complete disaster."

Gina pulled a face, clearly unimpressed with the report. "You have to give me more than that. What was he wearing, where did you go, does he still make your heart go pitter-patter?"

Charlie gave her friend a look. "Why would he make my heart go pitter-patter?"

"Because he's gorgeous and because you had a wild night with him and just because things are complicated doesn't mean you're blind and he's stopped being hot."

"Hello? Did you miss the bit where I got accidentally pregnant, and ambushed him to tell him he was going to be a daddy, whether he liked it or not?"

"I said it was complicated. But that doesn't mean it's impossible."

"Except this isn't a romantic comedy with Jennifer Aniston and some hot actor. This is a bad situation we are trying to make the best of. Him being hot or not is completely irrelevant."

"You don't think being attracted to the father of your baby would be making the best of a bad situation?"

Charlie's belly tensed thinking about it. "I think it's the worst thing that could possibly happen. Without question." She sliced a hand through the air to emphasize her point.

"Why? Is he seeing someone?"

"I have no idea. He could be seeing ten different someones for all I know."

"You didn't ask?"

"Why would I? He didn't ask me, either, by the way. Which should tell you something."

Gina cocked her head. "What should it tell me?"

"That our relationship is about one thing and one thing only—the baby."

"Do you like him?"

Charlie gave an exasperated sigh. She loved Gina's eternal optimism and rose-colored outlook most of the time, but sometimes her friend's refusal to accept reality could be a little frustrating.

"I don't mean sexually," Gina amended. "I already know you like him that way or you wouldn't have gone home with him. Do you like him as a person? Now that you know him a little better?"

Charlie took a moment to consider her answer. Gina filled the time by unwrapping the two enormous chicken-salad sandwiches she'd brought with her.

"I think he's a decent guy," Charlie finally said. "I think he's sincere about trying to make this work."

"But do you *like* him?"

Charlie reached for her sandwich. "I think it would be impossible not to. He's charming and funny and he has more charisma than you can poke a stick at."

He was aware of it, too. Not in an egotistical way, but he knew that he had the power to sway people if he put his mind to it. The knowledge was evident in the way he looked at her and the rest of the world, the way he walked, the way he spoke. Throughout their dinner last night she'd been aware of him working to put her at ease. The stories he told her, the light tone to his voice, his smiles... It had been subtle, but he'd been doing his best to charm her—and succeeding.

As she'd said, it was almost impossible not to like him. Certainly beyond her puny powers.

The important thing, as she'd reminded herself last night and as she would continue to remind herself, was that she not confuse all that charm and attention with anything more personal. Because that way lay disaster.

"Tell me about this big wedding you've been invited to," she asked her friend, sick to death of thinking about, talking about and worrying about her own problems.

For the rest of their shared lunch break they talked about Gina's cousin's wedding and Charlie's clients, Gina thankfully taking Charlie's unspoken cue to steer clear of more Rhys discussion.

After her friend had left, Charlie cleaned up and returned to her desk. The red flag was up on her in-box, signaling that she had email. She clicked on the icon absently while running her eyes over the pictures she'd been resizing before Gina arrived.

Her gaze sharpened when she saw the email was from Rhys. She opened the message.

Hey. You probably know already, but I saw this in the paper today and thought of you. If you go, let me know so I can tag along and learn something from an expert.

He'd included a link and she clicked through

to an article in the online version of the *Sydney Morning Herald* touting an upcoming exhibition of rare and vintage comic books at the Museum of Contemporary Art.

A slow smile spread across her face. Last night she'd mentioned she'd had an extensive comic-book collection as a child, an off-the-cuff comment. One of many little facts they'd traded over dinner. But Rhys had obviously registered it and remembered, and when he'd seen this article he'd thought of her.

Oh, he's good. No wonder his business is doing so well.

The cynical little voice wasn't enough to diminish her pleasure in his attentiveness and she pulled the keyboard close and started typing.

I hadn't seen this, but it looks great. I'd love to go if you're up for it, but you have to promise to send up a flare if I bore you to tears rabbiting on and on in nerdy detail.

She hesitated a moment before hitting Send, reading over what she'd written. She didn't want to sound too eager. Too pleased by the fact that he'd thought of her. She edited the email, deleting the word *love*. Her fingers hovered over the keyboard as she tried to come up with a suitable alternative to replace it. After a minute she shook her head and put *love* back and hit Send in a rush of exasperation.

It was one thing to be sensible where Rhys was concerned and another thing entirely to turn into a paranoid psycho who turned herself inside out overanalyzing every interaction with the man. She'd drive herself nuts if she kept double-thinking everything.

Her computer chimed quietly to signal the arrival of another email and the red flag went up on her in-box. She opened the message.

Done. Let's make a date closer to the exhibition opening. Don't worry about boring me—inside every man is a boy who once tried to jump off the top of the garage with a towel for a cape. (Yes, I broke my arm, but not badly.)
BTW, my sisters' birthday party is next Friday. We should probably aim to get there by 7, so I would need to pick you up by 6:30 at the latest. Cool?

The smile faded from her lips as she read about his sisters' party and him picking her up. She'd managed to forget his parents' invitation until that moment. Or, more accurately, she'd chosen to.

Even though she hated going anywhere without the security blanket of her car, it made sense to go with Rhys, so she fired back a quick response confirming his plan. The moment the email had left her in-box her stomach turned over with nerves.

There. She was truly committed now. A little over a week from now she would be meeting Rhys's family. All at once.

She was the first to admit that she wasn't at her best in large group situations, even under ideal circumstances—she was too much of a loner, or perhaps simply too used to being alone, to revel in rowdy group gatherings where people were expected to fight for the chance to be heard. And these were far from ideal circumstances. All Rhys's family knew about her was that she'd met him in a bar, gone home with him and now was pregnant with his baby. Rhys might claim that they wouldn't judge her for any of the above, but they would have to be an almost freakishly open-minded group of people not to have formed some idea of who and what she was.

There was no point kidding herself—meeting his family was going to be horrible and awkward and embarrassing, and she had no choice but to do it, even if her toes were curled inside her shoes the whole night. Rhys's brothers and sisters were going to be uncles and aunts to her child. Their children would be her baby's cousins, and Rhys's parents would be her baby's grandparents. She needed them to accept her. Or, at the very least, to accept her baby. She could live with their disapproval or dislike, as long as they loved her child.

Opening the calendar on her computer, she marked down the party for next Friday. Then she made a note to herself to buy a good bottle of wine and something nice for his sisters' birthday. And maybe she should get her hair cut. It had been a while, and it might help her feel a little more prepared.

Please. It's going to be a freakin' nightmare, haircut or no haircut. Nothing's going to change that.

But she would do it anyway. For her baby.

"THE THING YOU NEED to know about Mark is that even though he looks big and he talks loud, he's a complete pussycat underneath." Rhys changed lanes, preparing to make a left turn ahead.

"Okay."

"Don't talk about Wall Street and you'll be fine." He was aware of Charlie frowning as he signaled.

"Wall Street the place or the financial markets in general?" she asked.

"Both." He turned the corner.

"Right."

She sounded nervous. He'd be nervous, too, if he was her.

News flash, buddy—you are *nervous.*

It was true. He had no idea why. They were his family after all, not a firing squad. But there was no denying the tension in his chest and belly.

This felt like a big deal. Charlie meeting his family for the first time. The first of many meetings if things went well. The beginning of awkwardness and discomfort if it didn't.

He tightened his grip on the steering wheel. "Look, you'll be fine. They're nice people. A bit loud and rude sometimes but nice."

And Charlie was nice, too. Smart and funny in her own quiet way. The odds were good that everything would be fine.

A small silence fell as he drove through the dark residential street to his parents' house.

"When was the last time you brought someone home for dinner?"

He glanced at her, surprised by the question. She was watching him, a small smile on her lips.

"I don't know." He thought for a moment. "Maybe ten years ago. Why?"

"You seem a little out of practice."

He laughed, the sound loud inside the car. "Yeah. Maybe I am."

"Although the last woman you brought home probably wasn't pregnant, huh?"

"Not to my knowledge, no."

"Then I guess it's a voyage of discovery for all of us."

He found a spot in front of the neighbor's house and parked. He shut off the engine and turned to Charlie. Her face was in shadows and he could see the glint of her eyes but not the expression in them.

"You ready?"

"As I'll ever be."

"Then let's do this." He started to open the car door.

"Wait." Charlie's hand caught his sleeve. "How do I turn on the interior light?"

He reached across and flicked the map light on. She reached into her bag and pulled out a lipstick. He watched as she applied more color to her already pink mouth. It occurred to him that this was the first time he'd ever seen Charlie fuss over her appearance. Most women of his acquaintance—including his sisters and his mother—were constantly tweaking their hair or makeup or worrying about things like bra straps showing or visible panty line. But Charlie always seemed composed and confident within herself.

She wasn't a fussy dresser, either. Her black fitted shirt and tailored pants were well cut and conservative, and she wore no jewelry to speak of. He couldn't help contrasting her appearance with the way she'd looked that night at Café

Sydney. Sultry and sexy and mysterious. Looking at her now, it was almost impossible to believe that it had been the same woman. Not that she wasn't attractive and sexy in a far more subtle way in her current outfit, but there was definitely a Jekyll and Hyde thing going on as far as her appearance went.

"Is something wrong? Did I get lipstick on my teeth?"

He realized he was staring and that she'd finished checking her hair and makeup.

"No. You're fine. You look good."

She shook her head slightly in instant negation of his comment. "I wasn't fishing for a compliment."

"I didn't think you were."

She busied herself readying her handbag, but he'd have to be blind not to notice the pink flush on her cheeks.

"We should go in." She opened her door and slid out of the car.

He hesitated before following her. He wasn't sure what the blush was about. Self-consciousness? Discomfort because he'd all but admitted he found her attractive? Although how that could be a surprise to her after the night they'd shared together, he had no idea.

He climbed out and locked the car before joining her on the sidewalk.

"Careful of the crack on the pathway," he said as he led her toward the house.

She nodded, the movement a shadow in the darkness. He could smell her perfume, something that reminded him of orange blossom. Despite having already offered a warning, he couldn't stop himself from taking her elbow when they reached the crack in the walkway.

"Thanks," she said.

"These steps can be a bit tricky, too."

His parents had forgotten to leave the porch light on and the front of the house was dark with gloom. He guided Charlie up the steps with a hand on the small of her back, worried she'd trip.

"Thanks," she said again, but there was an unevenness to her tone that made him peer closer at her face.

Sure enough, she was smiling.

"What's so funny?"

"I'm pregnant. I haven't forgotten how to walk or climb stairs."

"Sorry." He felt stupid. Of course she could find her way up three concrete steps, even in the dark.

"I wasn't complaining. It's just…strange to be fussed over."

"Not much fussing in the R.A. Sigs?"

"Not really, no."

"I'm guessing there's going to be more fussing from everyone once you start to show."

"I'll work on getting used to it."

He was smiling as he reached out to give his customary arrival knock before opening the door. Warmth rushed out—as well as the sound of too many Walkers in one space.

"Brace yourself," he said as he led Charlie toward the back of the house.

She shot him a quick, startled look. Then she smiled, and it was only because he was beginning to know her that he understood she'd put on her social face and that the real Charlie was somewhere behind that small, easy smile. He felt a sudden, strong urge to put his arm around her, to guide her into his family in the same way that he'd guided her past the cracked pavement and up the steps.

Instead, he preceded her into the kitchen, stepping to one side so there would be room beside him. As he'd suspected, every eye turned to him and the volume dropped dramatically. His stomach gave an absurd, anxious squeeze and he turned to glance at Charlie. She was a little pale, but that small smile was holding and there was a determined light in her eyes.

"Everyone, this is Charlie Long. Charlie, this mob of reprobates, commie-pinko-lefties and mad people is my family."

He went on to introduce Charlie to his mum and dad, then his brothers and sisters and in-laws, and finally the children. Charlie shook hands and maintained steady eye contact and responded to every conversational sally that came her way in a clear, confident voice. He hovered at her side throughout, watching his brothers' and sisters' faces, ready to run interference if anyone said anything to make Charlie feel uncomfortable.

But everyone was on their best behavior and soon Charlie was having a glass of nonalcoholic cider pushed into her hand and the volume was rising as everyone broke into smaller conversations.

"I hope you like Italian, Charlie. Kim and Becky are suckers for pasta, so I always make my lasagna when it's their birthday," his mother said, drawing her to one side.

The better to interrogate her, Rhys suspected. He moved with them, determined not to leave Charlie to his family's tender mercies.

"I love Italian. I've actually signed up for a cooking course that one of the local restaurants is running in Balmain," Charlie said.

"Ah, so you enjoy cooking then?" his mother asked.

"I'm not sure," Charlie said with a small laugh. "To be honest, I'm not very good, but I've been trying to get better now I can't rely on the mess to make up for my deficiencies."

"That's right, Rhys mentioned you were in the army until only recently. It must be a big change for you, hanging up your uniform."

Rhys continued to hover as his mother and Charlie exchanged small talk. Out of the corner of his eye he could see his sisters checking Charlie out, taking in her clothes, her shoes, her hair. Again, he had to stifle the urge to put his arm around her shoulders. She was doing fine, and his family were maintaining the pretense that they were civilized. So far, so good.

After a few minutes his mother ushered Charlie into a chair and positioned a platter of antipasto in front of her.

"If you see something you like, claim it early," Rhys said. "Once the locusts move in you won't stand a chance."

Charlie gave him an uncertain smile before selecting a couple of olives. His brother engaged her in conversation about her web-design business, then Kim started to quiz her about her life in the army.

"So, is it true that it's a man's world in the defense forces? Did you ever feel as though you were discriminated against or not taken seriously?"

Charlie took a moment to answer. Rhys was

standing behind her chair and couldn't see her face.

"There's no getting away from the fact that it's a workforce made up predominantly of men, which means you're dealing and working with men all day. Personally, I didn't have a problem with that. I've always been pretty straightforward and most of the guys were up front with me, so it was all good. But I know some of the other women I worked with found it tough."

"But I'm sure I read somewhere that one of the best ways to gain promotion is to serve in active duty, which means that women are automatically behind the eight ball because they can't participate in combat," Kim said.

"There are lots of ways of participating in deployments that don't involve active combat. I was deployed to both Iraq and East Timor, for example."

"You were in Iraq?" Mark asked, his posture becoming more alert.

"I did an eight-month tour," Charlie confirmed.

Rhys was more than familiar with his brother's views on the war, thanks to the many arguments they'd "enjoyed" around the dinner table. He fixed his brother with a hard look, daring him to mouth off. Mark stared at him for a long second before refocusing on Charlie.

"That must have been interesting," Mark said.

Charlie murmured something noncommittal. Rhys rolled his shoulders as the conversation shifted to the movie his sister-in-law had seen during the week. Charlie waited until the conversation was flowing around her before turning in her seat and tilting her head to make eye contact with him.

"Could you tell me where the bathroom is?" she asked quietly.

"Out into the hall, second door on the right," his mother said before he could respond.

"Thank you," Charlie said, pushing herself to her feet. "Excuse me."

She offered his mother a small smile before exiting. Rhys was aware of all eyes turning to him the moment she left the room.

"What?"

"She doesn't need a bodyguard, Rhys. What do you think we're going to do to her?" Mark asked.

"I don't think you're going to do anything."

"So why are you following her around like she's had a death threat or something?" Becky asked.

"I'm not."

"You are. You haven't left her side since you walked in the door," Tim said.

Rhys resisted the urge—barely—to grind his teeth. "I'm trying to make her feel comfortable. Believe it or not, some people don't like being interrogated by a roomful of loudmouths all at once."

"Hello, Pot, I'd like you to meet Mr. Kettle," Becky scoffed.

"Charlie's not like us," Rhys said. "She doesn't have any brothers and sisters. She's not used to conversational guerrilla warfare."

"Thanks for the heads-up, Rhys. We're all so thick we didn't pick that up," Mark said.

"She'll feel more comfortable without you breathing down her neck," Kim said.

"Thanks for the advice. I know just what to do with it," Rhys said.

His mother held up both hands. "Not another word from any of you. Charlie is my guest, and I won't have any of you making her feel uncomfortable. Which means we all need to stop talking about her while she's out of the room, for starters. Honestly, you'd think you were all raised by wolves the way you behave sometimes."

"Thank you," Rhys said, crossing his arms over his chest, very satisfied that she'd set his brothers and sisters straight.

"That includes you, Rhys. Back off a little and give the poor woman some breathing room," his mother said.

Rhys opened his mouth to respond, but his father passed him a basket of garlic bread.

"Make yourself useful."

Rhys bit his tongue, but only because he was very aware that Charlie could enter the room again at any second. The last thing he wanted was for her to think they'd all been talking about her. Even though they had.

His movements stiff, he placed the basket of bread in the center of the table. When he turned away, he caught Becky studying him with an arrested, intent light in her eyes. He raised his eyebrows in silent question.

She shrugged. "I've never seen you like this about a woman before."

"I've never gotten a woman pregnant before, either."

Becky studied him a moment longer before nodding and reaching for her wineglass. Rhys moved closer to the door so that he'd be the first person Charlie saw when she returned to the room.

He didn't care what his mother or sister said. He wasn't abandoning her to their curiosity and interest, well-intentioned or not.

Stop being such a coward. Wash your hands and go out there and get to know the people who are going to become your child's family.

Charlie didn't budge from her perch on the toilet lid. She hadn't really needed to go to the bathroom—she'd needed a moment alone to get a grip on her nerves.

Rhys had filled her in on his family, but nothing could have prepared her for stepping into a roomful of tall, good-looking, confident Walkers, all of whom had started dissecting her with their eyes the moment she came through the door. If she'd thought about it, she might have anticipated that Rhys's family would be like him— dark haired and brown eyed, very attractive, with more than their fair share of charisma—but she hadn't. She'd been too busy being amused by his very obvious nervousness because it had made her feel that much better about her own nerves.

They're just people. No different from you.

It was true, but it was also a lie. She might be able to fake a reasonable facsimile of social ease, but she would never have the natural, bone-deep confidence that the Walkers all seemed to have been born with. Maybe it was genetic. Or maybe it was something their parents had instilled in them in their formative years. It didn't really matter, either way. She simply needed to get over this sense of intimidation and get her ass back to the kitchen where it belonged.

Hands on her knees, she pushed herself to her feet and crossed to the vanity. She washed her hands and tidied her ponytail before straightening her shirt unnecessarily.

Stop stalling, you big chicken.

She left the bathroom and walked the few steps to the kitchen door. Rhys was standing just inside the room, a frown on his face as he watched his brothers and sisters. His gaze swung toward her as he heard her footsteps and the frown faded from his face. He stepped closer and touched her arm as she entered the room.

"How're you coping? Need me to napalm the curtains yet?" he asked quietly.

His hand felt very warm on her arm, even through the fabric of her shirt. She looked into his deep brown eyes and was warmed in a different way by the very real concern she saw there.

"I'm fine."

He gave her a reassuring squeeze before dropping his hand to his side. She resumed her seat at the table and allowed herself to be drawn into a discussion about the pros and cons of the high Australian dollar between Tim, Rhys's oldest brother, and Meg, his sister-in-law. It wasn't long before more opinions were being offered and soon there were at least three competing conversations on the same topic swirling around her. Somehow she managed to follow all three. Rhys's siblings had strong opinions and weren't afraid to offer them up and stand their ground. They also weren't afraid to take shots at each other's logic or politics, and she found herself both shocked and amused by their take-no-prisoners verbal warfare.

"You're all wrong," a deep voice cut over the hurly-burly.

She glanced over her shoulder to where Rhys was standing, an amused, knowing light in his eyes.

"If any of you cared to befoul your pure minds by reading the *Financial Review* or following the market, you'd understand why the dollar is so high at the moment and why it's likely to stay that way." He proceeded to outline in crisp, decisive detail all the pertinent factors, talking over Tim when he tried to interrupt.

"So you can flap your gums all you like and stand on your soapboxes, but it's not going to change reality, my hand-knit-wearing, crunchy-granola-loving, ecowarrior friends," he concluded.

His delivery was so dry and droll and so obviously designed to insult and condescend that a bubble of appalled/admiring laughter burst from her mouth. Becky and Kim gave her matching reproving looks, their foreheads furrowed into identical frowns, even though Charlie had already worked out that, despite their similarity, they were fraternal and not identical twins.

"Don't encourage him, Charlie. He already

thinks he's the smartest person in the room. Our job is to keep him humble," Kim said.

"I think it might be too late for that," Charlie said, which earned her a round of laughter.

"She's got your number, Rhys," Tim crowed.

"Ever heard of loyalty?" a low voice said near her ear, and she turned her head so quickly she felt the brush of Rhys's five o'clock shadow against her cheek. She jerked away slightly and was aware of him doing the same.

"I'm very loyal," she said once she'd recovered her composure. "But I'm not delusional."

"Ouch," he said, but his eyes were laughing at her.

"Stop pretending you ever aspired to be humble. As if," she said, her own mouth curving into a smile.

He was about to say something in response when his mother spoke up.

"For heaven's sake, Rhys, go find a chair. You're right in the way where you are," Holly said.

"Since you asked so nicely..." Rhys said, straightening and taking a step away from the table to clear the path for his mother.

She flicked the tea towel she was holding at him threateningly and he rounded the table to where there was an empty seat diagonally opposite Charlie. She couldn't decide if it was a good thing or a bad thing that he wouldn't be sitting next to her throughout the meal. On the one hand, there was no denying that she found him distracting at the best of times. But he was also the only familiar face in what was shaping up to be one of the most challenging meals she'd ever endured.

"Please, everyone, eat while it's hot," Holly said as she ferried three plates of steaming lasagna to the table.

Ken followed her, a huge salad bowl in his hands.

The rich, almost overripe smell of tomatoes, onion and garlic hit Charlie as Holly slid one of the plates in front of her before heading back to the counter for more. Charlie looked at the stack of pasta sheets and oozing sauce and swallowed convulsively as a completely unexpected wave of nausea turned her stomach. Heat rushed up her neck and down into her body as bile burned the back of her throat.

Oh, God, please, not now.

How on earth could she have had absolutely no morning sickness whatsoever, only for it to strike now, of all possible moments? Surely fate could not be that cruel.

She swallowed again, reaching for her water glass. She took a small, careful sip. The burning eased in her throat. She kept her gaze glued to the glass, concentrating on the beads of moisture on the outside of the thick tumbler to avoid looking at the plate. Maybe if she waited a moment her stomach would settle. A few minutes ago she'd actually been feeling peckish, so maybe she was simply a little too hungry....

"Bread?" Tim's wife, Amber, asked, thrusting the basket of garlic bread beneath Charlie's nose.

Garlic and butter assaulted her olfactory senses and she took a gasping, panicky breath as her stomach rolled ominously.

"Are you okay?"

It was Rhys, rising from his seat. Charlie opened her mouth to assure him that she was fine, only to make the mistake of glancing at the red mess on the white plate.

"I'm so sorry," she said, shoving her chair back with a screech of metal legs on linoleum and clapping a hand to her mouth.

She turned toward the door, intending to race to the bathroom, but the distance she had to travel seemed like a long, long way and her belly was already tensing in rebellion. The thought of throwing up in front of Rhys's entire family only made her nausea more intense.

"Here."

Rhys urged her toward the closed door next to the kitchen sink. He twisted the handle and cool air hit her face as she stumbled down the steps and into the yard. She barely made it to the side fence before she bent and retched into the garden bed, the remains of her lunch burning up her throat.

CHAPTER NINE

A WARM WEIGHT landed on the small of her back.

"Are you okay?"

As stupid questions went, it was right up there. She didn't bother responding, simply remained hunched over, waiting to see if there would be a round two. Rhys seemed to get the message.

"Sorry," he said. "Ignore me."

Her stomach was still roiling, trying to decide if it was going to do another impersonation of Mount Vesuvius.

"Here. Give Charlie this."

She recognized Holly's voice, and the next thing she knew, a glass of cold water was pressed into her hand. She took it gratefully, rinsing her mouth out several times. Finally she felt able to straighten.

"I'm so sorry," she said as her gaze found Rhys's in the darkened yard. "That was…bad."

His expression was inscrutable in the shadows. "Are you feeling better now?"

"A bit." She didn't sound very convincing, probably because she wasn't one hundred percent certain that her stomach had finished torturing her for the evening.

"Maybe try some more water."

She followed his suggestion, taking sips from the glass and actually swallowing them this time. Her stomach didn't seem in immediate danger of exploding and she gave a small, relieved sigh.

"Better?"

"Yes." Except for the bit where she'd humiliated herself by almost hurling in front of his entire family. Other than that, everything was just dandy.

"Sit down for a second," Rhys said.

His gesture drew her attention to a low-lying lounger that was angled across the patio. She sank onto it cautiously, not wanting to excite the nausea again. Rhys sat beside her, his long legs bent awkwardly to accommodate the lounger's low height.

"I thought you said you hadn't been sick," he said after a few seconds.

"Until two minutes ago, I hadn't."

"So that's the first time?" He sounded incredulous. As well he might be.

"I was fine right up until I looked at that lasagna."

He made a small, muffled sound. She glanced at him, and even though his face was poker straight she knew he'd swallowed a laugh.

"It's not funny."

"You feeling sick isn't. But you've got to admit, the timing is awesome."

Maybe tomorrow, or next week, she'd think it was funny. Right now she was too busy feeling queasy and embarrassed and miserable.

"God knows what your mother thinks of me." And the rest of them. She could still see their shocked faces as she pushed away from the table.

"Kim and Becky both practically lived with their heads in the toilet bowl during their pregnancies. And Mum will tell anyone who sits still long enough that I gave her hell for the first four months of her pregnancy. Apparently they even thought about calling me Ralph at one stage."

Charlie smiled slightly, despite her still-churning stomach. "No wonder your business is doing so well."

"Sorry?"

"You're too charming for your own good."

"I'm not sure that's possible."

She gave him a wry look. He reached out and encouraged the glass toward her mouth again.

"Drink some more water, and stop worrying about my family. You weaseled your way into their good books with that crack about me not being humble. You're home free from here."

"If only it was that easy," she said ruefully.

"Trust me, it is. They're a cheap crowd."

She smiled again, very aware that he was working overtime to put her at ease—the way he had last week at the restaurant. Now that she was getting to know him, she suspected it was a purely instinctive reaction for him, as natural as breathing.

"I bet people don't say no to you much, huh?"

There was a small giveaway pause before he responded. "Not often, no."

"So I really didn't have much of a chance that night, did I?" she said. "Once you'd engaged your tractor beam." She'd been joking, but she could feel him tense beside her.

"You make it sound as though it wasn't something you wanted," he said. There was a question in his voice and she realized she'd thrown him off balance.

"I was joking," she said. "Not very well, apparently."

"So you don't regret it, then?"

She turned to look at him. He was leaning forward, his elbows on his knees, but he faced her. For a long moment their eyes met and held.

Suddenly her head was full of images from that night.

His hands on her breasts.

His weight pressing her into the bed.

The hard planes of his chest and back, smooth and warm beneath her hands.

Sitting in the dark with him with the faint, sour taste of bile in her mouth, it all seemed like a lifetime ago. As though it had happened to another person. But it hadn't, it had happened to her. To them. For one night she'd thrown all her inhibitions, self-doubt and beliefs about herself and the world out the window and simply allowed herself to *feel*.

And it had been good. It had been *wonderful*.

"No. I don't regret it. Not the going-home bit, anyway." Maybe she was crazy, but despite everything, she didn't have it in her to regret the hours she'd spent in his bed.

She swept her hand in front of her in an all-encompassing gesture. "This bit—the bit where we've been forced into a relationship with each other for the rest of our lives because of a faulty piece of latex—I could do without."

"It could have been worse, you know."

She gave a small snort of disbelief.

"It's true," he insisted. "You could have been a psychotic bunny boiler without a single sensible thought in your head, and I could have been a slacker, stoner loser on unemployment with a killer marijuana habit."

She shook her head. "No. There's no way I

would have gone home with that guy. Even if I was a bunny-boiling head case."

"You wouldn't have had a choice. I would have trapped you in my tractor beam, remember?"

"I don't think slacker, stoner Rhys has a tractor beam."

"No?"

"No. I think the tractor beam is all yours."

"I wasn't sure I liked the tractor-beam idea at first, but it's growing on me. I'm going to take that as a compliment."

She huffed out a little laugh.

"How's the nausea?"

She did a swift body check. "Better."

"Good."

She glanced over her shoulder toward the house. "We should probably head inside."

"Why?"

"Because they'll be wondering what's going on."

"It'll give them something to talk about. Besides, it's nicer out here. Quieter."

She peered at him in the darkness. "I can't tell if you're joking or not."

"Not. But we can go inside if you really want to."

She gauged her own wants and needs against what she knew was the polite thing to do.

Rhys sighed theatrically and pushed to his feet.

"Come on, then, if you insist on doing the right thing." He offered her his hand. His fingers were firm around hers as he helped her to her feet.

"I hope I haven't ruined your sisters' birthday party," she said.

Now that she was standing she could see through the kitchen window to where the Walkers were still gathered around the table.

"Are you kidding me? You made it a red-letter event. This will go down in the annals of Walker family history as the night Charlie nearly tossed her cookies on the table. You're officially a legend, immortalized forever."

She smiled, mostly because she knew she was meant to. Rhys wrapped an arm around her shoulders.

"It's not a big deal. Honestly."

"If you say so."

"I do." He looked at her, a warm light in his eyes.

Something tightened in her chest as she gazed into his handsome face. Not because he was good looking, but because he was so *nice*.

Nice—and funny and quick and smart. He smelled good, too, and the arm around her shoulder was hard with muscle. The rest of him was, too, she knew. His thighs and his belly and his chest…

She shrugged out from under his arm. "Better not keep them waiting."

She didn't look at him again as she headed for the back door.

IT WAS ONLY WHEN Charlie slipped out from under his arm that it hit Rhys that he had no right to touch her so familiarly. That they didn't have that kind of relationship.

Yet all night he'd been fighting the need to touch her, to protect her, to literally shield her with his body.

Clearly, there was more than a little caveman blood running in his veins.

He was half a second behind Charlie as she reentered the kitchen, in time to witness his smart-ass family offering her a rousing round of applause.

For a long beat Charlie's face was a study in shock then her mouth curved into a slow, appreciative smile. She glanced at him, checking to see what he made of his family's antics, and he rolled his eyes.

"They think they're funny," he said.

His mother ushered Charlie to her spot at the table, minus the plate of lasagna. He resumed his own seat, watching with satisfaction as his parents refused to accept Charlie's apology for something that was clearly beyond her control. If anyone was to blame, they said, it was the person who'd created this situation in the first place. At which point all eyes turned his way for the second time that night. He was about to defend himself, when Charlie beat him to it.

"It wasn't Rhys's fault," she blurted.

All eyes swiveled to her. Rhys watched, fascinated, as color climbed into her pale cheeks.

"I mean, it wasn't anyone's fault. Or maybe it was both our faults. But really it was an accident. It's the twenty-first century. Condoms are supposed to work, right?"

The moment the word *condoms* slipped out of her mouth her eyes widened and her gaze shot to the children's end of the table. Meg snorted wine out her nose while Rod choked on a piece of garlic bread. The rest of the table erupted into laughter—which was almost loud enough to drown out Garth's youthful, carrying tenor.

"What's a condom, Mum?"

Charlie dropped her head into her hands as the laughter cranked louder. Rhys waited until he spotted the smile hidden behind her hands before allowing himself to grin.

"Let me get you some salad, sweetheart," his mother said as she wiped the tears from her eyes. She patted Charlie comfortingly on the back as she went to fetch a clean plate.

The rest of the evening went smoothly—or

as smoothly as any Walker family gathering ever did. Charlie managed to eat a little salad and a handful of crackers, then they cleared the table and dimmed the lights before bringing out Kim and Becky's birthday cake. Gifts were offered and accepted, and soon the table was covered in torn wrapping paper and discarded envelopes.

Rhys kept checking in with Charlie, catching her eye across the table to gauge how she was doing. Her color remained good and she seemed to be enjoying herself—although he had to admit that sometimes it was hard to tell with Charlie. She was adept at keeping up appearances. But her laughter and smiles seemed genuine to him, and there was no doubting her sincerity when she pulled two small, beautifully wrapped boxes from her handbag and offered one each to the twins.

"Just a little something," she said as she handed them over.

"You shouldn't have—but that doesn't mean I'm giving this back," Kim said, her fingers already untying the colorful ribbons.

"I couldn't have said it better myself," Becky agreed.

Almost in unison they unwrapped their boxes and each extracted a bracelet, silver with intricate beading, Kim's in dusky-blue tones and Becky's in sea green. Rhys could tell by the way the other women of his family oohed appreciatively that Charlie had made good choices.

"The woman in the shop said the artist lives in the Blue Mountains," Charlie said. "There were other colors, so if these don't suit I'd be happy to swap them—"

"It's lovely. Beautiful," Kim said. Standing, she walked over to kiss Charlie's cheek. "Thank you."

Becky followed suit. Rhys watched as Charlie fussed with her handbag, making a big deal out of hanging it over the back of her chair again to cover her self-conscious pleasure at his sisters' reactions. Her cheeks were very pink and she ran a hand over her hair as though checking to make sure all was in order. Then, while he watched, she settled herself and took a steadying breath and slowly but surely composed herself.

It was an impressive feat of self-control. He'd already noted how self-contained she was. How disciplined.

She hadn't been self-controlled in his bed that night, though. She'd been wild and willful and passionate. Abandoned, even. So much so that it had taken him weeks to get her out of his head.

"Who wants coffee or tea?" his father asked.

Rhys realized he was staring at Charlie, so he stood. "I'll take care of it."

The small domestic task kept him busy for the next several minutes. The coffee mugs had barely been drained when his siblings started making leaving noises. While they gathered their children, he made eye contact with Charlie and cocked an eyebrow, asking if she was ready to go. She shrugged and nodded, which he took to mean she was happy to leave when he was.

He turned to his mother, ready to say goodbye.

"Can you help me take the rubbish out before you go?" she asked before he could get a word out. She had that look in her eye again. The one that said she had something to say to him.

"Sure." No point trying to put off the inevitable. His mother was as ruthless as the KGB when she wanted something.

"Won't be a second," he said to Charlie.

He collected the bulging bag from beneath the sink and made his way outside. His mother followed him, carrying a token juice container to justify their joint excursion. Rhys dumped the garbage in the bin and turned to face his mother.

"What's up?"

"Why does anything need to be up?" she asked.

"Mum. Please. Subtlety was never your thing. Play to your strengths." He watched as she tried to decide whether to pretend to be offended or to simply cut to the chase and start the inquisition.

"Charlie's waiting," he prompted her.

She gave him an exasperated look. "You know,

I can't wait till this baby of yours is old enough for you to understand how I feel right now."

"My child will never have sex," Rhys said. "I've already decided that. So he or she will never be in this situation."

His mother's smile was nothing short of patronizing. "Of course not. He or she will be perfectly polite and obedient, too, of course."

"Naturally."

"She's not what I imagined, you know."

The smile faded from Rhys's lips. Finally, they'd come to the point.

"When I heard how you met, I had a picture in my head. A cliché, I guess. Big hair, short skirt, platform heels, too much makeup—"

"Thanks, Mum." As a comment on his taste in women, it wasn't very flattering.

"But she's nothing like that, is she? I can see now why you believed her when she said the baby was yours."

"She's not a liar."

"No. She isn't."

His mother fixed him with a determined look. "You should know that I'm going to ask for her number and I'm going to stay in contact. Not just because I want to be a part of this baby's life. She hasn't got any family, and she might have questions and I want to let her know that we're here for her if she needs us."

Rhys frowned. "It's a nice idea. But she's a very private person, Mum."

"I want her to know she's not alone."

"She already knows that. She's got me."

His mother patted his arm. "Not in the way that I had your father. I know you're doing your best, but it's not the same as knowing that you've got someone by your side who loves you and is as excited about the baby and what happens next as you are."

He stared at her, wanting to deny her words while, at the same time, knowing she was right.

"Charlie will be wondering what's taking so long."

He entered the house, heading to the bathroom to wash his hands. The kitchen was empty when he returned, but he could hear voices in the adjoining room. Charlie, his sisters and sisters-in-law. He collected his coat and went to join them.

He arrived in time to watch his mother press a scrap of paper with her number on it into Charlie's hand, which, of course, necessitated that Charlie offer up her own. He swooped in before the other women of his family could get the same idea.

"Time for us to hit the road. I've got an early meeting tomorrow," he said.

Charlie focused on his mother. "Thank you for

a lovely meal. And I'm sorry about the, uh, sickness. The lasagna really did look beautiful."

"It was our pleasure, Charlie," his mother said.

"Thank you for our lovely presents," Kim said.

Charlie lifted a hand in an awkward wave, but his mother stepped close and gave her a warm hug.

"It was lovely meeting you. I hope we see you again soon."

Charlie blinked rapidly a few times as she drew back from his mother's embrace. A few more farewells, and then they were on the porch, the door closed behind them.

Charlie was quiet as they made their way to his car. He waited until they were both buckled in and the engine running before speaking.

"Well. We survived. Mostly intact, too."

"You have a nice family."

"I have a loud, overbearing, opinionated, rude family. But it's nice of you to say so."

She smiled faintly but didn't say anything else. He thought about what his mother had said about Charlie feeling alone. It was almost impossible for him to put himself in her shoes. Frankly, he was having enough trouble dealing with his half of this situation. But he wasn't the one who would be carrying a baby to full term, and while his life was about to change significantly, it wouldn't change as profoundly as Charlie's.

He tried to find something to say that would bridge the gap between them. But there were no words that could undo the child that was growing inside her, and there was no magic wand he could wave to change their relationship. It was what it was.

Imperfect. Inconvenient. Unconventional.

Beside him, Charlie yawned, one hand lifting to cover her mouth politely. "Sorry."

He put the car in gear. "Let's get you home."

CHARLIE'S "EVENING SICKNESS," as Rhys soon dubbed it, was not a one-off occurrence. As she entered her tenth week she became far too familiar with the queasy, uneasy feeling that gripped her like clockwork the moment the sun went down. It didn't take her long to learn that from approximately 6:00 p.m. onward she was good for nothing but lying on the couch with one of her many baby books, nibbling on dry toast or a banana.

She told Rhys as much when she canceled their second get-to-know-you dinner and he insisted on swapping out for a lunch so she would have her evenings free to wallow in her misery—his words, not hers.

"That's very generous of you," she said.

"Thank you. I thought so, too."

She didn't need to see him to know he was

smiling. She leaned back in her chair and put her feet up on the corner of her desk.

"I think a really generous person would volunteer to swallow several tablespoons of syrup of ipecac, to show his true solidarity," she said.

"An interesting idea. Let me think about it for a few weeks and get back to you."

"Some women believe the human race would have died out long ago if men had to have babies, you know," she said. "What with all the varicose veins and morning sickness and episiotomies."

"I would totally be up for it if it was possible. But, sadly, it isn't."

She liked the way his voice got a certain note in it when he was teasing her.

"You'd better hope they don't make a huge leap in reproductive science in your lifetime," she said.

"No kidding."

She was still smiling when she ended the call a few minutes later, and the next day he made her smile some more when they met in Surry Hills to try the Mexican restaurant she'd read about. They discussed the biography of Steve Jobs she was reading over bowls of fresh guacamole and crispy corn chips, sharing a pitcher of fruity nonalcoholic punch. Conversation shifted to his family as they shared a platter of fajitas, with Rhys filling her in on the various romances and courtships that had led to his siblings' marriages.

"I still think it's weird that you're the only one who isn't married yet," she said as she used the last of her tortilla to mop up her plate.

"Just as weird as you not being married."

Her response was out of her mouth before she could think it through. "It's not the same. Not by a long shot."

"Why not?" His gaze was direct and questioning.

She shifted, regretting her unthinking words. "I'm really thirsty. Do you want some more punch?"

Rhys cocked his head. "Am I missing something here?"

"No." He didn't need her to point out how good looking he was and how average she was and how that affected their respective chances for attracting the opposite sex. The man had eyes in his head.

The topic changed and she heaved a silent sigh of relief and made a mental note never to discuss Rhys's marital status again. It was none of her business, anyway.

Still, she found herself wondering about his love life as he settled the bill at the bar. Probably because the waitress was pouring on the smiles as she served him.

There was no way that a man like him didn't have a woman in his life, even only on a casual basis. Every time they'd gone out together he turned female heads—yet he'd never mentioned another woman in her presence.

So what? He doesn't have to offer his whole life up to you on a platter. And you don't have to offer everything up to him, either.

Not that there was much to hold back. But the principle was sound.

The following week Rhys couldn't make lunch, so he compensated by coming to her place on Friday night with a bunch of bananas and a DVD. She was more touched than she should have been that he'd remembered bananas were one of the few things she could stomach.

They wound up talking through the DVD and eventually she turned it off so they didn't have to do battle with the sound track. She told him about the coffee date she'd had with his mother, an event that could have been awkward and horrible but had been thoroughly enjoyable. Rhys warned her that his mother had a sixth sense for anything remotely private. Charlie put on her best poker face and told him that she'd already told Holly all the juicy details about their one night together. Rhys fixed her with a knowing eye and refused to rise to the bait. As the evening wore on he told her all the choice exploits he and his brothers had gotten up to when they were younger and she reciprocated with hair-raising tales from recruit training.

"I don't know how you stuck it out," he said when she'd finished telling him about how she'd had to complete a ten-kilometer hike—with a ten-kilogram pack—twice in order to accomplish it in under the required time limit. "I would have told them where to stuff their stupid requirements."

He was lounging in the Eames chair, feet propped on the ottoman, his shirt open at the neck and pulled out from the waistband of his trousers. His shoes lay unlaced on the floor beside his chair. He looked big and rumpled and supremely at ease sprawled across her vintage furniture.

"If you want in, you have to pay the price of admission."

He made a derisive sound. "Who told you that bull? One of your sergeants?"

"My father, actually."

He winced. "Open mouth, insert foot. Sorry."

"It's all right. I can understand how it might sound a bit slogany to someone who didn't know him."

"He was in the army, too, right?"

She nodded. "He was in the engineers corps. Right up until when I was born. Then he had to take a compassionate discharge."

"Because of your mum."

"Yes. There wasn't anyone else to take me." She stirred, swinging her legs from the couch to the floor. "Would you like a coffee? Or a cup of tea?"

He eyed her steadily. "It's all right. We don't have to talk about him if you don't want to."

"I don't mind talking about him."

"Okay."

She didn't like the idea that he thought she was running away from something or avoiding a difficult topic. She'd offered him coffee because she'd thought they'd exhausted the subject of her father.

"Ask me anything. What do you want to know?"

"What was he like?"

"Hardworking. Loyal. Dedicated."

"I meant as a father. Were you friends?"

She rested her hands on her knees. "We didn't have that sort of relationship."

"So you didn't get on, then?"

"We didn't not get on, either. I guess, if I had to say anything, I'd say that we didn't really know each other very well. But that's hardly surprising, really. As he said more than once, it would have been much easier if I'd been a boy instead of a girl."

"He said that to you?" Rhys sounded offended on her behalf.

"He didn't mean it in a bad way. He simply

didn't know what to do with a girl, that's all. Still, the plus side was that I knew how to tune an engine by the time I was twelve. You'd be surprised how often it comes in handy." She stood. "Sure you don't want a coffee?"

"A glass of water would be great, thanks."

She nodded and headed for the kitchen. Her movements were stiff and tight as she moved around and she almost spilled the first glass of water when she pulled it away from the tap with too much force.

She shook the water off her hand, aware of an irritated agitation within herself. She dried her hand on the tea towel and returned to the living room with a glass for each of them.

She handed one to Rhys, but he caught her wrist before she could retreat to the sofa again.

"I didn't mean to upset you, Charlie."

"I'm not upset." The high pitch of her voice belied her words.

Rhys held her gaze and after a second she looked away. She pulled her wrist free and returned to the sofa, setting her water on the coffee table. She stared at her hands for a long beat before looking at him again.

"The truth is, I don't like talking about him because it feels like unfinished business and I know it will never be finished because he's dead now. Which is stupid, really, because it would never have been finished even if he'd lived to be a hundred and fifty."

She dropped her gaze. Rhys didn't say anything and she felt an unexpected surge of gratitude for his sympathetic silence.

"I've thought about it a lot over the years, and I think the thing is, he was a man's man, you know? A soldier. He didn't talk about his feelings. Ever. God knows how he managed to meet and woo my mother, because he was a man of very few words. But I guess he did woo her, or I wouldn't be here, would I? And maybe he was different before she died." She shrugged. "Either way, I think he was probably one of those people who should never have been a parent. He had no natural instinct for it. So he did his duty, but that was about it."

"Did you join the army for him or for you?"

She gave a tight smile. "Good question. At the time I thought it was for me. But then I kept waiting for some sign from him that I'd finally got it right. Whatever 'it' was supposed to be. It never came, of course. But by then I'd worked out that the army and I weren't a bad fit, after all. You work hard, they reward you. That made sense to me."

"How did he die?"

"Pancreatic cancer. He didn't tell me until the end. And even then it was one of the nurses who called me. He died the next day, before I could get compassionate leave to come home."

"Hard yards, Charlie." There was a world of sympathy in his voice.

"It wasn't great. But it wasn't awful, either. There are a lot of people with uglier stories to tell."

Rhys frowned. "I've always hated that argument. As though just because you can find someone in the world worse off than you, your own stuff isn't supposed to count or hurt."

"I was trying to appear stoic, if you must know."

"Walkers don't do stoicism. We wail, we complain, we gnash our teeth and bitch and moan. We kick up a stink and rock the boat. You should try it sometime."

"Maybe I will."

His eyes were very warm as they watched her and she could only hold his gaze for a few seconds before she had to look away again. His phone beeped to signal an incoming email. She watched as he slid his phone from his pocket to check it. He put it away again almost immediately.

"Real estate agent," he explained when he saw her surprise. "I looked at an apartment he was selling on the Finger Wharf at Woolloomooloo a few weeks back and he hasn't stopped bugging me since."

"You're not interested?"

"Nope."

He stretched his arms over his head, straining the buttons on his shirt. Charlie caught herself staring and made herself look away.

"I should head home. Let you get to bed." Rhys started to lift his legs from the ottoman. *"Ow."* He leaned forward, gripping his calf, his face creased with pain.

"What's wrong?"

"Cramp. Get it all the time," he said through gritted teeth.

Charlie crossed to his side. "You need to stop clenching. Flex your foot," she instructed, batting his hands away.

She dug her fingers into his calf, massaging the spasming muscle. He groaned and she dug a little harder, reaching for his foot. Gripping it, she arched it toward his body, then away again so his foot was extended. She repeated the motion and after a few seconds she felt his muscle loosen beneath her fingers.

"Better?"

"Yes. Man, that's a killer."

She dug her thumb into his muscle one last time before letting go and straightening.

"You need to stretch more."

"That's what my personal trainer says."

"He's right." She was standing so close the outside of her thigh was pressed against his knee. She told herself to move, but Rhys looked at her with an appreciative smile and her legs ignored her.

"You have strong hands," he said.

"Thanks. I think."

"That was a compliment, in case you missed it."

"I'm not sure it is."

"Sure it is. I didn't say you had man hands."

"God forbid."

His smile broadened. Of its own accord, her gaze drifted below his neck. She could see the dark curls of his chest hair through the open collar of his shirt, and a small patch of his flat belly where his shirt had ridden up. His knees were slightly bent and the fabric of his trousers hugged his legs, outlining his powerful thigh muscles.

She knew what those thighs looked like. She knew what lay between them, too.

Suddenly he shifted, dropping his legs to the ground. She took a hasty step backward as he stood. Her heel caught on one of his shoes and she lost her balance.

Rhys's reflexes were lightning fast as he steadied her with one hand at her waist and the other on her upper arm.

"Sorry."

His eyes were very dark as he looked at her. "I think this is officially déjà vu."

It took her a moment to understand he was referring to the night they'd first met. Looking into his handsome face, she felt a bittersweet pang of regret for the excitement and promise of that night.

"Did you ever get that shirt cleaned?"

"Nope."

"I left you money."

Her gaze dropped to the strong column of his throat. Not so many weeks ago she'd kissed him there. She'd pressed her face against his skin and inhaled the lovely smell of him. Spice and man and heat.

"I know. I have to say, I thought you were a little on the stingy side. Took a while for my ego to recover."

She started then saw his smile and realized he was joking. She smiled sheepishly. "I never thought of it *that* way."

"I should hope not."

"If I had I would definitely have left a bigger tip."

He laughed. His fingers flexed lightly into

the muscles of her shoulder and waist, almost as though he was encouraging her to step closer.

Maybe.

Hot desire flooded her as she contemplated taking that step. The urge was so powerful it stole the breath from her lungs and made the backs of her knees, the creases of her elbows and the nape of her neck instantly damp with sweat.

A long-drawn-out second passed as they stared at one another. Then another.

She had an out-of-body experience as she imagined how they must look to a fly on the wall, standing so close, him holding her as though he was about to kiss her.

As though they were lovers.

Maybe.

She sucked in a shallow, inadequate breath and forced herself to step backward instead of forward. He let go of her slowly, reluctantly—or so it seemed. And then she took another step and common sense returned with a rush of cool objectivity and she shook her head at her own foolishness.

"I'll get the DVD for you." She walked to the player, crouching to hit the eject button and collect the disk. Out of the corner of her eye she saw him sit and grab his shoes. By the time she had the DVD in its case he was on his feet again.

"Thanks for coming over," she said, careful to

keep her voice absolutely neutral as she passed him the DVD.

"Thanks for having me."

They walked to the front door in thick silence.

"I'll call you on the weekend," Rhys said as he faced her across the threshold.

"Okay."

He turned toward the stairs.

"Drive carefully," she said.

She pushed the door shut between them, only letting out her breath when she'd twisted the lock. She stood very still, listening to his retreating footsteps. Then she walked into the bathroom and flicked on the overhead light. She stood in front of the mirror and stared herself in the eye.

"Don't be an idiot."

The woman in the mirror stared back at her. Her hair was a straggly mess, her lipstick long gone, her complexion unflatteringly pale. She looked tired and very, very plain.

As she always did.

Far too plain for a man like Rhys Walker to want.

"Don't be an idiot," she said again. Because it was good advice and it bore repeating.

She reached for her toothbrush and prepared for bed—brushing her teeth and washing her face before smoothing on moisturizer. She walked into the bedroom and stripped off her jeans and sweater then pulled on her pajamas.

Right from the start she'd been very clear with herself about what she wanted from her relationship with Rhys—security, love and stability for her child. Another pair of loving hands. Extended family.

What she didn't want was to develop some kind of ridiculous unrequited crush on a man who was around only because of contraceptive failure. She had spent the first ten years of her life craving something from her father that he had never given her, and she'd learned her lesson as far as that sort of pointless, soul-destroying yearning went. By the time she was twelve she'd understood that happiness was about setting her sights on the things that were possible, the things she could earn and achieve herself without relying on anyone else.

Rhys was not one of those things. She could not win him with her attention to detail and her conscientiousness. She could not earn him with her staying power and determination and smarts.

Therefore she would not want him. She simply refused to. Refused to set herself up for failure and pain by buying into a ridiculous fantasy that would never come to be.

She climbed into bed and turned off the light. She closed her eyes and instantly she was in her living room, staring into Rhys's face, feeling the pull of desire, every inch of her skin lighting up in anticipation of his touch.

Her lip curled into a sneer at her own foolishness, but she didn't force the memory away. Instead, she fixed it in her mind, going over and over it, forcing herself to imagine what Rhys had seen when he'd looked into her face—her neediness, her desire, her hope. Forcing herself to see the scene as it had really played out, and not through the hazy, gauzy filter of wishful thinking.

Heat washed through her—embarrassed, self-conscious heat this time instead of desire.

Thank God she hadn't obeyed the voice screaming in her head and taken a step forward. Thank. God.

Tugging the covers higher around her shoulders, she rolled onto her side, her hand sliding to cover the barely-there bump of her belly.

After long moments the tight feeling in her chest eased.

The small person growing beneath her hand was what was important right now. Nothing else.

Good to remind herself of that.

CHAPTER TEN

WHAT ARE YOU DOING, MAN?

Rhys asked himself that question all the way home from Charlie's place.

He'd almost kissed her tonight. If she'd been any other woman, he would have. He would have pulled her into his arms and kissed her and seen where it took them—but there was no "seeing where things go" when a woman was pregnant with your child.

Through some miracle, he and Charlie had formed a friendship over the past month. Out of potential disaster they had discovered a shared sense of humor, common values and, he hoped, mutual respect. On a very basic, human level, he liked her. He liked her a lot.

He liked her calm, no-nonsense, straightforward approach. He liked her honesty and quiet courage. He liked her slow smile and her dry wit. He even liked her quietness. With Charlie, there was no pointless chatter. She said what needed to be said. She listened. And when she did say something, it was always worth hearing.

If they'd met under any other circumstances he would have been intrigued and attracted by her. But they hadn't. They'd had one fiery night together, and now she was carrying their baby.

All of which meant she was out-of-bounds. Big-time.

The relationship they were forging would be tested in a hundred different ways over the coming months. There would be stress and sleeplessness and a million other doubts and domestic crises—he'd seen what happened when a baby was thrown into the mix with his brothers and sisters. Tempers were short. Sleep was precious. Time was at a premium.

He and Charlie were going to need every scrap of goodwill toward one another that they could muster. What they didn't need was a failed romance lying between them. Hurt feelings and guilt and anger and sadness. It would be tough enough without making their lives more complicated.

Of course, there was always the chance that a romance might work between them. He'd never embarked on a relationship yet that he hadn't hoped would lead to marriage—he didn't know anyone who did. What was the point, after all, if you didn't think things would go all the way? But as his current single status so eloquently proved, none of those relationships had worked out, for a variety of reasons. And there were no guarantees one would work out between him and Charlie, either.

For starters, he had no idea where her head was at in regard to him. Sometimes she looked at him and he was sure he saw an echo of the intense attraction they'd shared that night. Other times she was unreadable and utterly unknowable. If he'd given in to his instincts tonight and kissed her, in all honesty he had no idea if she would have kissed him back or pushed him away.

She stepped away, remember?

So maybe that was his answer. Which meant that he was mulling over a problem that didn't even exist. If Charlie wasn't attracted to him the way he was attracted to her, he was spinning his wheels and giving himself a hard time for nothing.

Except...

There had been *something* in her eyes tonight. Desire. Need. Want. Maybe all of the above. Surely he hadn't simply imagined that, projecting it on to her because, no matter what else lay between them—the baby, the future—for the life of him he couldn't forget the night they'd had together.

And it wasn't only about good sex. Okay, *great* sex. It was about the whole night. The conversation they'd enjoyed before they went to his place and those moments in the small hours when they'd talked and laughed, lying skin to skin in his bed.

The only way he could explain that came even close to doing it justice was that he'd felt an unspoken connection with her. As cheesy and clichéd as that sounded. No, he hadn't heard birds singing or a choir reaching for high notes. But it had been real. He'd felt as though they'd *seen* each other. It definitely hadn't been just a roll in the hay.

For you, maybe. But she left without waking you. Remember?

Rhys pulled into his building's underground parking garage and cut the engine. It hit him for the first time him how incredibly un-Charlie-like it had been to sneak off like that. He'd watched her gird her loins prior to meeting his family. He'd seen her gumption and spine and been on the receiving end of her clear-eyed, sharp gaze. Charlie wasn't a slinker or a sneaker. She stared things in the eye and dealt with them head-on.

So why had she left that night? It had bugged him then, and it bugged him now. He'd asked her once and she'd given him a nonanswer. A really unsatisfying nonanswer.

He made his way to the elevator. The doors opened when he hit the button and he stepped inside and swiped his security card before punching the number for his floor. The car stopped on the first floor, the doors sliding open then starting to close almost immediately.

Maybe he should tackle Charlie on the issue again. Maybe—

"Could you hold the lift, please?"

He stuck his arm out to stop the doors. He heard the clatter of heels, then a woman appeared, her face flushed, a small rolling suitcase trailing behind her. She was slim and blonde, late twenties, early thirties, and wearing one of those jaunty little neck scarves that he always associated with flight attendants. His gaze dropped to her tailored, discreetly sexy dress and he realized she *was* an air hostess. Complete with name tag—Heather—and uniform.

"Thanks," Heather said as she dragged her bag over the gap between the lift and the floor. "Huh. We're on the same floor. How's that for a coincidence?" She pushed a strand of wavy blond hair out of her eye and gave him a friendly smile as she offered him her hand. "Heather, apartment 4A. I moved in last month."

"Rhys, 4D. Been here awhile," he said as they shook hands as the lift began to ascend.

"Ah, so you must know where I can find a decent cup of coffee around here. Because the café around the corner—"

"Sucks hard. I know. Don't worry, everyone

gets conned at least once. Try the place up the hill. The one with the orange sign. They do a mean single origin."

Heather's smile broadened. Her gaze flicked down his body in a lightning-fast appraisal before finding his face again. "Orange sign, up the hill. Got it."

A pinging sound announced their arrival on the fourth floor. Rhys stood back while Heather maneuvered her suitcase out of the elevator.

"Thanks," she said. "You'd think I'd be better with this thing, after all these years but I think I must be suitcase challenged."

They paused in the hall. His apartment was to the right, hers to the left.

"Well, nice to meet you, Rhys," Heather said.

"You, too."

Rhys was turning away when she spoke again.

"Maybe we could have coffee or wine some-time and you can fill me in on the other local se-crets."

She fiddled with the suitcase handle as she waited for his response. He was so fixated on what had almost happened with Charlie that it took him a moment to realize that Heather was signaling her interest—in the nicest possible way.

"Um, yeah. Sure. Why not?" he heard himself say after a slightly-too-long pause.

She nodded uncertainly, clearly picking up

on the ambivalence in his lukewarm response. "Okay. I guess I'll see you around." She hesitated a second as though she was waiting for him to say something else, then she waved and headed up the corridor.

Rhys walked to his own apartment and let himself in. He shrugged out of his jacket, slinging it over the back of the nearest chair.

He was very aware that Heather had been waiting for him to name a time and place for them to get together. Which he hadn't done because the first thing that sprang to mind when he thought about having a coffee with another woman was that it would be a betrayal of Charlie.

Which was pretty much crazy. Especially considering the lecture he'd been giving himself in the garage not five minutes ago. He and Charlie were friends, and they were about to become parents. He owed her his support and his patience and his time. He did not owe her his emotional or sexual loyalty. They had a relationship, but they weren't *in* a relationship. And the odds were good they never would be, for all the reasons he'd already listed. There was too much at stake.

So he could have said yes to Heather. Apart from a lackluster blind date that Greg's wife, Jessica, had set up for him a few weeks after that fateful night at Café Sydney, he hadn't been out with anyone since Charlie. He'd been too busy with work to socialize. And, if he was honest with himself, he'd been a little thrown after his experience with Charlie. The intensity of it, followed by the fact that she'd simply bailed on him the next day. He hadn't exactly felt like diving into the dating pool.

He ran his hand through his hair, very aware that the real reason he hadn't set up a date with Heather—and the reason why he wasn't knocking on her door now to do so—was because, as attractive as she was, he really wasn't that interested.

His head was too full of Charlie. And not only because of the baby.

Better get past that, buddy, because it's never going to happen.

Stripping off his shirt, he strode through the bedroom into the en suite. He shed the rest of his clothes and stepped beneath the shower, washing away the day's labors.

Not so long ago, his life had been simple. He'd known what he wanted, and he'd had a plan to get it. Now…he had no idea what he wanted. And half the things he'd once thought were important had lost their shiny allure. The wharf apartment, the European sports car, the high-roller lifestyle.

That apartment was no place for a baby, let alone a toddler. There was no outdoor space, and the thought of combining even a moderately enterprising kid with some outdoor furniture and a balcony frankly freaked him out. The sleek Aston Martin Vanquish he'd been stalking for the past few years… It wasn't as though the designers had put a lot of thought into how to fit a car seat into one of those things. When he got a new vehicle, it was far more likely to be a sedan with a good safety rating. He didn't think he could go as far as a van—he still had his pride, after all—but a new Audi or BMW would probably hit the mark. And when he moved out of this apartment, he would probably look for a house with a yard, instead of a slick bachelor pad.

He shook his head. Six weeks ago, if someone had told him that he'd relinquish long-held ambitions so easily, with so little regret, he would have laughed in their face.

And yet here he was, mentally scrapping the wharf, the Vanquish, and walking away from a potential date with a hot blonde flight attendant. All because of Charlie and the baby.

A brave new world, indeed. One that he needed to get a grip on ASAP, because it was doing his head in.

CHARLIE SPENT THE WEEKEND not waiting for Rhys to call. On Saturday she went to Paddington Markets on Oxford Street and spent several hours checking out handcrafted jewelry, leatherwork, clothes and artwork. She bought her first purchases for the nursery—a carved wooden monkey with arms and legs that moved, thanks to leather thongs at its shoulder and hips, and an elephant with a bright red trunk.

Afterward she bought a big bowl of chicken and mango salad from a nearby deli and took it to the Royal Botanic Gardens. Sitting on the grass in the warm afternoon sun, she ate her lunch and watched the ferries and pleasure boats steam across the harbor. She didn't check her phone once, and she left it at home when she went to the movies with Gina and her boyfriend, Spencer, that night.

On Sunday she contemplated tackling the box of her father's belongings, actually going as far as sliding it out from beside her desk before shoving it back and heading to Bondi to tackle the five-beach trek to Coogee. The winding, twisty path followed the coastline from Bondi Beach past Tamarama and Clovelly to Coogee and took up to four hours return to do properly. Charlie walked for forty minutes before turning back, her face glistening with sweat and her thighs and butt sore. She hoped the baby enjoyed the bumpy ride. It felt good to use her body—and breathe the ocean air—after a week of sitting hunched at her desk.

When her phone rang that evening she was

pleased to feel nothing but a mild fillip of pleasure when she saw Rhys's name on the display. Just as she would if it were Gina or Yvonne or Hannah or one of her other army friends.

She told him about her weekend and he told her about his, then she reminded him that she had her twelve-week ultrasound on Thursday morning and he assured her he'd be there. They were both friendly, but there was a certain constraint evident in how carefully they chose their words, and they wound up the call earlier than usual.

Just as well, Charlie told herself. There was a definite danger in allowing Rhys too close. Arm's length was much smarter and more manageable.

The early part of the week slipped away thanks to a tight deadline for one of the sites she was working on. She was feeling gritty eyed and sleep deprived when she stepped into the shower on Thursday morning. She'd stayed up late inputting some last-minute client changes, despite the fact that the site had already gone live, and waking at her usual time had been harder than it should have been.

"I blame you," she said, glancing in the general direction of the baby. Her eyes widened. Overnight, her stomach had popped and suddenly there was a very distinct convex curve to her lower torso. She actually looked pregnant. Very early-days pregnant, but pregnant nonetheless.

She'd been wondering when her body was going to declare its status. So far her pregnancy symptoms had been limited to "evening sickness." No thickening of the waist, no sore or suddenly huge breasts.

But as of today she had a baby bump. A tiny baby bump, with the promise of bigger things to come.

She ran her hands over the rounded shape, imagining the little kidney bean growing inside her. Today, she was going to see him or her for the first time. She was going to see arms and legs and a heart. She was also going to find out if there was anything wrong with her child.

She'd read through the ultrasound sections in her baby books. She knew that at thirty-two years old she had a higher chance of something being wrong with the baby than if she were twenty-two—not significantly, but there was still a difference—and a little tickle of nervousness made her take a deep breath as she stepped out of the shower.

She and Rhys hadn't discussed the medical purpose of the scan. It occurred to her that if something was wrong with their child they were not prepared.

There aren't going to be any problems, The Bean is fine.

She hoped the voice in her head was right, but someone had to draw the short straw.

She dressed in her jeans, deriving an almost perverse delight in the fact that they were suddenly snug. She pulled on a blue sweater and dried her hair before pulling it into a ponytail. By then there was just over an hour until her appointment. She went to the kitchen, dutifully measured a liter of water then systematically drank it over the next twenty minutes. Then she drove to the radiology clinic in Glebe. Her bladder started to complain as she parked. She checked her watch. Another ten minutes until her appointment. For the sake of her bladder, she hoped they weren't running late.

She half expected Rhys to have arrived ahead of her, but there were only strange faces in the waiting room. She settled into her chair and glanced toward the parking lot.

Fifteen minutes later, she was feeling distinctly uncomfortable and Rhys was late. She checked her phone for the tenth time in as many minutes and resisted, again, the urge to call him to check if he was on his way. The most likely explanation was that he was stuck in traffic and she didn't want to force him to answer his phone when he was driving.

She shifted in her chair. Would it be considered beyond the pale if she undid the snap on her

jeans? It was either that, or she would have to use
the bathroom. She shifted to the edge of the chair
and eyed the door to the ladies' room wistfully.

"Charlotte Long?"

She glanced toward the white-coated woman
standing in front of the reception desk.

"That's me," Charlie said, standing. She
glanced toward the entrance, willing Rhys to
arrive, but the doorway remained resolutely
empty.

"This way, please." The woman led her up the
hall.

Charlie shot one last glance over her shoulder
before following. There was precious little she
could do, after all. She couldn't stall until Rhys
arrived—the waiting room was full of people
waiting for their scans. He'd have to make do
with the DVD she'd been told she would be given
afterward.

Disappointment thunked in her belly as she
entered a treatment room dominated by an examination table and a portable computer worksta-
tion. It wasn't until this moment that she realized
how quickly and completely she'd bought into the
notion that she wouldn't be doing this on her own.

*Better wake up from that little fantasy, Cinder-
ella.*

Because Rhys was not her husband. He wasn't
even her boyfriend. They didn't share a house or

their lives, and they would not be sharing every aspect of this journey.

So this was a timely wake-up call, really.

"Shoes off, jeans unsnapped and unzipped," the woman instructed as Charlie placed her handbag on the chair beside the exam table. "Did you drink your liter of water?"

"Oh, yes," Charlie said meaningfully, offering the other woman a rueful smile.

The woman remained po-faced as she wrote something on a form. "The technician will be with you in a moment."

She left, closing the door behind her.

Charlie bent to untie her shoes and was placing them neatly beneath the chair when a small knock sounded at the door.

"Come in," she said.

The door opened to reveal Rhys, a chagrined expression on his handsome face. His gaze zeroed in on her socks, then the examination table.

"Shit. Don't tell me I've missed it? Bloody traffic."

Charlie grinned, unable to quell her bone-deep pleasure and relief that he was here. They would be sharing this experience after all.

"You're fine. We're about to start. That's if my bladder doesn't explode first."

"Right." A small frown signaled his confusion about her reference to the status of her bladder.

"They make you drink a liter of water to help with the imaging," she explained.

"A liter? Wow." He glanced around. "Lucky there's no running water in here then, huh?"

She laughed, feeling unaccountably buoyant. "Yeah."

She climbed onto the crinkly paper covering the table and settled against the raised backrest. Her hands went to the snap on her jeans—and suddenly she remembered that the last time she'd undone her pants with this man he'd helped pull them off.

Then he'd tumbled her onto his bed and made her forget her own name with his skilled, intense lovemaking.

A wave of heat washed up her chest and into her face. She forced her fumbling fingers to undo the button, carefully not looking Rhys's way, then she slid her zip down. Out of the corner of her eye, she was aware of Rhys glancing away, obviously as uncomfortable as she was.

"Don't worry. I have a no-nudity clause," she joked.

"I wasn't worried."

A knock sounded then the door opened to admit a different woman. Tall, dark haired and very slim, she wore a pair of heavy, dark-rimmed glasses on the end of her thin nose. Charlie guessed she was in her late thirties, maybe early forties.

"Hi. I'm Sally. I'll be doing your scan today."

Rhys offered his hand. "Rhys. And this is Charlie."

"Hi," Charlie said.

"Nice to meet you both. So, shall we take a peek at this baby of yours?"

It was a rhetorical question, and neither she nor Rhys answered it. Sally busied herself at the computer, typing Charlie's details before turning to her.

"I'll get you to fold your jeans back, Charlie, and roll your top up, too, please."

"Sure." Charlie did as instructed, exposing her pale belly and the upper edge of her black cotton panties. Her bump sat proudly between her hips, a gentle molehill that would soon become a mountain.

"Look at that. You're pregnant," Rhys said. He sounded a little surprised.

"It happened overnight. I woke up and it was there."

She was aware of Sally shooting a glance between the two of them, obviously trying to work out their relationship now that Charlie had revealed that they didn't live together. When she spoke, though, she was all business. "Okay, this has been in the warmer but it might still be a little on the cool side. Sorry about that."

She proceeded to squirt a bluish-colored gel over Charlie's belly. It *was* on the cool side, but she'd had worse.

"Okay?" Sally checked.

"All good."

"Then let's say hello to this little person."

Rhys drew up the chair beside the table as Sally used the mouse to click something on the screen. She swiveled in her chair, bringing the ultrasound wand close. Then, her gaze on the screen, she began to glide the wand over Charlie's abdomen.

"Searching, searching... Ah, there we are."

A small white shape appeared in the blackness of the screen, surrounded by what looked like static. Charlie held her breath as Sally tapped the keyboard some more and the magnification increased.

And there, filling the screen, was The Bean.

"Oh," Charlie said. An unexpected rush of emotion washed over her as she looked at her baby's tiny curled body.

"Okay, before we go any further I need to ask if you want to know the baby's gender. Sometimes we can't see it at twelve weeks but your baby is perfectly positioned."

Charlie looked to Rhys. "We haven't really talked about it, have we?"

"Now seems like a good time," Rhys said with a faint smile.

"Yeah."

"And?"

"I think I'd like to know."

"Me, too."

They both turned to Sally.

"You're having a little girl," she said simply.

Charlie swallowed against the sudden tightness in her throat. She hadn't really thought about her baby's gender. She certainly hadn't had a preference. But a little girl suddenly felt extraordinarily right.

A little girl she could lavish love on. A little girl she could assure and nurture and guide. A little girl who would always, always know that she mattered.

"Hey," Rhys said quietly. His hand gripped hers as she sniffed away the tears flooding her eyes.

"Sorry," Charlie said.

"Nothing to apologize for," Rhys said, and she saw that his eyes were shiny with unshed tears, too.

"For the record, I'm more than happy for you to call the baby Sally," Sally said.

They all laughed and the tightness in Charlie's throat eased. Sally spent the next ten minutes taking them on a tour of their baby, showing them the whirling miracle of her tiny heart, her limbs, her developing organs. They watched, awestruck, as the baby lifted a tiny arm, almost as though she was waving at them.

"Hey, there, baby girl," Rhys said.

After taking some measurements, Sally informed them that there was a very low risk that their baby suffered from Down syndrome. She went on to check for spinal abnormalities before inspecting the placenta and declaring that everything looked healthy and normal.

Charlie only realized that she was still holding Rhys's hand when Sally ducked out of the room to organize their films.

"That was freaking amazing," he said.

She tugged on her fingers and he glanced down as though he, too, had forgotten they were holding hands.

"Sorry," he said, relaxing his grip.

"Your mum will probably want to look at the scan. I wonder if we'll be able to copy the DVD?"

It was strange, but she felt oddly shy after the intensity of the past few minutes. As though she needed a few minutes alone to compose herself.

"We can ask when Sally comes back. But you're right, Mum will go nuts over this." He pushed his hair back from his forehead, a relieved smile on his face.

"I don't mind telling you, I was a bit nervous

on the way here. I checked out some sites this morning and there's some scary stuff on the Net about what could be wrong at twelve weeks."

"I know. But we're lucky," she said quietly.

Sally reentered the room, her white coat billowing behind her. "Okay, that's all sorted. We'll get you cleaned up, Charlie, and the films and your DVD should be out to you within ten minutes."

The other woman used special tissues to clean the gel off Charlie's belly before disposing of the debris and washing her hands. Charlie zipped and buttoned her jeans.

"Here," Rhys said, offering up her sneakers.

"Thanks." She tied the laces hurriedly, very aware of the need to use the bathroom now that the excitement had passed.

"Good luck with everything," Sally said as Charlie stood and reached for her bag.

"Thank you. Will we have you next time we come?" Charlie asked.

"It depends on the roster, but you can always request me," Sally said with a wink.

Rhys shook hands with her again before they both exited to the corridor.

"We should—"

Charlie held up a finger. "Hold that thought. I'll be back in a second."

She resisted the urge to break into a run as she

headed for the ladies'. Rhys's low laughter followed her up the hallway.

Five minutes later, she joined him in the waiting room, taking the seat beside him.

"Better?" he asked.

"Yes, thank you," she said primly.

He grinned.

"I'm glad you find all the peccadilloes of pregnancy so amusing," she said.

"So am I."

His dark brown eyes were dancing and she suddenly realized that her shoulder was flush against his and that the whole left side of her body was being warmed by his. It was always like that with Rhys, though. She was lulled by his charm and the forced intimacy of their situation, then the next thing she knew, she was thinking things she had no business thinking, and feeling things that were plain stupid.

Trying to make the movement seem as natural as possible, she leaned forward to adjust her handbag on the floor, shifting farther to her right so that their bodies were no longer in contact. Rhys glanced at her, a question in his eyes. He seemed on the verge of saying something when the receptionist called Charlie's name.

She shot to her feet, grateful for the interruption. Just as well they would be going their separate ways in five minutes' time. Clearly she was hormonal and sentimental and stupid after the scan—not a good state to be in when she was within a three-mile radius of Rhys Walker.

CHAPTER ELEVEN

CHARLIE WAS SIGNING the credit card slip at the reception desk when Rhys joined her. He frowned when she handed the slip to the receptionist, but he didn't say anything until they were outside.

"I thought Medicare covered all this."

"Mostly, they do. I'll get a lot of that back."

"I don't want you being out of pocket." He reached for his wallet.

She gave him a look. "What are you doing?"

"Making sure you aren't footing the bill for my mistake."

She flinched at his choice of words.

"I didn't mean it like that," he said immediately.

But she knew he did. And technically he was right—this baby was a mistake. She certainly wasn't planned. But from the moment Charlie had seen the poster depicting her baby's development in the GP's office, The Bean had become very real to her, and she'd become even more real now that Charlie knew her baby was a girl.

"There's no point you simply handing me

money willy-nilly from your wallet," she said. "If you want to be that gung-ho about it, I'll create a spreadsheet. We can track every expense down to the cent."

Her disdain for the notion must have been evident, because Rhys gave her a frustrated look. "What else do you suggest we do, then?"

She knew he was right. As much as she hated having to treat her pregnancy and their child like some sort of joint project, the reality was that if they were truly going to share responsibility, they needed to keep track of expenses and contributions. It wasn't pretty, but it was practical.

"It's just…hard," she said, trying to convey how she felt. "The Bean is a person in her own right. Not some piece of furniture we're going halves in."

His eyebrows arched. "The Bean?"

"That's what I call her. Even before I knew she was a she. There was a poster in the doctor's office that said at eight weeks the fetus is the size of a kidney bean." She shrugged, feeling more than a little foolish. "It stuck in my head."

"The Bean. I like it. The Bean Walker has a real ring to it."

As always, his silliness made her smile.

"It will look great on business cards, that's for sure," she said.

"And on a desk plate. Engraved in brass."

A woman was approaching the entrance, her big pregnant belly leading the way. They both stepped to one side to let her pass. Rhys pulled back his cuff and checked his watch.

"You probably need to go," Charlie said, checking her own watch.

Somehow, what had felt like only fifteen minutes had chewed up nearly an hour.

"What are you doing now?" Rhys asked.

The sun was behind him, causing her to squint as she looked at him.

"I've got some page flats and some coding I need to sort out. Why?"

"I was thinking we could grab lunch." He glanced toward the clear blue sky. "It's such a great day, seems a shame to waste it."

"What about your work?"

He shrugged. "My afternoon is clear. I can play hooky for a few hours. How about you?"

Her stupid, stupid heart gave a little jump at the prospect of spending a sunny afternoon with Rhys—a very good reason for her to make an excuse to put him off.

"Come on. I'll put in a good word for you with the boss," he said in his most charming, wheedling tone.

She found herself nodding, despite the sensible voice in her head. "Okay. Sure, why not?"

"Great. We can leave your car here and pick it

up later. Where do you want to go?" His started toward his BMW, confident and relaxed.

"Um. I'm not sure. Maybe somewhere near the water. I got takeout and went to Mrs Macquarie's Chair on the weekend and that was pretty nice."

"Let's do that," Rhys said.

She couldn't help smiling at his enthusiastic decisiveness.

Rhys made a quick call to the office to let them know his plans, then they stopped in Glebe to buy takeout from a macrobiotic-food store Charlie had recently discovered. Afterward, they drove across the city and into the Domain. They weren't the only Sydneysiders who thought a bright day was the perfect excuse for a picnic and they had to park halfway around the loop and walk back to the point that offered the most sweeping harbor views. Rhys found an old beach towel in the back of the car and they spread it out on the slope facing the Harbour Bridge, the wind in their hair and the sun warming them.

"This was a good idea," Rhys said as she pried the lids off the various plastic containers. He glanced at the food and his eyes narrowed suspiciously. "The food I'm not so sure about."

"Wait until you taste it. It's so good you'd swear it was bad for you."

"How bad? Hamburgers-and-French-fries bad? Deep-fried-chicken-wings bad?"

"You'll have to try and see."

"You sounded like a mum then."

"I did not."

"You did. Gave me a little mum look, too. Next, you'll be asking if I have a hankie in my pocket."

She passed one of the tofu burgers to him. "Try not to talk with your mouth full." It was the only motherly thing she could think of on the spot, but he laughed anyway.

He bit into his burger and made a surprised sound. She raised her eyebrows, waiting.

"Okay. I'll eat my words, as well as this burger. This is delicious."

She smiled in what she hoped was a smug way and resumed eating her own burger.

They ate the salad and the dairy-free cheese-cake, then lay back on their elbows in sated, companionable silence as they soaked up the view.

"It's good to be the king," Rhys said after a few minutes.

She smiled. The sun was on her face, warm and life affirming. She knew she should probably be running for the shade, worrying about her complexion, but instead she settled onto her back and closed her eyes and basked like a lizard.

"Guess we're going to have to start a list of girls' names," Rhys said beside her.

He sounded as drowsy and content as she felt.

She was suddenly very glad that she'd agreed to share lunch and the sunshine and this view with him.

"Actually, I have a name picked out already. An old family name," she said without opening her eyes.

"Yeah? What is it?"

"Gertrude," she said, absolutely straight-faced. She cracked an eye so she could see Rhys's reaction. He was frowning, and she could almost hear him trying to formulate a diplomatic response. Then he caught her watching him and a slow smile curved his mouth.

"Nice one. Almost had me."

"*Almost?* You were fully on the hook."

"But I was still wriggling."

"On the hook is on the hook."

He rolled onto his side so he faced her. "You're a tough customer."

"Former army, don't you know."

He smiled, his gaze scanning her face before dropping below her neck. "You look good in that color."

She glanced down at herself. She'd had the sweater for years and had long ago stopped thinking of it as a piece of fashion apparel.

"What color would you call that? Periwinkle blue?" Rhys asked.

"I have no idea what a periwinkle even is."

"Hot-summer-day sky blue. That's what we'll call it."

"That's quite a mouthful."

"When you're aiming for accuracy, brevity has to be sacrificed." He said it very solemnly, almost pompously, and she laughed.

His gaze moved over her features lazily, idly. "I guess our little girl will look like you, won't she?"

She made a face. "God, I hope not."

He looked surprised. "You think that would be a bad thing?"

"I think she'd be better served taking after the Walker side of the family." She lay a hand on her stomach. "Do you hear that, Bean? Think Black Irish and you can't go wrong."

"Hang on a minute. Let's not rush to the Walker side just yet. I think The Bean would be doing herself a disservice if she missed out on your nose. And she definitely needs your mouth." His gaze dropped to her lips.

"Fine. But she has to get everything else from you. Including your hair."

"Again, what's wrong with your hair?"

"It's dead straight. And it's the color of a well-known rodent."

"It's brown. Mink brown."

"Minks are rodents, too."

His gaze was intense now. "You're serious, aren't you?"

"Your sisters are beautiful. Why wouldn't I want her to take after them?"

"You're beautiful, too."

Charlie let her gaze slide over his shoulder. She knew what he was doing—being kind, his usual charming self.

"Thank you," she said stiffly, because she'd read somewhere that it was always polite to acknowledge compliments. Not that she'd had a lot of practice, but still.

"You don't believe me, do you?" Rhys asked, his frown deepening.

"I think—" She jerked to the side as a big fat bee flew into view and hovered near his shoulder. *"Shit."*

"It's okay. He won't hurt you if you don't hurt him."

"I'm allergic," she said tightly, pressing herself into the ground.

Rhys immediately rolled onto his back, luring the bee with him. She watched as he shooed it gently away, and finally it flew off to search for less vigilant prey.

"Thanks," she said. "He probably wasn't going to hurt me, but being stung still worries me."

Rhys resumed his position, took one look at her and started laughing. She blinked.

"I'm beginning to think you have a twisted sense of humor."

"Sorry. You got some grass in your hair just now, that's all."

She gave him a look. "How old are you?"

"Old enough to appreciate when someone looks funny. It looks as though a little bird has made his home on your head."

She reached up to brush the grass away. "Has it gone?"

"Nope, not all of it."

He was enjoying himself hugely at her expense. She started to sit up.

"Relax. I'll get it." He reached across and brushed at her hair. Unable to hold his gaze at such close quarters, her eyes drifted to his jaw, then, somehow, to his mouth. She traced his full bottom lip with her eyes, marveling that it could be both masculine and soft looking at the same time. Sometimes, if she closed her eyes and let herself be very foolish, she could still remember how he tasted. How it had felt to have those lips on her skin…

She realized that Rhys had long since stopped brushing her hair and she lifted her gaze. He was watching her, his dark eyes intent.

"Charlie," he said, his voice very low.

His thumb brushed her cheek, then he lowered his face toward her. She acted in instinctive, panicky self-defense, lifting a hand to his chest to halt his descent.

"What are you doing?" she squeaked.

"Kissing you?"

"No."

He pulled back a few inches. "You don't want me to kiss you?"

"I think it's a really bad idea."

He tilted his head a fraction of an inch. "That's not the same as not wanting me to kiss you."

"It might as well be."

"Are you telling me that you haven't thought about it? About us, together?"

An image popped into her mind, inspired by his words. Rhys between her legs, filling her with his heat and hardness, his mouth at her breasts.

"No," she lied.

He stared at her. He was leaning over her, blocking out the sun, filling almost all her vision, and it was impossible to avoid his searching gaze.

"No," she said again.

Then, because she was afraid that what willpower and common sense she possessed were hanging by a rapidly unraveling thread, she pushed him away and wriggled to the side until she could sit upright without banging heads with him.

"We should go." She collected the empty containers, stuffing them all into the bag they'd come in. Then she rose and started up the hill.

She didn't look back. She knew exactly what she was walking away from. She knew she was doing the right thing, too. But knowing didn't make it any easier.

RHYS WATCHED CHARLIE walk away from him and tried to work out what had happened between them. She had wanted him. He'd seen it in her eyes. Yet she'd lied to him, told him she never thought about the two of them together.

"Bullshit," he said under his breath. He scrambled to his feet, scooped up the beach towel and went after her.

She was dumping their garbage in a bin when he caught up with her.

"We need to talk about this. Even if just to clear the air," he said.

She looked at him, her face shuttered. "There's nothing to talk about."

"Yeah, there is. There's a bloody huge elephant in the room, and we've been dancing around it for weeks."

"We haven't been dancing around anything."

He refused to let her sidetrack him. "The reason you're pregnant, Charlie, is because we had sex. And we had sex because we're really into each other."

She crossed her arms over her chest. "That was three months ago. And it was one night. And we were both drunk."

Rhys flinched. "I knew exactly what I was doing and who I was with. Are you saying it was different for you?"

Color flooded Charlie's cheeks, but she didn't say a word. Taking the Fifth, obviously.

"Why did you leave that night without saying goodbye?" He'd promised himself that he wouldn't ask her again, that he wouldn't harangue her like a lovesick teen, but the words were out his mouth before he could stop them.

Her arms tightened around her body. "Because it was a one-night stand. We both knew that."

"I didn't."

She stared at him, her regard so intent that he felt as though she was searching for his soul. After a long moment she looked away. "I did."

"You didn't have a good time?" Hard to ask, but he needed to know if he'd been kidding himself about her right from the start.

The glance she sent him was almost resentful. "You know I did."

"Then why leave?"

Charlie threw her hands in the air. "I don't even know why we're having this conversation."

"Because we almost kissed."

Charlie blinked. Then her chin came up. "I would like to go back to my car now, please."

She didn't wait for him to respond, turning on her heel and walking toward where they'd parked. For the second time that day Rhys stared at her retreating back. Everything in him wanted to keep pushing, to demand she be honest with him about how she felt and what she wanted. He took a step, ready to go after her yet again.

Then it hit him that she *had* told him what she wanted. She'd told him she didn't think it was a good idea that they kiss. She'd told him that their one night had always been only one night in her mind. She'd told him that her priority was the baby. And only the baby.

She'd told him a number of times in a bunch of different ways what she wanted. He simply didn't like what she was saying.

She's not interested, mate. Accept it, suck it up and move on. Otherwise you'll start looking like some obsessive stalker head case.

He turned and looked at the view, inhaling deeply through his nose before exhaling again in a frustrated, resigned rush. High overhead, a seagull squawked. He glanced at it as it wheeled against the bright blue sky.

Shaking his head, he dug deep into his pocket and found his car keys. He started toward the car. He could see Charlie, standing beside the passenger side, her face and body in profile to him as she stared out toward the naval base in Wool-loomooloo Bay. She looked slim and strong and very alone.

He waited until he was a few feet from the car before activating the remote lock. She opened the door and slid in without saying a word. He climbed into the driver's seat. He didn't start the car. No way was he driving back to Glebe and letting her go home with this sitting between them.

"If it makes you uncomfortable, if you're not interested, I won't raise the subject again," he said quietly.

She glanced at him for a second before fixing her gaze on the car ahead.

"I think it's for the best," she said.

He had no idea what that even meant, but he'd told her he'd drop it, so he started the engine and signaled before pulling out. After a few minutes of silence Charlie brought up the DVD of the scan, telling him she would attempt to burn copies this evening, one for him, one for his parents.

"I know they'd appreciate that," he said.

Conversation continued in fits and starts, both of them making an effort to get back on an even keel. When he stopped at the radiology clinic, Charlie released her seat belt and collected her bag from the floor.

"Lunch was nice. Thanks for playing hooky with me," she said.

She didn't kiss him goodbye. Instead, she touched his forearm briefly before opening her door and slipping out of the car.

He was halfway to the office when he realized work was the last place he wanted to be.

It had been a long time since he'd felt that way.

He called Julie and told her he wouldn't be in at all for the rest of the day, then headed for home. His workout gear had been kicked into the corner in the spare room, and he changed into shorts and a tank top and jogged the two blocks to the gym. He sweated on the weight machines and treadmill for a good hour, working out his frustration and confusion.

He wasn't used to being in the dark this way. He liked to have a plan. He liked to have goals he could aspire to. He liked certainty.

There was nothing certain about Charlie. She slipped through his fingers, constantly confounding him, letting him close then pushing him away.

Her choice—she had a right to keep him at a distance if that was what she wanted. But it didn't mean the rest of his world needed to remain in flux. He'd been reacting—reeling in shock, really—ever since he'd learned he would be a father. It was time to get back into the driver's seat.

He made plans as he jogged home. He'd call

around a few real estate agents first thing tomorrow and see how much house his money could buy him in the Eastern Suburbs. He'd be happy in Paddington and Woollahra, maybe even Rose Bay. All suburbs at the pricey end of the property market, but the Finger Wharf had been, too. He might have adjusted some of his priorities, but he didn't need to give up all his aspirations.

He'd investigate trading in the BMW, too. Start setting himself up for the next phase—the baby phase. Anticipating, rather than simply waiting for, the next curveball life threw his way.

He was sweaty and hot by the time he entered the foyer of his apartment complex, but for the first time in what seemed like weeks he felt as though he had a bead on things.

A woman was collecting her mail from the boxes next to the elevator and she glanced over as he crossed the marble floor.

"Rhys. Hi," Heather said, a friendly smile curving her mouth as she faced him. She wore a pair of slim-fit jeans with red boots and a snug red sweater.

He paused, using the back of his forearm to wipe the sweat from his brow. "Hey. How are you?"

"I'm good. Not quite as virtuous as you, since I haven't been to the gym in weeks, but good. I tried that coffee place you recommended, by the way." She kissed her fingers. "I owe you."

"Glad you liked it."

"I loved it. You saved my life. I'm a complete write-off until I've had my caffeine hit in the morning."

"I know the feeling." He glanced toward the elevator, keen to get out of his damp clothes.

"I won't hold you up," she said, gesturing for him to keep moving. "I just wanted to say thanks."

Her smile was bright and uncomplicated. An image popped into his mind—Charlie standing beside his car, looking out to sea. Distant and unknowable and closed off.

He focused on Heather. Made himself really look at her. She was an undeniably attractive woman. Friendly. Intelligent. Not so long ago, he would have asked her out without hesitation.

So what's making you hesitate now? And if the answer is Charlie, you need to get your head checked. Pronto.

The pushy bastard in his head was right.

He smiled at Heather. "You're not holding me up. I almost forgot I promised to word you up on some of the local secrets, didn't I?"

"I don't think it was exactly a promise."

"An offer, then. There's a bar in the café strip

closer to Kings Cross that does a mean mojito if you'd like to hook up some night this week...?"

She pulled a face. "I'm about to head off on a long haul. I won't be back until late Friday."

"What about on the weekend, then?"

She looked a little sheepish. "Saturday and Sunday nights are booked already."

He smiled. Clearly, she was a woman in demand. "How about lunch on Saturday?"

"Saturday lunch I can do."

"Phew."

She laughed.

"Shall I swing by and pick you up?" he asked.

"Sure. You remember my apartment number?"

"It's 4A, right?"

"That's right." She looked pleased that he'd remembered.

"I'll see you on Saturday," he said.

"You will."

He stepped into the lift. The doors closed and he was confronted with his reflection in the polished steel. The smile faded from his lips as he leaned forward and punched the number for his floor.

He didn't owe Charlie anything—so there was absolutely no reason for him to feel guilty about making a date with another woman.

No reason at all.

CHARLIE DROVE HOME on autopilot, her mind whirling as she tried to process what had happened.

She shouldn't have said yes to lunch. She should have stuck to her guns and played it safe and kept Rhys at a distance.

We had sex because we're really into each other... I knew exactly what I was doing and who I was with.

She shook her head, trying to shake Rhys's words loose.

Until he'd spoken, she'd been sure she understood what had almost happened between them as they lay on the grass—it had been an emotional morning, the sun had been shining, Rhys had gotten caught up in the moment…

But then he'd said all those things…and he'd pursued her.

Charlie sat at a red light, clenching and unclenching her hands on the steering wheel as she tried to reconcile what he'd said with what she knew—what the world had shown her, again and again—to be true. Men like Rhys Walker were not attracted to women like her.

He was gorgeous, smart, funny. He walked into rooms and heads turned. He spoke and people listened. He could have anyone. *Anyone.*

So why would he choose her?

Someone behind her leaned on their horn and she realized that the light had changed. She put her foot down, forcing herself to concentrate on the road. She drove past the turnoff for Balmain and into the neighboring suburb of Rozelle. She pulled into the guest parking spot at Gina's workplace ten minutes later. She turned off the engine and pulled out her phone, dialing her friend.

"C. What's up?" Gina asked.

"Are you busy? Do you have time to talk?"

There was a small, telling pause. "I can make time. Do you want me to come over to your place?"

"I'm out front."

"Five seconds," Gina said.

Charlie had barely put her phone in her handbag when Gina exited the building, phone in one hand, bag in the other. She opened the passenger door.

"Please tell me everything's okay with the baby," Gina said, her face a study in concern as she peered in at Charlie.

"She's fine. Healthy and moving and complete."

"Thank God. It was the first thing I thought of." Gina slid into the car and pulled the door shut. Then she suddenly smiled, her eyes brightening. "You said *she*. Does that mean you're having a little girl?"

Charlie nodded.

"Hey, that's so cool," Gina said. "A little girl."

"Yeah."

Gina shifted so that her body angled more toward Charlie. "So if the scan was okay, what's up?"

Charlie tried to work out what to say, where to begin. After a few seconds she shrugged. It was all such a mess, there was probably no easy place to start.

"Something happened today. With Rhys. And I don't know what to do with it."

"What sort of thing? A good thing or a bad thing?"

"He tried to kiss me."

Gina cocked her head. "Since when do you not know what to do when a hot guy tries to kiss you?"

Charlie dropped her gaze to where her hands were clasped in her lap. "Rhys isn't just a hot guy."

"But you agree he's hot?"

Charlie made a frustrated noise, but Gina held up a hand to silence her.

"I'm not yanking your chain by asking you that. Believe it or not, whether you're still attracted to Rhys is kind of a big deal in this situation." Gina cocked an eyebrow. Waiting.

"I'm attracted to him," Charlie said quietly. "But that just makes me one of about a million, from what I can tell."

Gina frowned. "Why do you keep doing that?"

"What?"

"Deflecting. Or maybe it's distracting. Every time I ask if you like Rhys or are attracted to him you tell me that it would be impossible not to like him and that, of course, you find him attractive, because who wouldn't? I want to know what *you* think, Charlie. What *you* want."

Charlie couldn't hold her friend's gaze.

"Do you even know?" Gina asked after a moment, her voice low with sympathy.

So many thoughts and feelings were jumbled inside Charlie's head, she knew she couldn't even begin to articulate them.

"I'm not setting myself up for failure."

"Why would you be setting yourself up for failure by acknowledging you're attracted to a man who tried to kiss you? Call me crazy, but it seems to me that he's kind of flagging a few things here. You know, like the fact that he wants to kiss you."

Charlie made a dismissive gesture with her hand. "Under any other circumstances, Rhys wouldn't even look twice at me, but we're trapped in this situation. I don't want to be some kind of consolation prize. I don't want to be convenient."

"You are not a consolation prize, Charlotte Long, and you are definitely not convenient. You are a beautiful, smart, capable, resourceful, funny woman. If I was a man, I would give Rhys a run for his money. I'd make him fight for you."

Charlie shook her head, instinctively rejecting her friend's words. Gina was being kind. It was what she did. Telling Charlie what she thought she needed to hear.

"You don't need to pump me up. I know how the world works. I'm not stupid."

"You have no idea how the world works. Not if you think I'm flattering you without cause and if you think Rhys would kiss you just because you happen to be the woman he's with at the time." Gina looked a little angry, her face flushed with color.

"Maybe we should talk about this another time," Charlie said. "You sounded busy when I called. I don't want to keep you from your stuff."

Gina studied her, her gaze sharp, assessing. "You know, I was scared spitless of you when we first met at recruit training. You were so bloody cool and reserved and determined. No one was as tough as you. Remember when you cut your hand on that can of stew when we were on a training exercise? I would have screamed for a chopper to take me to the nearest hospital, but you merely wrapped it up and told everyone you were fine."

"I *was* fine."

"You needed five stitches when we got back to base."

"I was still fine."

"I thought you were the bravest person I'd ever met. I used to feel like such a wimp every time I got scared or tired. I'd look at you and tell myself that if you could do it, so could I."

Charlie frowned. That wasn't how she remembered recruit training. She'd been terrified of failure. It wasn't until later—once she understood that the army had been her last, desperate bid to win her father's love and approval—that she'd understood why.

"I was scared all the time, too," she said.

"I know. I just worked that out."

Charlie rubbed at the thin white scar on the back of her left hand, the legacy from that incident during training.

"Tell me what you're afraid of now, Charlie," Gina said, her voice very soft.

Charlie remained silent, staring at her scar.

"Is it too hard? Or are you afraid that if you start, you won't be able to stop?"

Charlie's gaze shot to her friend's face. Gina watched her steadily. Patiently.

Charlie's chest was tight. Everything in her told her to open the door and walk away from this conversation she never should have initiated. She should have done what she always did—circle the wagons, protect herself and wait for the storm to pass, for whatever had happened between her and Rhys to blow over.

After all, there was no risk of rejection if you didn't put yourself out there in the first place.

"I'm not brave. Not by a long shot." The words came from her gut, raw and honest.

"How about we suspend the value judgments for a few minutes? How about you let yourself be a human being for once?"

Charlie's throat got tight as she stared at her friend, as though a lifetime of repressed fears and thoughts and feelings had suddenly rushed up all at once, wanting out. Wanting to be free.

Ever since she was very young she'd kept her own counsel, grieving her personal failures in private. While she was growing up, her father had been distant, disengaged. Later, as an adult she'd never had a truly trusted confidante.

But now Gina was inviting her to share, offering her friendship and understanding and empathy. Offering to know all of Charlie, and promising not to turn away, no matter what she revealed. She took a deep breath. Gripped her hands together tightly.

"What if I fall in love with him and he doesn't love me back?"

CHAPTER TWELVE

CHARLIE'S VOICE SOUNDED small and choked. Gina took her hand, her face creased with sympathy.

"Everyone takes that risk when they fall in love, Charlie. Everyone."

But Charlie knew that some people were better at being loved than others. At being lovable. Some people simply had the knack for it. Gina and Rhys, the whole of Rhys's family… But not Charlie. She'd always had to work hard to be loved. And it seemed to her that the harder she'd worked, the more she'd wanted it, the harder it had been to hold on to.

"I don't think I'm enough for him."

"What does that mean? Enough what?"

"Beautiful enough. Smart enough. Interesting enough."

Gina's frown deepened. Her fingers squeezed more tightly. "It kills me to hear you say that. How can you not know how special you are?"

More than anything in the whole world, Charlie wanted to believe what her friend was saying. Wanted to believe that the lessons life had taught her were wrong, that she'd somehow been mistaken all these years.

But the lessons had been too harsh, and too hard hitting. They sat in her bones, a part of her. Incontrovertible.

"Here's how special I am—when I was thirteen, Billy Hendricks wouldn't go in the cupboard with me when we were playing Spin the Bottle. When I was seventeen, I was the only girl at my school who didn't have a partner for the debutante ball. When I was five—" Charlie swallowed and took a deep breath, very aware of the hot pressure building behind her eyes. No way was she sniveling self-pityingly, not when she was already exposing herself so fully. "When I was five, my father asked my aunt to take me in, but she refused and he was stuck with me. When I was eighteen, he told me it was time for me to leave home and stand on my own two feet. I know you're trying to be kind, and I love you for it, but I am not a special person, Gina. I don't know what I am, but I am definitely not that."

"Charlie." Gina's hand tightened painfully on hers as she blinked away tears. "Those people are all *stupid*. Your father… I don't even know what to say about a man who was willing to give up his own child. But I know that whatever it is, it's about him, not you. You are *lovely*, Charlie. Lovely and extraordinary and smart and loyal and so many good things that I can't even begin to list them. I was thrilled when you took me up on my offer of the spare room, because it meant I'd lured you to Sydney and I'd get to see you more often. Those three years we lived together were some of the best of my life." A tear slid down Gina's cheek.

"I didn't tell you any of that stuff so you'd feel sorry for me," Charlie said. "I just want the truth. All my life, that's all I've ever wanted. I don't want people to pretend or be polite or kind. I'd rather know what's what, and get on with things. I don't want to be some sort of obligation or duty."

Gina wrapped her arms around Charlie. "I don't pity you. I feel sad for you. I feel angry for you—angry that life can be so bloody sucky to good people sometimes. You deserve a whole lot better than the shitty hand you've been dealt, Charlie. But your father's failure as a parent does not define you. It certainly doesn't mean that you should stop trying and believing."

Charlie rested her head on her friend's shoulder, suddenly incredibly weary. She was so sick of fighting all the time. Of being strong. Of pretending she didn't care.

She cared. She cared too much. She always had.

After a minute Gina released her and pulled back.

"I want you to promise me something—the

next time Rhys tries to kiss you, promise me you'll let him."

"It probably won't happen."

"I'm betting it will. And I want you to believe in it, Charlie. Don't push him away because you think he's being kind. Men don't kiss women to be kind. They definitely don't have sex with them because they're being kind. I want you to give Rhys a chance to prove himself to you. I want you to give *yourself* a chance."

Charlie started to shake her head. Gina was asking too much. Rhys was so overwhelming, so…*everything.* If she allowed herself to believe that she might have a future with him and nothing came of it… She had no idea how she would recover.

"It's too messy. We have to think of the baby. If things didn't work out, it would be horrible."

"But what if they did? What if you fell in love with Rhys and he with you?"

"It's a fairy tale. Too convenient and twee to be real."

"I bet it's happened in the history of the world. Why can't it happen for you and Rhys?" Gina's gaze was challenging.

A thousand reasons why it couldn't happen for her and Rhys circled her mind.

Because I'm me.

Because life doesn't work like that.

Because it would be too perfect. Too much.

"Sometimes you have to take a leap of faith. You are the gutsiest woman I know. You can go on this journey with Rhys. I know you can. Give yourself a chance to be happy."

Charlie shook her head, but there was no conviction behind the gesture. "I don't know. I don't know what I want. I need to think about this…"

Gina didn't say anything and when Charlie finally met her eyes, she saw understanding there.

Gina knew she was lying. She knew what Charlie wanted. She also knew Charlie was too scared to reach out for it.

"I love you, C," she said simply.

Charlie's chest squeezed all over again and she blinked rapidly. "I love you, too."

Her voice sounded rusty. How long had it been since she'd dared to say those words to another human being?

Gina's phone beeped, the sound incredibly loud and unnaturally bright in the small space. She checked the display.

"Shit. I have to go in. There's a problem with the oysters we ordered for tomorrow's wedding." She looked at Charlie. "Are you okay? Do you want me to come over after work?"

"I thought you were seeing Spencer tonight."

"I can see him another time."

Charlie smiled faintly, touched by her friend's

loyalty and concern. "I'll be fine. I need to do some thinking, anyway. Sort a few things out."

"Okay."

They said their goodbyes, then Gina slid from the car with a wave and headed inside.

Charlie drove home, Gina's words whirling in her mind.

Her friend thought she was brave. The gutsiest woman she knew. She also thought Charlie was lovely and funny and smart and interesting. Gina wanted Charlie to take a leap of faith. To believe that all the things she wanted in her heart of hearts were possible.

That Rhys might be attracted to her in the way she was attracted to him.

That they might have a future.

That he might fall in love with her, the way she was sure she could fall in love with him.

It wasn't until she climbed the stairs to her apartment that she realized she'd been frowning the entire drive. She lifted a hand to her forehead, easing the muscles with her fingertips.

She didn't have to make any decisions today. It wasn't as though Rhys was going to burst in the door right now and try to kiss her again. She had time to mull over her friend's words. To try to take on board what Gina had said.

Charlie walked into the study and her gaze went straight to the dark corner where she'd shoved the box from the hospice, drawn like iron filings to a magnet. She still hadn't gotten around to unpacking it. Had been avoiding it, if she were honest.

She strode across the room and dropped to her knees and pulled the box toward herself. She closed her eyes, trying to imagine what she would find inside. Preparing herself.

Some papers, maybe. Some books. Possibly her father's old transistor radio.

She opened her eyes and folded back the flaps and peered inside. Two pairs of folded pajamas sat on top—plain, serviceable blue cotton. She pulled them out, resting them on her knees. The weight felt wrong and she delved between the two tops and slid free an old metal picture frame with a black-and-white shot of her parents on their wedding day. It was the same photograph that had graced her father's bedside table all her life and she wasn't surprised that he'd taken it to the hospice.

She studied her mother's face, a small, pale oval with dark eyes and hair and a bright, hopeful smile, and felt only the same dull, distant ache that she always experienced when she thought of her. It was impossible to truly miss or grieve someone you'd never known. Her gaze shifted to her father, very upright and proud in his dress uniform. He looked impossibly young. She could see her own reserve in his expression.

They looked happy. Expectant. As though they were ready for life's next adventure. Sadly, her mother had only lived another two years before she'd bled out after a difficult labor and delivery.

The silver frame was tarnished and Charlie took a swipe at it with her sleeve before placing it on her desk. Perhaps she'd buy a new frame for it sometime.

She turned back to the box. Her next find was a narrow case, which, when she opened it, revealed her father's reading glasses. They were the same frames he'd had for years and she had a flash of him wearing them, sitting in his favorite armchair, reading one of the many biographies he'd enjoyed. If she'd interrupted him, he'd always taken his time before looking up from his book, fixing his cool blue gaze on her over the tops of the lenses. Letting her know that she had his attention only temporarily.

She put the case to one side. Next she found a handful of pens and a foolscap manila folder. A quick inspection revealed that the folder contained word puzzles her father had clipped from the newspaper. Again, she set it all to one side. As she'd predicted, her father's transistor radio was next, the yellowed power cord wrapped neatly around it. There was only one item left, a book lying facedown. She pulled it out, turning it over. She stilled as she realized what it was.

When she was ten years old, her father had celebrated his fortieth birthday. Even though he wasn't a very social man, she'd known it was an important occasion, and she'd wanted to give him something meaningful to commemorate it. After weeks—months—of reconnaissance, she'd settled on a book on Gallipoli she'd heard her father discussing with a friend. She'd claimed coins from the couch cushions, sacrificed a portion of her lunch money and sold some of her most precious comic books to a neighbor, Jimmy Chandler, to afford the purchase. Her father had opened the gift in his usual methodical manner, easing the tape from the paper, folding it away from its contents carefully, painstakingly. Twenty-two years later, she could still remember the rising excitement she'd felt as he'd revealed the book. She'd watched his face, waiting for understanding to dawn.

Waiting for him to understand how much love and planning and care and anticipation had gone into this gift.

His eyes had scanned the title. Then he'd opened the book and spent a few seconds flicking through the first chapter or so. Then he'd met her hopeful, yearning gaze and nodded. Once.

"It's a good book. Thank you," he'd said.

He'd stood, crossed the room and put it on the bookshelf. And, to her knowledge, he'd never taken it down again. He also hadn't pulled her into his arms and told her that she was a good girl and that he loved her, or that he knew how much she loved him. He hadn't said any of the things that she'd dreamed of him saying. That he was glad she was his. That she made him happy. That she was important to him. That she mattered.

She had cried herself to sleep that night, heartbroken that he hadn't recognized her love. That he didn't seem to want it or value it. At some point in the small, dark hours she'd come to the understanding that life had reinforced again and again throughout her lifetime: love could not be earned, and just because one person loved did not mean that that love would be reciprocated. In fact, in her experience, it almost seemed the opposite. The more she loved her father, the more distant and unattainable he'd become.

Yet he'd kept this book. He'd cleared out the house and sold it once he'd been diagnosed and knew the prognosis, determined to leave nothing but a bank account, a will and a corpse behind when his illness got the better of him.

He'd disposed of everything he'd ever owned, passing his belongings to friends or local charities—except for this book.

She lifted the cover. Inside she found her own

childishly round writing, as perfectly formed as she could make it at the time.

Dear Dad,
Happy birthday.
With all my love,
Charlotte (Charlie), your daughter

She shut the cover again and rested her hand on the glossy jacket, trying to figure out why he kept this book—other than for the reason that she wanted him to have kept it, of course. But for the life of her she couldn't come up with a single explanation other than the fact that it had meaning for him, right up until the end.

It was something. In a lifetime that had been short on sentiment and approval, it was something. Especially in light of what had almost happened with Rhys and the discussion she'd had with Gina and what she'd challenged her to do.

Charlie stood and added the book to her bookcase among her reference and design manuals. It looked out of place with its big, thick spine and larger format, but that was okay. She could live with it.

Before she could think it to death, she reached for the phone and called Rhys.

"Charlie. Hi," he said carefully.

"I wanted to make sure you got home okay."

She immediately felt stupid—as if he couldn't travel ten kilometers across the city without supervision.

"I did. Thanks."

Idiot. Say what you mean for a change. Be brave.

"I was wondering what you were doing on Saturday? That comic-book exhibition you mentioned starts on Friday. If you wanted, I thought we could maybe go see it then have lunch together afterward."

She stared at the wall as she waited for what seemed like a long time for Rhys's response.

"I've actually got something on this Saturday. But maybe we could go on Sunday?"

"Sure. Sunday is good for me, too."

"Shall I swing by and pick you up?"

"What if I pick you up for a change?"

"Okay. Good."

She wrote down his address and they discussed options for lunch before deciding to simply check out the offerings near the gallery.

Charlie felt ridiculously buoyant when she ended the call. She was seeing Rhys again, sooner than their usual weekly lunch appointment. She'd made the first move. And if he tried to kiss her again… She'd cross that bridge when she came to it.

She could almost hear Gina chastising her and

urging her to be bold and brave, but Rome wasn't built in a day.

Anyway, Rhys might never try to kiss her again. She may have blown her one chance with him, rejecting him the way she had.

In which case, it wasn't really a chance, right?

It was a little shocking how disappointed she felt as she considered this prospect. Which went to show what a huge, messed-up hypocrite she really was.

Sunday. Just wait till Sunday, idiot.

Not the worst advice she'd ever given herself.

THE FOLLOWING SATURDAY, Rhys hit the gym before showering and getting dressed for his date with Heather. He'd almost canceled twice during the week, but both times common sense had prevailed. He owed Charlie his support and friendship, but he didn't owe her his entire life. And she'd made her own feelings more than clear. There was no point in him sitting at home twiddling his thumbs, trying to second-guess Charlie when he could be moving on with his life.

He glanced in the mirror before heading for the door. Polo shirt, jeans, a pair of dark brown boots, his leather jacket in case it got cold. He strapped on his Hugo Boss watch, avoiding looking himself in the eye.

He grabbed his keys and wallet and locked up

before walking up the hallway to Heather's apartment. He knocked, and after a few seconds she opened the door.

"Hi."

"Hi." He gave her an appreciative once-over. She was wearing a pair of skinny jeans that made her legs seem to go on forever. On top she wore a soft-looking pale blue sweater that accentuated her full breasts. Like him, she carried a leather jacket.

"You look like you're ready to go," he said.

"I am."

"Then I guess we should go."

She matched his smile with one of her own before locking the door. He allowed her to precede him to the elevator and his gaze slid to her backside. Between Tuesday and now he'd somehow managed to forget how attractive she was—and sexy. She'd clearly gone to a lot of trouble to prepare for their date, too—her hair was a smooth, glossy fall down her back, her makeup was perfect, she smelled good.

She looked great. Really great. And she seemed like a nice person. Fun. Bubbly. This was going to be a good afternoon.

Who are you trying to convince, buddy?

"So, where are we going?" Heather asked as they rode the lift to the garage.

He hadn't really given the venue for their date

much thought. Quickly he plucked a restaurant from the air. "I was thinking the Icebergs at Bondi."

The restaurant was perched at the top of the cliff beside Bondi Beach and offered sweeping views of the bay, as well as the saltwater Olympic-length pool that was part of the fitness club located beneath the restaurant. It was a good, solid first-date option. Definitely a safe bet.

"Perfect. I love it there. I especially love that you can watch people sweating it out in the swimming pool below while you lounge around with a drink in your hand."

"A recreational voyeur. Nice," he said.

"I'm a lounge lizard, in case you couldn't tell. If I didn't have good genes, I swear I'd be the size of a house."

They talked easily on the drive. He learned that Heather had two older brothers, and that she was thinking of quitting the airline to go back to university to study law.

"That's a bit of a sea change," he said as they turned the corner into Bondi Parade.

"I know. Especially at my age, but I always wanted to study law. I let myself get talked out of it when I was younger by my mother. She was a hostie before she married and loved the lifestyle. She said there wasn't a better way of seeing the world, and in many ways she was right."

"But?"

"But I don't want to be handing out coffee and tea when I'm fifty. And there are only so many times you can see the Eiffel Tower or the pyramids or the Golden Gate Bridge and feel excited about it, you know?"

He found parking on a side street and they walked across the Parade and down a short stretch of residential road to the club entrance. They were shown a table on the balcony and they both put on their jackets to defeat the cool breeze.

"We can ask for a table inside if it's too cold for you," Rhys said.

"The sea air is nice and fresh. I like it."

They continued to talk as they ordered food and a bottle of wine, a little stiffly at first but with increasing ease as the meal progressed. He couldn't help thinking of his first meal with Charlie. She'd been so tense, nothing like Heather with her air of casual confidence. But there had been a lot more at stake then, too. The baby, the tenor of their future relationship.

He realized that Heather had stopped talking and was looking at him expectantly, obviously awaiting a response. He replayed the previous few minutes in his head but drew a blank.

"You have no idea what I said, do you?" Heather asked, amused.

"Sorry. I drifted off for a second."

"I asked if you wanted dessert here or if we should go for cake someplace else? There's this little place I know in Rose Bay that makes awesome chocolate brownies."

"Sounds great," he said.

He pushed Charlie to the back of his mind, where she belonged, and signaled for the bill. When it came, he slid his credit card in the folder. Heather didn't so much as bat an eyelid. A refreshing change from the constant battle of wills with Charlie.

Although, as he'd pointed out to himself on several occasions, his outings with Charlie had never been dates.

"There's a place my friends told me about in Annandale that we should try next time," Heather said as the waiter came to take his card away. "Really good Italian, apparently."

There was an assured assumption behind her words. Rhys hadn't projected beyond today's outing in his head, but he forced himself to do so now, trying on the idea of seeing Heather again.

She was fun and a good conversationalist. Sure, they hadn't touched on any deep or serious subjects, but it was a first date, not a counseling session. And she was undeniably an attractive woman—more than one head had turned when they'd walked in the door.

He became aware that he was essentially talking himself into a decision that should have been a no-brainer. Because of Charlie, of course. Because he felt responsible and beholden.

The waiter returned with his card, then he and Heather stood and headed for the door. The wind whipped their faces as they exited to the street.

"Wow. The building must have really been protecting us, hey?" She laughed as her long hair swept out behind her like a flag.

"I guess. Or maybe the wind's just picked up." He glanced toward the sky, but the only clouds were very high and a benign fluffy white.

"I love the wind. It's so energizing. Don't you think?"

He was about to respond when he spotted a tall, willowy woman fifteen feet ahead of them. She was in profile, about to step onto the road from the concrete steps that led to the beach. His subconscious mind registered who it was a split second before Charlie glanced to her left to check if the path was clear before stepping onto the road. He knew the exact second that she recognized him—her eyes lit from within, full of warmth and unexpected pleasure, and her mouth curved into a delighted smile. She lifted a hand, and seemed ready to call out a greeting.

Then her gaze slid to Heather and her smile froze. Charlie's gaze traveled back to him, and the pain and hurt and betrayal he saw literally took his breath away, as real and visceral as a blow to the solar plexus. Suddenly he realized that he'd been fooling himself by taking Heather out, fooling himself hugely in relation to Charlie.

He took a step forward, searching for the words to convince her that this was not what it looked like. That he wasn't seeing another woman. That this had nothing to do with them, with her.

"Charlie."

She whipped her head around, her body following jerkily as she walked away from him.

"Charlie!" He lengthened his stride, charging ahead of Heather.

After a few steps Charlie stopped. Her shoulders lifted, then dropped, and she turned to face him.

Her smile was perfectly judged—friendly, a little surprised, not too effusive. Her eyes were opaque, giving nothing away.

"Rhys. I almost didn't hear you. This is a coincidence."

He stretched out a hand to touch her, needing to comfort her, to soothe away the hurt he'd seen—the hurt he'd caused. She shifted deftly to one side, her gaze focused over his shoulder.

"Hi," she said.

He glanced back as Heather walked the final few feet to join them. She was laughing, one hand attempting to stop her hair from flying across her face. She looked model perfect and beautiful and utterly desirable—and again he cursed himself for a fool for thinking that she could act as a substitute for Charlie. It was an insult to both women, not to mention completely futile.

"Isn't it a great day?" Heather said.

"It is. Really nice," Charlie agreed, smile still firmly in place.

There was so much pride and courage in that smile... It hurt him to look at it, especially when he'd seen the pain that lay beneath her mask.

"You look like you've been making the most of it," Heather said.

"My second attempt at the Bondi-Coogee track. Still not quite up to the full return trip yet. I'm Charlie, by the way."

"Heather. Nice to meet you."

Rhys watched as the two women shook hands. Heather glanced at him, but for the life of him he couldn't think of anything to say. All he could think about was what he'd seen in Charlie's eyes.

"I'd better keep moving," Charlie said. "I don't want to hold you up."

He stepped forward to block her path. "Charlie. I'm sorry, I should have told you."

She met his eyes, her expression completely neutral. Her soldier's face, controlled and calm. "Your private life is none of my business."

She stepped around him and he started to go after her.

"Am I being thick or am I missing something here?" Heather said.

He stopped in his tracks. He couldn't chase Charlie and leave Heather here to cool her heels. He'd already been enough of an asshole for one day. He glanced at her, taking in her bemused expression and defensive body language.

"Please tell me that wasn't your girlfriend, because I am really going to hate myself if I'm the other woman," she said.

"Charlie isn't my girlfriend."

Heather's eyes narrowed. "But she was, right?"

"No."

Charlie had been his for one night only.

"Then what was all that about?" Her tone sounded a little pissy.

Fair enough. He deserved it. And Heather deserved the truth. The problem was, every fiber in his being was straining to go after Charlie. To comfort and reassure her. To explain.

If she'd let him.

He cast a look up the hill. Charlie was crossing the road, her step brisk, her head high. Graceful and dignified and strong, as ever.

"If you want to go after her, just go," Heather said, shooing him off with a dismissive gesture.

He wasn't stupid or rude enough to take her at

her word. "Come on, I'll take you home," he said. "And I'll explain."

"An explanation would be good." She looked at his face then shook her head ruefully. "Although I have a feeling I'm not going to like what I hear. So much for the cute guy in 4D."

He attempted a smile and willed her to start walking. He needed to get her home then he needed to find Charlie and talk to her.

If she'd let him.

CHAPTER THIRTEEN

CHARLIE WALKED TO her car in a daze. Once, during training, she'd been standing too close when a mortar shell had exploded. She hadn't been injured, but for a whole day afterward her ears had rung and she'd walked around in a haze.

That was how she felt now. Her ears weren't ringing, but she felt numb. Utterly numb.

For weeks she'd been telling herself that she was smart and pragmatic. She'd even rejected Rhys when he'd tried to get closer. She'd told herself he was charming, but that she was strong, that she could resist his appeal because there was so much at stake—The Bean, her and Rhys's relationship as coparents, her own continuing happiness.

And yet she'd fallen in love with him anyway.

It had taken seeing him with another woman to alert her to her own foolishness. For the rest of her life she would remember those few seconds when she'd mounted the last step from the beach and seen them walking together, smiles on their faces.

Of course, a voice had said in her mind. *Of course he's seeing someone else.*

Of course.

But the rest of her had been reeling. Primitive, instinctive jealousy had burned through her like acid, closely followed by a searing sense of betrayal. She'd said no to Rhys, held him at arm's length, but deep in her heart she'd allowed herself to imagine something different. To hope. Stupidly, she'd thought she had time, that he would wait—as though any man had ever waited for Charlie Long, let alone a man like Rhys.

Her car was up ahead. She broke into a run, suddenly desperate to be somewhere small and private. Somewhere safe. She yanked the door open and scrambled in. Then she pressed her hands to her face in a futile, ridiculous attempt to contain the grief and hurt rising inside her.

She'd done all the right things. She'd abandoned Rhys's bed after their one night. She hadn't lingered or indulged the hopeful idiot inside herself by leaving her contact details. She'd left, a clean break. When she'd discovered the pregnancy, she'd had no choice but to contact him, but even then she'd been so careful. She'd warned herself, she'd kept a close, tight watch on herself.

And yet she had still wound up here, hunched over her steering wheel, trying to contain the pain of a loss that felt more profound and encompassing than anything she'd experienced in her life before.

She pressed her hands harder against her face, digging her fingers into her scalp, but there was no holding back the tide of emotion. Her breathing choppy, she started to sob, a potent mix of anger and grief sending scalding tears down her cheeks.

In her mind's eye she kept seeing them—seeing *her*—walking over. Charlie didn't need to ask herself why Rhys had chosen the other woman. She had eyes in her head, she could see. And no doubt Heather of the gorgeous body and face had never pushed Rhys away or been prickly or difficult. No doubt Rhys had chosen to be with her of his own free will, rather than being forced into something he didn't want by a faulty piece of latex that had changed his life and taken away his choices.

A horn sounded in the distance and Charlie became aware that while her car offered the illusion of privacy, the reality was far different. Any second now Rhys and Heather might walk past. The thought of them seeing her sobbing had her sliding the key into the ignition and blinking away her tears and buckling her seat belt. Using her sleeve to mop her cheeks, she took a deep breath and pulled out into traffic. All the way across town she had only one goal in mind—to get home where she could hide her shame and hurt and sadness from the world.

That was what she did, after all. Put a brave face on it, play the stoic, then let her pain off the leash when she was alone. Her father had been deeply uncomfortable around displays of emotion and so Charlie had waited until she was alone and private in her bed at night to allow her true feelings to surface. From the age of five, she had ceased to cry in front of him. It had become a point of honor for her, and eventually it had become the habit of a lifetime. The discipline of a lifetime.

She worked hard to keep her mind blank as she drove. She flicked on the radio and forced herself to listen to the news report. She studied the cars ahead and in the rearview mirror as assiduously as if she were taking her driving test. Then she turned onto her street and saw her building ahead and the wall she'd constructed inside herself crumbled and she started to cry again. She parked and took the stairs two at a time. Then she was inside her apartment, and she was safe.

She wrapped her arms around herself as she sank onto the edge of the couch, then after a few seconds stood again. She didn't know where to put herself. Her chest ached with misery, her eyes burned. She walked into the bedroom and kicked off her sneakers and crawled beneath the quilt. She curled tightly into herself and closed her eyes, wanting to block everything out. Wanting not to feel.

Not to love.

I wish I'd never met you, she told Rhys in her head. *I wish I'd never let Gina talk me into doing that lap of Café Sydney. I wish I'd never suggested we go to the bar. I wish I'd taken that taxi home with Gina instead of going home with you. I wish our bodies and biology hadn't betrayed us. God, how I wish...*

Even as she thought it, her hand slid down to cover the barely-there bump of the baby, a silent apology for wishing her out of existence. It wasn't The Bean's fault that things were so screwed up.

After a while the tears stopped and all that was left was a pervading sense of her own stupidity and naiveté. She'd been fretting over their near kiss in the park, even though she'd told herself it was nothing—told him it was nothing, too. She'd rushed to Gina's and dissected the whole thing and allowed Gina to talk her into hoping. Into believing. After thirty-two years of caution, she'd been ready to give it a shot. To lay it on the line and to believe that maybe she had got it wrong all these years.

And all along Rhys had been seeing another woman. Not just any woman, either. A woman with shampoo-commercial hair and hot-summer-day sky-blue eyes and a body that belonged on a *Sports Illustrated* cover.

They looked good together. A study in light and dark. They looked like a match set.

Charlie opened her eyes and stared at the wall. She felt empty. No hope, no plans, no dreams. A passing feeling, she knew—people didn't die of broken hearts, after all. And she was tough. She'd made herself tough. She might be indulging herself right now, but soon she would get up and she would soldier on. That was what she did. It was what she'd always done. It was what she'd continue to do, especially because it wasn't only herself she had to fight for now. The Bean deserved better.

So Charlie would get over this thing with Rhys. She would move past it. Eventually, she might even consider it good that the situation had come to a head and her own self-deception had been dragged into the light. Better to be done with it, stare it in the eye, than to go on pretending and fooling herself. A quick, surgical strike—painful but fast—then on to recovery.

She closed her eyes again. Maybe in a few days or weeks she would get to that place. But not yet. She pulled the quilt higher over her shoulders and burrowed into the pillow. Sleep seemed like a great option right now. A bit of peace. A respite.

The phone rang, the sound echoing through the

apartment from the study. Charlie didn't move. Instead, she listened until it stopped.

Whoever it was could leave a message, call back later. She wasn't ready to face the world yet.

Barely two minutes later, a knock sounded on her door. Her eyes popped open and she sat up.

There weren't many options: Gina or Rhys. Her gut squeezed nervously.

She knew who it was. And she didn't want to see him.

"Charlie. I know you're in there."

Rhys's voice echoed down the hallway. He started to knock again almost immediately, a continuous, persistent pounding. Any thought she had of ignoring him in the hope that he'd go away went out the window. She swung her legs over the side of the bed and stood. Her face felt stiff from her tears. She walked toward the door and peered through the spy hole. All she could see was Rhys's shoulder.

"Charlie. I'm not leaving till I've spoken to you," Rhys yelled.

Anger surged inside her. This was her place, her space. She'd come here to be safe. To think and consider and to recover from what had happened today. He had no right to follow her here and demand entrance so he could assuage his conscience. Because she had no doubt that was what this was about. He'd said as much to her at the beach, hadn't he? *I'm sorry. I should have told you.*

She didn't want his apology or his pity. She didn't want anything from him except what he owed their baby. Which was the way it should have been right from the start, before she'd allowed herself to believe in fairy tales.

Still, there was no time like the present to set things straight. Chin high, she twisted the lock open.

RHYS FELT THE DOOR give beneath his fist, then Charlie was standing there, her face pale and tear blotched, arms wrapped tightly across her chest.

"I do have neighbors, you know," she said.

"I want to explain."

"You don't need to explain anything to me."

She was very calm. Very controlled. But behind the blankness in her eyes he knew she was hurting. That he'd hurt her.

"Yes, I do, Charlie."

"It's none of my business. We don't own each other. We made a baby together. That's the end of our mutual obligation."

"What you saw today was a first date. And I went on it only because I was trying to get you out of my head."

Her chin jerked back a little.

"Not very noble, I know," he said. "But there it

is. I was pissed after the park the other day and I ran into Heather and… It was a mistake, Charlie. A stupid, dumb mistake."

She lifted a shoulder in a fair imitation of an unconcerned shrug. "I don't know what I'm supposed to say to that."

He took a step closer, crossing the threshold. Her chin came up even higher, but she held her ground.

"How about 'Rhys, I can't get you out of my head, either'?"

She started shaking her head before he'd even finished speaking. But he hadn't expected this to be easy. Charlie would never give up her secrets without a fight.

"Does that mean you don't think about me?"

She stared at him then her gaze dropped to his shoulder. "It means I don't see the point of this conversation."

"That's what you said at the park, too." He took another step toward her. This time she retreated. "Tell me why we shouldn't talk about our feelings for each other, Charlie. Tell me why that's pointless."

For the first time he saw emotion behind the mask—surprise, swiftly followed by denial.

"Because of the baby. Because things are complicated enough."

"I don't care."

She seemed startled by his instant rebuttal.

"I used to think that stuff was important, Charlie, but it isn't. You're important—very important—to me. I want you to be happy. I want to make you happy."

She blinked, as though she couldn't comprehend what he'd said. She looked so lost, so bewildered that he couldn't stop himself from reaching for her.

"Charlie, I'm sorry. You have no idea how much." He tried to draw her into his arms, but she placed a hand on his chest, her elbow locked straight to keep him at a distance.

"This is a bad idea."

"I used to think so, but I'm starting to think it might be the best idea I've ever had."

"What about when things go wrong?"

"What if they don't? What if they go right?"

Her breath left her on a shuddery exhale and for a moment—the barest fraction of a second—there was so much yearning in her eyes it broke his heart. She opened her mouth to say something—to reject him again, no doubt—but he spoke over her.

"Don't you ever get sick of fighting, Charlie?"

He saw the answer in her eyes. He slid his hand from the nape of her neck to the curve of her jaw.

"You don't need to fight me. I swear it."

She closed her eyes. The arm keeping him at

bay relaxed. He didn't wait for a second invitation. He pulled her close and kissed her the way he'd been wanting to for weeks. There was the smallest of hesitations then she kissed him back, her body straining toward his almost desperately. She tasted of salty tears and need and he tightened his arms around her, wanting to take away the pain he'd caused her, needing to make things right between them. He tried to slow the kiss, to control it, but Charlie tugged his shirt from his jeans, smoothing her hands up his chest, her hips pressing against his urgently, provocatively.

Everything else fell away as he walked forward until her back hit the wall. There was only him, and her. Still devouring her mouth, he slid a hand onto her breast, his thumb finding her already-hard nipple unerringly. Her fingers dug into his chest as he pinched her then soothed her. His other hand moved to cup her backside, resting her more snugly against his hips. They rocked together, savoring the torturous friction. He released her backside and slid his hand between her legs. She arched against his palm as he stroked her through her yoga pants. He could feel how hot she was, how wet, and he groaned into her mouth.

"Charlie," he said, reveling in the way she trembled in response.

It was the way he'd remembered—only better,

because he knew her now, and he understood how precious she was. How strong and brave.

Suddenly Charlie wrenched her mouth from his. She was panting, her brown eyes dilated as she looked at him.

"I need you. I need you so badly," she said, her voice a low husk.

He spotted what he hoped was her bedroom doorway. "Come on." He urged her ahead of him.

His gaze slid to her round, firm backside as he followed her. He yanked his polo shirt over his head and let it fall to the ground, his hands dropping to the buckle on his belt. He had it open and was working on the stud of his jeans when he entered her bedroom.

Charlie tugged off her long-sleeved T-shirt, revealing full, creamy breasts cupped in white lace. She reached for the rear clasp, but he beat her to it, slipping it free and then cupping the warm, heavy weight of her in his hands. She pressed her backside against his erection, her head dropping against his chest as he teased and soothed her breasts.

"You're so damn hot," he whispered in her ear. "I've been dreaming about you for weeks, Charlie."

She slipped a hand between their bodies to grip him through his jeans. She stroked her hand up and down the hardened length of him. He pressed forward, his hands tightening on her breasts. After a torturous minute, she released him and stuck her thumbs into the waistband of her pants, pushing them down. He forced himself to take a step away and felt himself get even harder as she removed her panties, bending to offer him a perfect view of her ass.

She glanced over her shoulder, her ponytail swishing against her pale skin, her eyes alight with heated desire. She stepped forward and crawled onto the bed, offering him an even better view. He realized he was standing like a dodo, his pants half undone. He dragged his zipper down, shoving off his jeans and boxers. Seconds later he followed Charlie onto the bed, stalking her across the mattress. She rolled onto her back and welcomed him as he covered her body with his.

"I need you inside me," she said against his mouth as he kissed her.

She hooked a leg around his hips and urged him closer. He found her entrance, and she arched her hips at the same time that he thrust inside her. He closed his eyes as he slid home—the rightness of it, her heat, her scent, the feel of her skin against his. He'd needed this, craved this for so long, and he hadn't realized, hadn't understood.

"Charlie," he whispered against her skin as he started to move. "You drive me crazy."

She dug her hands into his backside, urging

him to go harder, faster. She met him thrust for thrust, her need feeding his, until finally she cried out, her body shuddering around his, her face distorting with pleasure-pain. She pushed him over the top into his own climax and for precious seconds he forgot everything except the rush of sensation bombarding his body and mind.

Only afterward did he notice they were both panting raggedly, their bodies slick with sweat, and—more important—that he hadn't used a condom. Then he remembered the baby—crazy, but she'd slipped his mind in his mad rush to be a part of Charlie again—and he let his head drop to Charlie's shoulder.

After a minute or two she stirred beneath him. He rolled to one side.

"Did I squash you? Sorry." He brushed a damp strand of hair from her forehead, admiring the purity of her skin, the fullness of her mouth.

She looked at him and he could see the doubts beginning to crowd behind her eyes again.

"You need to stop thinking for a moment," he said.

"I can't."

"Yes, you can." He curled his body against hers, one arm wrapped across her waist, one leg thrown over hers, his face pressed into her neck. "Just breathe. And think about how good this feels. How right."

Despite his words, he felt the tension returning to her body, degree by degree.

"It's going to be okay, Charlie." He pressed a kiss to her neck.

"I need to know what happens next."

"We date," he said simply. "We see what happens. The way normal couples do."

"But what if it doesn't work out?"

"What if it does?" Because he was holding her, he felt the ripple of tension that washed through her at his words. He drew back a little so he could look into her eyes.

"This is real, Charlie," he said. "Let's trust it. Have some faith in it."

She swallowed. "I don't know how to do that."

"We'll do it together."

He swept a hand down her body, resting his palm against her sternum before sliding it to the small, soft swell that was their baby. In the heat of the moment he'd forgotten about The Bean—it had been all about Charlie, only Charlie—but now he mapped the gentle slope, brushing his palm over her warm skin. He'd wanted to touch her this way ever since the scan. Wanted to feel for himself what was happening inside her.

"I like you with a little belly."

"It won't be little for long."

"No. I guess it won't. I suppose we'll need to get inventive then."

Color flooded her cheeks. Her gaze dropped to where he was already growing hard again, her eyelashes momentarily concealing her eyes from him. When she met his gaze once more, he could see the hunger there—and the doubt and the hope.

He would do his damnedest to live up to that hope. He figured they had as much of a chance as anyone. He wanted Charlie—had never stopped wanting her—and he admired her and enjoyed her and liked her. He had a reasonable suspicion that the feeling was mutual. It felt like a hell of a lot in their favor.

"There's something that's been bugging me for months now," he said, dropping a kiss onto her full bottom lip.

"What?"

He sucked her lip into his mouth, abrading it gently with his tongue.

"Last time, we were so mad for it, we rushed everything. We did everything at breakneck speed."

"Did we?"

He smiled as he felt the subtle arch of Charlie's body as she shifted. His gaze fell to her breasts.

"You know we did. Like we did just now." He moved so he could kiss her breasts, sucking one nipple into his mouth and tonguing it until she squirmed. His hand remained on the swell of her belly, fingers spread. Grounding her and himself.

"I want to take it slow, Charlie. I want to lick and suck and touch you till you beg for it. I want to make you come so hard you forget everything except the two of us and what's good between us."

She inhaled sharply as he switched his attention to her other breast.

"I think you already did that." Her voice was thready, breathy.

"No. Not yet."

He tongued her nipple again, taking it in his mouth before biting ever so gently. Another surge of her hips, another gasping breath. He slid his hand from her belly into the silky hair between her legs. Her thighs fell open eagerly and he delved into slick, wet heat. He made an approving sound, tracing her lightly, deftly, paying attention when she stopped breathing and when her hips jerked involuntarily.

After a few minutes he lifted his head and looked into her face. She was flushed, her eyes half closed. Her hair had come loose from the ponytail, the strands a tousled nimbus around her head. She looked like a beautiful, aroused angel.

Holding her eye, he moved down the bed, his hand gliding from her belly to her hips. Finally he settled between her thighs, lifting one of her legs so it draped decadently over his shoulder.

Her hands were already fisted in the quilt, her eyes hot on his. Then he lowered his head and started to make good on his promise to drive her wild.

CHARLIE COULDN'T THINK. Rhys was between her legs, his mouth on her, his tongue doing things that made her want to shriek with need. She tensed, clutching at the quilt, trying to quiet the tide building inside her.

It was all too much. The shock of seeing him with another woman. The despair of finally acknowledging how deeply her own feelings ran. Then Rhys almost knocking down her door to get to her, to tell her that she was the one he wanted. That he'd wanted her ever since that night.

She gasped then bit her lip to stop herself from being any more vocal as Rhys slid a finger inside her. He continued to lap at her, his tongue rough and smooth at the same time, so hot and crazy making. Tension built inside her, coiling tighter and tighter. He changed the tempo, becoming more urgent as he sensed her growing need.

He slid a second finger inside her and his name hissed from her lips, escaping her tight control. Then she was lost, her body arching off the bed, one hand gripping Rhys's shoulder, anchoring her. She forgot to breathe for long, long seconds, lost in the darkness behind her own eyelids, her world reduced to nothing but pleasure. Then her climax was over and he shifted, coming over her, sliding inside her still-throbbing body, and before she knew it, she was coming yet again, panting and calling out his name.

Afterward, he withdrew and made her roll to the side so he could pull the quilt from beneath them. Its warm weight settled over them and Rhys wrapped his body around hers and kissed her shoulder.

"Rest. You're going to need it," he murmured against her skin.

She smiled, so drugged by sex and satisfaction that she couldn't keep a grip on all the reasons why this was never going to work. Warm and sated, wrapped in Rhys's arms, she drifted into sleep.

She woke in darkness, Rhys's body warming her side. He'd shifted in his sleep, withdrawing his arm but remaining on her side of the bed. She lay blinking in the dark, suddenly horribly aware of how much she'd risked by sleeping with him, by letting this happen. By letting down her guard.

Everything, really.

It had been bad before when she had loved him with no hope of ever having him, but now...

He'd offered her the dream—her fantasy—on a

silver platter. The two of them together. A couple. Raising their child together. A family.

The fairy tale, essentially. The one she'd told Gina she didn't believe in. The one she'd craved in her secret heart for more weeks than she cared to count.

Cold anxiety washed through her, constricting her belly, her chest, her throat. She swallowed, hugging her arms tight to her breasts, willing the feeling to go away. It didn't, and after a few minutes she slipped from the bed and made her way into the living room. A blanket was folded over the edge of the couch and she wrapped it around herself and huddled in the corner of the sofa, knees pulled tightly to her chest.

She stared into the shadows, trying to calm her panicky thoughts and gain some perspective.

Rhys had made love to her with a single-minded intensity. He'd said all the right things—told her she was beautiful, that she drove him crazy, that he'd been thinking about her for weeks. He'd said that they were real, that he trusted them, that he wanted to see where this took them.

If she'd scripted it herself she couldn't have done better. Yet here she was, shivering with an overdose of flight-or-fight anxiety.

Resting her forehead against her knees, she ac-knowledged at last that there was nothing Rhys could say to her that would make her fear go away. There was nothing anyone could say or do because it was *her* fear, as old as she was, born the moment her mother died and she was left with a father who had never truly been a father.

Talking to Gina earlier in the week, Charlie had started to see how profoundly that relationship had shaped her life and who she was. Her reserve and caution had been hard-earned thanks to necessity, and as she'd grown toward adulthood she'd held on to the incidents and memories that reinforced her view of the world and let go of the good things, the memories and moments that spoke of connection and love and her worthiness as a human being.

It was so much easier to believe the bad stuff when you'd been taught that believing the good stuff only set you up for failure and rejection. It was so much easier to believe the worst, full stop. She didn't know why that was, she only knew it was true.

She wanted to hang on to the good things that had happened today. She wanted to remember the sweaty, sexy things Rhys had whispered against her skin while he was inside her. She wanted to hang on to the way he'd gripped her so tightly, as though she was as essential to his happiness as he was to hers. She wanted to preserve the safe, surrounded feeling she'd experienced when he'd pulled her body against his and soothed her to sleep.

She wanted to believe. She wanted to grab the fairy tale by the throat and hang on for grim life. She wanted to be brave enough to reach for happiness.

"Hey. What are you doing out here?"

She lifted her head as Rhys padded barefoot and naked into the room. His body was a masterpiece of muscle and sinew, a study in light and shade as he approached.

"I couldn't sleep."

"You should have woken me. Come back to bed."

He didn't wait for her answer, simply caught her arm and urged her to her feet. He wrapped himself and the blanket around her from behind and made her smile as they tried and failed to match their steps for the short walk to the bedroom. The bed was still warm and he encouraged her to lay her head on his chest while he caressed her shoulders.

"If you want to ask me anything, or if there's something you want to say, I'm up for it," he said after a while.

She knew what he was really asking—why she'd been out on the couch, brooding in the dark.

"It's been a while since I shared a bed with someone, that's all," she lied. She kissed his chest, loving him for asking, for wanting to know, even though she couldn't tell him.

Not yet, anyway. Maybe one day, when her belief in all this was a little more solid.

There was a long silence.

"I've been a planner all my life, even when I was a kid." His voice was low and deep. "I had a plan to get Boyd Taylor to swap his salami-and-cheese sandwich for my peanut butter one. A plan to wrest the bottom bunk from Tim. A plan to buy a car, to kiss Sophie Goodwood, to start my own business." He paused to catch one of her hands, threading his fingers through hers. "But I never planned for you, Charlotte Long. I had this vague idea that I'd meet someone sometime, that all the usual stuff would happen, but I didn't have a clue."

He almost sounded as though he was talking to himself, thinking out loud, but his words warmed her soul. When she looked at him, she saw confidence and good looks and charisma. She saw a man who attracted her in every possible way. It was good to know she'd rocked his world as much as he'd rocked hers. She needed to believe that.

He continued to talk, telling her about one of his childhood schemes. Slowly she let herself be eased toward sleep, his voice rumbling through her body.

A thought pierced her before sleep took her

completely—this was the happiest she could ever remember being.

Another thought came hard on its heels.

Don't screw it up. Whatever you do, don't screw it up.

She tensed, but Rhys's hand swept in a comforting arc across her back and after a few tense seconds she relaxed again and finally fell asleep.

RHYS WOKE with the warmth of sunshine across his face and Charlie's head on his chest. One of her hands was curled loosely over his heart and he could feel the warm weight of her breasts pressing against his side.

He blinked a few times, memories from last night flashing across his mind's eye. Charlie arching beneath him. Charlie calling his name. Charlie huddled on the couch in the small hours.

It had killed him to find her like that, hiding like a little kid. It had killed him even more when she hadn't trusted him enough to tell him what had driven her out of bed.

She was so self-contained. Even when they made love there was a part of her that was always on guard. It was only toward the end, when she started to lose it, that she let herself go completely. It drove him a little crazy every time he watched her pack away her feelings so neatly and comprehensively. And every time she assured him she was fine when he knew she wasn't. Partly because he wanted to know—really know—all of her, and partly because he knew she did it to protect herself, which meant she didn't trust him.

Lying in the sunshine in Charlie's bed, he thought about what he knew of her, what she'd told him and what he'd observed.

He knew she'd grown up without a mother. He knew her father had been distant and disinterested—to the point that he'd left notifying his only child he was dying till the last minute. It was impossible for Rhys to imagine a childhood without brothers and sisters and two parents who were warm and interested and engaged. But he tried because he wanted to understand Charlie.

He thought about all the times when his parents or siblings had been there for him and tried to imagine what it would have been like to navigate those moments alone. He thought about the Christmases and birthdays, the family holidays, the shared memories, the in-jokes, the love.

Charlie had had none of that. She'd been so starved of affection that she'd joined the army in an attempt to win her father's approval. Rhys had a vision of her enduring the hell of recruit training, gritting her teeth and telling herself that it would be worth it, that she had to make it through so as not to disappoint her father. Then, after a while, understanding there was nothing she could do to bridge the gap between them.

What had she called it that night when he'd asked about her father? *Unfinished business.* A relationship that had never given her what she wanted. What she needed.

Was it any wonder that Charlie was slow to trust, slow to reveal herself? Was it any wonder that she always held something in reserve? She'd had no experience of trust, and Rhys suspected she hadn't had nearly enough love in her life.

His arms tightened around her and she stirred against him. He fought the need to pull her closer again, to kiss her and come inside her and show her that she was valued and beautiful and loved.

Because he'd loved her for a while now. He hadn't admitted it to himself until he'd seen the hurt in her eyes yesterday afternoon and known that he was responsible and understood that she was the last person he ever wanted to hurt or harm.

He'd fallen for her in slow degrees, seduced by her quiet humor and quick tongue and intelligence and sexy, slender body. She had more integrity in her little finger than most people had in their whole body. And she had courage and determination by the bucketful.

He wanted to be a part of her life. He wanted to earn her trust. He wanted to make her happy.

Resolve hardened inside him. He'd told Charlie that he hadn't planned for her advent in his life. It was true, but he would plan for her now. He would do his damnedest to get her to drop her guard. He would chip away at her reserve until she let him in.

He would love her until she let herself love him back. If it was his life's work, he would do it.

Charlie stirred again, and this time he gave in to need and ran a hand over her, cupping a breast. He was painfully aroused, craving connection with her, and he waited only until she'd blinked open her eyes and smiled before kissing her and rolling on top of her. They made slow, intense love in the morning sunlight. He told her with his body all the things he knew she wasn't ready to hear yet and told himself that there would come a day—soon, he hoped—when he *would* say it all out loud.

They showered together, and then he took Charlie out for breakfast before taking her to the comic-book exhibition. They walked hand in hand from one display to the next and he watched her face light up as she found old favorites or discovered a much-longed-for rarity.

"Tell me if I'm talking too much," she said as they moved from one superhero section to the next.

"I will. You're not even close."

She smiled her slow, shy smile and he used their joined hands to pull her close and kiss her. She tasted like the cinnamon-ginger pikelets she'd eaten for breakfast and he made an approving sound and deepened the kiss.

Charlie drew back, her cheeks red. "Rhys," she said, her eyes darting first left, then right.

"This is the modern-art gallery. Kissing is not only acceptable, it's encouraged."

She laughed, even as she shook her head at him and told him he was incorrigible. When she started to fade midafternoon he insisted on taking her home so she could catch up on the sleep they'd lost last night. They lay on top of the quilt fully clothed and dutifully closed their eyes, but after twenty minutes Charlie asked if he was still awake and when he confirmed he was, they wound up peeling each other's clothes off and fooling around until they both drifted into exhausted, sated sleep.

It was eight at night when they woke again. Charlie made them a quick dinner and they sat on the sofa, arms and legs entwined while they watched an old James Bond movie. He stirred when the credits started to roll, checking his watch.

"I should probably go. I have an early start tomorrow," he said apologetically.

He waited for Charlie to suggest he stay the

night and go home to change in the morning, but she simply nodded and disentangled herself. He watched as she collected their glasses and carried them to the kitchen, frustrated with her and annoyed with himself for being such a sulky little kid. She'd spent the day with him. She'd laughed at his jokes, responded to his kisses, returned his affection. It was day two. He needed to cultivate some patience.

She returned from the kitchen, stopping in the doorway. She was wearing a pair of stripy pajama pants and a T-shirt with no bra, her hair mussed around her face. Her mouth was pink from his kisses. She crossed an arm across her stomach and gripped the opposite hip and attempted to look casual, even though he could see the tension in her body.

"I was thinking, we could catch up one night during the week. Maybe grab a movie or something?" she suggested.

He smiled, all his frustration evaporating. He joined her in the doorway, sliding his arms around her waist. He loved that he was allowed to touch her now. Loved the feel of her strong, slender body against his own.

"I was thinking more than one night," he said.

Her mouth tilted up at the corners. "That's a little presumptuous, isn't it?"

"Presumptuous is my middle name. As well as Andrew."

"How many nights were you thinking?"

"How many have you got?" he asked.

"I'm having dinner with Gina on Tuesday night."

"Then I'm thinking four nights. Unless Gina doesn't mind me tagging along, then I'm thinking five."

She looked a little uncertain. As though she wasn't sure if he was joking or not. He kissed her.

"This is real, Charlie," he said seriously.

She stared at him then kissed him back, a fierce, passionate kiss that had him hard in seconds.

When she stopped they were both breathing heavily.

"I'll ask Gina if she minds sharing me with you."

He tucked a strand of hair behind her ear. "You do that." He turned reluctantly toward the door. "I'll call you tomorrow, okay? We can work out what we want to do tomorrow night. See a movie."

"Or stay in."

He glanced at her. She raised her eyebrows, innocent as a newborn lamb. He smiled.

"Or stay in," he agreed.

They lingered on the doorstep, each kiss extending into another, then another. Finally Charlie slipped free and laughingly pushed him away.

"At this rate you'll never go," she said. "And you need to get up early."

"Okay." He walked down the hall. "I'll see you."

"Yes."

He glanced at her as he reached the stair landing. She watched him, an unreadable expression on her face. She waved, and he followed suit. Then she slipped inside her apartment and shut the door.

He paused for a moment, fighting the urge to go to her.

You are not fifteen, she is not your first girlfriend, and you will see her tomorrow. Man up, buddy, and get your ass home.

He kept walking to his car then he drove to his place.

He would see Charlie tomorrow—and the day after that, and the day after that. He'd keep seeing her for as long as she'd have him, and he would win her trust and wipe the uncertainty from her eyes.

He would make it his mission because he loved her, and he wanted her to be happy.

CHARLIE BRUSHED her teeth then slipped between sheets that smelled of him and turned off the light. She buried her face in his pillow and inhaled the scent of his aftershave and shampoo and allowed herself to be warmed by the memories of their weekend.

It had been perfect. Better than perfect. He'd been funny, tender, teasing, sexy, generous... He'd been her fairy-tale prince, and he hadn't put a foot wrong.

Her smile faded as she contemplated the week ahead. He wanted to see her every night. She'd psyched herself up in the kitchen before asking him if he wanted to catch a movie one night and he'd come right out with a request to see her every night. *Every night.*

She gave in to instinct and pulled Rhys's pillow closer, wrapping her arms around it. It didn't come even close to substituting for him, but it was something.

This is real, Charlie.

She wanted to believe him very badly. She would try very hard to do so. And she would pray to all the gods and fates and the universe that he was right, that this was real, that this was going to work for her and him and The Bean.

Her arm wrapped around the pillow, she fell asleep. She woke to the ring of the telephone. She blinked blearily at her alarm clock before staggering from the bed in search of the phone.

"Morning," Rhys said, his voice deep and low.

"Hi." Stupid, but she felt a little breathless, simply because he'd called. "Is everything all right?"

"Just making sure everything is okay at your end."

"It is."

"You slept okay?"

"Yes. How about you?"

"I slept."

She waited for him to tell her why he'd really called, but as they kept talking it slowly occurred to her that he'd missed her. The notion was heady, almost intoxicating.

Don't get ahead of yourself.

She repeated the same mantra to herself hundreds of times over the following weeks, determined to give happiness a chance but also to maintain some sense of perspective.

Just in case things didn't work out.

AFTER THE FIRST COUPLE of weeks Charlie and Rhys settled into a routine of sorts. Most nights were spent at her place, since Rhys claimed she had a lot more style than him and that his place was really a glorified walk-in closet. They double-dated with Gina and Spencer on Tuesday nights, but most of the time it was only the two of them, the way Charlie liked it. Maybe she was greedy, but she loved having Rhys all to herself, and he seemed to feel the same way about her.

The sex got better and better, even though the baby was definitely making her presence felt. Charlie quickly grew out of all her old clothes and moved beyond the point where an elastic stretched between button and hole, and a long T-shirt could help her skate by. She was in her sixteenth week and contemplating a shopping trip for maternity clothes when her breasts seemed to grow a cup size overnight—much to Rhys's unashamed delight.

"Who am I to look a gift horse in the mouth?" he said when she commented on his near obsession.

Her enlarged breasts were exquisitely sensitive, too, but he was gentle and tender with her and their lovemaking took on yet another dimension. That same week, Rhys's mother celebrated her birthday and they attended their first Walker family gathering as a couple.

Charlie had thought that she'd been nervous the first time she met Rhys's family, but she was almost beside herself at the notion of showing up as his girlfriend. She'd spoken to Holly twice since she and Rhys had started seeing each other, but both times she'd been unable to find a way to reveal their new relationship to his mother. She suspected that Holly would be thrilled, but Charlie wasn't sure and she didn't want to lose the sense of connection that had been growing between them.

"Relax, Charlie. They already love you. Make a few cracks about what a money-grubbing capitalist pig I am and you'll have them eating out of both hands," Rhys said as they walked up the front path.

"This is so stupid. Why am I so nervous?" she asked herself out loud.

Rhys hooked an arm around her neck and drew her close. "Because you have no idea how lovable you are," he said easily, pressing a kiss to her mouth. "That's why."

She was still blinking in confusion when the door opened and his father ushered them inside to join "the rest of the horde."

"No lasagna tonight, Charlie," Holly announced as they entered the kitchen. "Oh, my, haven't you popped!" Her gaze went from Charlie's belly to the arm Rhys had draped around her shoulders.

Charlie was very aware of Rhys's siblings doing the same, but no one said anything, and pretty soon she was being pressed into a chair and handed a drink and a handful of crackers.

"Actually, the nausea stopped a couple of weeks ago," Charlie explained when Meg made a big deal about moving the dip platter out from under Charlie's nose in case it upset her stomach.

"Oh, good. I had a salad for you, just in case, but this is much better," Holly said. She rested her hand on Charlie's shoulder for a few seconds and her eyes were warm as they met Charlie's.

The tension inside Charlie unraveled as she saw the unquestioning acceptance in the other woman's eyes. As she'd hoped, Holly was pleased. One less thing to worry about.

Later, after a dinner of roast beef and vegetables and lemon meringue pie for dessert, Kim, Becky and Amber took Charlie aside and offered her bags of maternity clothes they no longer needed, before taking turns touching her belly.

"You'll feel her move soon," Becky said. "The strangest feeling in the world. Like an eyelash brushing against your skin—only on the inside."

Charlie frowned and Kim gave her sister a shove in the arm. "Don't freak her out. It's nothing like that. It's more like a goldfish swimming around."

"Oh, that's much better," Becky scoffed.

"It's fine. I don't freak easily," Charlie said.

"Of course you don't. You're with a Walker— if you freaked easily, you'd have run a long time ago," Amber said.

Charlie laughed and thanked them all for their thoughtfulness. Glancing across the room, she caught Rhys's eye. He was watching her, unashamed lust and admiration in his gaze. Even though it had been nearly a month, she still had the urge to pinch herself and glance over her shoulder to make sure it was really her he was looking at with so much heat and possessiveness.

As he kept telling her, this was real, this thing between them.

She caught herself yawning as Holly handed out coffee and Rhys immediately stood. "Charlie's tired, I'm taking her home."

His oldest brother gave him a disgusted look. "Have a little bit of dignity, mate. We all know you can't wait to get her alone, but there's no need to be that obvious."

Charlie felt her face go up in flames as the rest of the Walkers started to rib Rhys. He laughed, fended them off and stuck to his guns, encouraging her to her feet.

"Think what you like. Charlie and I are going home."

In the car five minutes later, the maternity clothes stowed in the trunk, she pressed her hands to her cheeks in an attempt to cool them. "That was embarrassing. If I could, I would have disappeared down an escape hatch, no questions asked."

"Mark's an idiot. And way too observant for his own good. Come here."

He kissed her across the console, his hands soon wandering to her breasts. When the windows started to steam up, she broke their kiss and gave a small laugh.

"In case you're wondering, I'm way too big to do it in the car."

"Really?" He sounded genuinely disappointed.

"Plus, we're in front of your parents' place, and your brothers and sisters will be walking past any second now."

"A far better point," Rhys said. "Let's go home."

She sat back in her seat and tried not to reveal how much his choice of words had affected her. *Home,* he'd said. *Let's go home.* She was past pretending those three words didn't mean an enormous amount to her, that the notion of sharing a home—a life—with Rhys hadn't become bigger and more real and more possible in her mind with each passing day.

True, he hadn't said he loved her yet, but this very night he had said that she was lovable, and that was close enough to almost make no difference....

She studied his profile in the reflected light of the dashboard as he turned onto the freeway. She found him just as handsome today as she had all those months ago when she'd spilled his wine at Café Sydney. More so, really, because she knew that there was enormous character and intelligence and drive behind his gorgeous face, which only made him more appealing.

She glanced out the window and saw that they were driving past the turn off for McMahons Point.

"Take this exit," she said impulsively. "Let's go sit at the Point and watch the ferries."

He glanced at her curiously but didn't say anything as he signaled and took the exit ramp. When they pulled into the small parking bay at the Point, the shadow of the Harbour Bridge high overhead, they were the only car in the small gravel parking lot.

"Park over there," Charlie said, pointing to the darkest corner.

Again Rhys glanced at her, but this time there was a knowing glint in his eye. She waited until he'd cut the engine before tugging off her stretchy leggings.

"I changed my mind about being too big."

Rhys pushed his seat back and she clambered awkwardly over the console and straddled him. He grinned at her, his eyes very dark in the dim interior.

"I've been wanting to do this to you all night," he said, his hand between her legs.

She closed her eyes as he caressed her, moving her hips in rhythm with his stroking fingers. She heard the clink of his belt buckle, then the hiss of his zip. She opened her eyes and reached between them to grasp his erection, freeing it from his boxers. He was big and hard and velvety smooth in her hand. She watched his face as she stroked him and he stroked her, then she positioned him and slid down to the hilt. They sighed simultaneously, his hands finding her hips. She started to rise and fall and it didn't take long for them to both find their peak, their gasps and moans and murmured imprecations filling the small space. When she finally collapsed on top of him she was limp, her thighs quivering with exertion.

"God, I love you, Charlie," Rhys panted against her neck.

She tried not to react, tried not to take it for anything other than what it was—a throwaway comment at the height of passion—but something must have given her away because Rhys's hand found her chin and tilted her head so that she was looking him in the eye.

"I do, you know. I love you. I love you with everything I have."

His eyes were steady on hers, his body still inside her, his hands on her skin. She wanted to believe him. So badly. She wanted to tell him that she loved him, too. That he had made her happier than she thought she could ever be. That she loved how he made her feel, how he made her laugh, how he'd made her braver and bolder and smarter and funnier.

She couldn't, though, the old fear still holding her in its grip. If she didn't want it quite so much, if she didn't hold on to happiness so tightly, maybe it might last this time—that was what the voice in the back of her head said.

Maybe she wouldn't screw it up.

Rhys was waiting for her response, and because she couldn't give him words, she gave him actions, kissing him with all the pent-up fervor and love and passion and adoration in her. He kissed her back, but she could feel the disappointment in him and she couldn't quite look him in the eye when she broke the kiss and scrambled to her own side of the car.

The windows were fogged up and Rhys wound them all down and blasted the windshield with the heater. She struggled into her leggings, aware of the loaded silence in the car. Waiting for Rhys to say something. He steered toward the parking lot exit. After he'd found his way back to the highway, he reached for her hand and brought it to rest on his thigh, his own hand on top of it. She dared a glance at him, and he offered her a small smile.

"It's hard for me. But I'm trying," she said, the words bursting out of her.

"I know," he said simply. "There's no rush."

Gratitude filled her, along with a wash of love for him. He was so much bigger and better than any of her imaginings had made him. He was the man of her dreams.

CHARLIE DIDN'T THINK things could get better, but the next month slipped past in a haze of happy days and long, steamy nights. She'd thought the passion between them might die off after a while—all good things faded with time—but their chemistry only seemed to burn brighter and higher. He told her he found her burgeoning body erotic and sexy as hell and she could only believe him since he backed up his claims with lots of solid evidence.

They were together when The Bean first made her presence felt at seventeen weeks, sending a ripple of sensation across Charlie's belly. She gasped and nearly leaped off the sofa, scaring Rhys half to death before she explained what had happened. Her eighteen-week scan confirmed that everything was progressing normally with their little girl and they began to discuss names in earnest, finally settling on Beth Emily Walker.

"Although she will forever be The Bean to me," Rhys said.

They were nearing the end of June when Gina began making noises about Charlie's birthday. Her birthdays had never been a big deal in the

Long household, her mother's death being inextricably linked with the date. Traditionally Charlie marked the day by buying herself an indulgent slice of cake and a bunch of flowers. Gina, however, had other ideas.

"I want to throw you a party. You could invite Trish and Yvonne and Hannah—I'm sure they'd love an excuse to ask for leave, and who doesn't love Sydney? You can invite Rhys's family and Spencer and any of your clients you like enough to break bread with."

They were in Gina's kitchen, polishing off the last of a batch of scones Charlie had made as part of her continuing quest to master the art of cooking.

"I don't know," Charlie said doubtfully.

"Give me one good reason why it's a bad idea for all your friends and loved ones to celebrate the fact that you came into the world," Gina challenged.

"Well, for starters, it's the same day my mother died," Charlie said quietly. "And I've always felt…I don't know…ungrateful for getting excited about my birthday. Plus, I haven't told Rhys it's coming up and I know his family will want to make a big deal, too, and I'm really not sure about any of it."

Gina pulled a face. "Sorry. I forgot about your mum."

"It's okay."

"But that doesn't mean that we shouldn't have a party for your birthday, Charlie. I bet your mum would hate to think that you've never allowed yourself to have a special day because of her. If I were a mother, that would really piss me off."

"I think if you were a mother, you'd say *ticked off*," Charlie said.

"Stop deflecting. I promise it won't be over the top or too in your face. We'll have nice food and some music and everyone can dance attendance on you and worship your big fat belly."

"Gee, thanks."

"Come on. You know everyone wants to touch it. I can barely keep my hands off it and I know how private you are."

"You can touch it if you want," Charlie said shyly.

"Yeah?"

"If you put your hand right here, you might even feel her moving around. She's been active this afternoon."

Charlie guided her friend's hand to a spot to the left of her belly button. She felt the baby surge inside her—she'd decided after a few weeks it felt like corn popping, not an eyelash brushing her skin or a fish swimming around—and watched Gina's face.

"Can you feel her?"

"I think so. Like a tiny little earth tremor. Hey there, little lady."

They exchanged smiles. Gina reversed their grips, catching Charlie's hand in hers and giving it a squeeze.

"Let me throw you a party, Charlie. Please, pretty please?" Gina put on her best beseeching expression.

Charlie glanced at her belly, thinking of all that lay ahead. Thinking of the birthdays her little girl would enjoy one day. She would want her to celebrate. To be happy, no matter what.

"Okay. But please don't go to too much trouble. And you have to let me contribute."

Gina did a little happy dance and kissed Charlie's cheek. "You will do no such thing. And you also won't worry about anything. Leave it all in my capable professional caterer's hands."

Rhys picked her up half an hour later and she rather sheepishly told him about the party as they drove the two blocks to her apartment.

"You didn't tell me your birthday was coming up," he said blankly.

"I usually don't make a big deal out of it. It's Mum's anniversary, too, and it's always felt weird. But Gina wants to throw me a party. And I think I want to let her."

Rhys's gaze was understanding as he looked at

her. "Then you should. You know my family will want to come, right?"

"I'd love for them to be there."

"Try to keep them away. Now I have to come up with a suitable gift for you."

"Like I said, I don't usually make a big deal out of my birthday."

"I promise not to go too over the top."

She eyed him suspiciously. He had his teasing face on, which could mean anything.

"Promise me you won't spend a lot of money or do something crazy."

"Can't do that. But I will promise that it will be good. Whatever it is."

She bit her tongue, swallowing the urge to protest. He'd only dig his heels in and become even more cryptic and mysterious. One thing she'd learned about the Walker men was that they loved a good tease. The more prolonged and infuriating the better.

"Good girl," Rhys said smugly.

"Wait till it's your birthday."

"I will."

As usual, she felt a peculiar little thrill over the fact that she'd made a reference to the future and Rhys hadn't pulled her up short or pointed out that what she was talking about was weeks, maybe even months, away and that they had no business planning that far ahead. It was stupid—

and yet another example of how she couldn't seem to let go of the deeply ingrained lessons of her past—but she was aware that a part of her tested Rhys every time she referenced the future. As though one day she would catch him and he would be forced to admit that he'd been playing her for a fool all along.

She didn't believe that, not in her heart of hearts. When she lay next to him in bed at night and he reached for her in his sleep, she knew that he meant it when he said he loved her. He phoned her at least once a day, usually at lunch to check on how she was doing, and every morning he opened his eyes and smiled when he saw her looking at him.

He loved her, and she loved him. They made each other happy. There was absolutely no reason for her to still be carrying around the gnawing sense that, any moment now, her happiness could blow away like so much dust. She told herself every day to get over it, to move on, and while the sense of fragility and uncertainty had diminished, there was always a nagging little voice in the back of her head urging her to be cautious and careful and wary.

Maybe when the baby was born the voice would go away. Or maybe she was doomed to carry it around with her for the remainder of her days. Maybe it was the legacy of a sterile child-hood, an absent mother and a distant father.

Or maybe it would simply take more than a couple of months of Rhys in her life and in her bed for her to accept that she was loved and that this really could be her future.

THE DAY OF HER PARTY brought with it leaden clouds and a cold, bone-chilling breeze. Rhys woke her with kisses and breakfast in bed, followed by a hot shower and even hotter lovemaking. Only when she was lying flushed and limp on the sheets did he place a small box on her belly.

"Happy birthday, Charlie," he said quietly.

She stared at the small, square velvet box, her heart leaping into her throat.

Surely he hadn't…?

He couldn't possibly have. They were still finding their feet together.

No. He wouldn't.

"This looks interesting," she said, forcing a bright note into her voice.

Rhys didn't say anything, although she could feel him watching her, weighing her reaction. She willed her hands not to shake as she opened the hinged lid on the box. A pair of intricately worked silver-and-gold earrings nestled against white velvet. Charlie recognized them as the work of the same artist who had made the bracelets she'd bought for Kim and Becky's birthday.

She looked at Rhys, enormously touched that he'd come up with such a thoughtful gift.

"Thank you," she said simply. "They're beautiful."

"I love you, Charlie."

Warmth filled her chest. She reached out and wrapped an arm around his neck, pulling him close so that she could press her face against his shoulder. She inhaled his scent and rubbed her cheek against his.

"I love you, too."

It was the first time she'd been able to voice her feelings—the first time she'd felt safe enough to. His arms tightened around her and they lay together for a long moment, holding each other. Loving each other.

After a few minutes the baby made her presence felt with a powerful kick, almost as if she sensed that the outside world was preoccupied with something other than her for a change.

"Wow. I felt that," Rhys said, pulling away from her to stare at her belly.

"She's going to be a fighter, our Beth," Charlie said, hands pressing the taut curve of her abdomen.

"Like her mum," Rhys said.

The phone rang then and the rest of the morn-

ing was consumed with getting ready for her
party and helping Gina out with a few last-minute
details, like picking up some flowers and extra
bottles of wine. They arrived an hour before everyone else, but Gina insisted on Charlie putting
her feet up while she and Rhys finished the prep-
arations.

Gina had cleared off the covered patio and
borrowed some clear marquee walls from work
in order to make the space weather tight. Giant
gas-powered jet heaters sat in opposing corners,
already making the space toasty. A long trestle
table groaned with food, again courtesy of Gina's
work. Charlie had insisted that her friend let her
pay for the party, but Rhys and Gina had over-
ridden her. Her job, she had been told more than
once, was to sit back and lap it up.

A hard task for someone who had always
prided herself on being a team player. She wasn't
used to being the center of attention, but as guests
started to arrive she became so absorbed in greeting and talking that she forgot that this day was
all about her. The Walkers were their usual bois-
terous selves, and there was much laughter and
hugs when her army friends arrived from inter-
state. She was particularly touched that Yvonne
and Hannah had flown all the way from Perth—
no small feat—and spent a good half hour huddled in a corner with them catching up on their

news and allowing them to feel her belly. As Gina had predicted, her bump was the star of the show.

"I'm starting to get worried about what it'll be like when I get really big," she said in an aside to Rhys.

"Complete strangers will accost you in the street. That's what happened with my sisters."

"Lucky I know self-defense, then."

Wine flowed and conversation swelled and Charlie felt as though she was awash in a sea of friendship and affection. She was enjoying a quiet moment alone, watching everyone talk and laugh around her, when Gina sidled up.

"Told you it would be fun, didn't I?" she said.

"You did. Thank you. This is really, really nice."

"I give good party, what can I say? And you have good friends."

Gina waited until the trestle table was being cleared in preparation for dessert before clinking a fork against her wineglass to get everyone's attention.

"Okay, people, it's that time of the day when we get to embarrass Charlie. Come on up here, birthday girl."

Rhys urged Charlie forward with a hand in the small of her back, and she took her place beside Gina, standing on the rear step.

"Look at you, all aglow with your pregnancy hormones," Gina said.

Everyone laughed. Charlie looked out at the sea of smiling faces and felt her throat close up with emotion. One of the things she'd loved the most about being part of the army was the sense that she belonged—not a particularly startling observation, given her background, and probably one of the reasons why she'd chosen to serve for so long. Much of her nervousness about becoming a civilian had been anxiety at the loss of that sense of belonging and identity, but looking out at her gathered friends and Rhys's family, she understood something that she'd never really allowed herself to register before—family wasn't defined only by blood ties and the accident of birth. Family could be made, too, held together with bonds of friendship and shared experience and love and goodwill.

"Brace yourselves, I'm about to get maudlin," Gina said. "I met Charlie during recruit training more than fourteen years ago. At the time, I was freaking out over the fact that I'd signed my life away. Recruit training was hard and demanding, and after the first few days I started to think I'd made the biggest mistake of my life. Then I got paired with Charlie for an orienteering exercise."

Gina glanced at Charlie, her eyes dancing with mischief. Charlie shook her head, knowing it was pointless to try to stop her friend from telling tall stories.

"To this day, I don't know how I got paired with her, because everyone wanted to be with Charlie. We'd all worked out on the first day that she was the only one who knew what she was doing. She was fit and she was tough and she never, ever complained. She made me feel like the saddest, wimpiest princess ever."

"She's exaggerating," Charlie interjected.

"She's right, I am. She did complain one time—she told me I was holding her back when I asked to stop for a rest break."

Everyone laughed. Charlie caught Rhys's eye and pulled a "can you believe this?" face. He had his arms crossed over his chest and his gaze was affectionate as he watched her. She flashed to this morning—the feel of his arms around her, the scent of his skin, the words *I love you* hanging in the air between them. As lovely as all this was, she had a sudden craving to be back in her bedroom, only the two of them.

"Once training was done we all went our separate ways and I didn't run into Charlie again until we were both posted to Townsville. The moment I heard she'd arrived at the same time as me I suggested we share digs together. I'm not stupid, right? I'd learned my lesson the first time—find the smartest and the strongest and copy her for all you're worth."

Charlie bumped Gina with her hip, embarrassed by her effusive praise. Gina tucked her arm through Charlie's but didn't stop talking.

"The three years we lived together were some of the best of my life. I learned that not only was Charlie the best soldier I knew, she was also the best friend a woman could have. Loyal, generous, supportive, honest—and she wasn't afraid to hand out a bit of tough love, either. She's also the woman least likely to hog the limelight, least likely to demand credit for her accomplishments and least likely to ask for help when she needs it, even though I can name dozens of people who would fall over themselves to provide it.

"Needless to say, I am thrilled to death that Charlie allowed me to throw her this party today because I have been waiting for years to spoil her and make her squirm." Gina turned to face Charlie, her eyes suspiciously shiny. "Think of it as payback for all those sit-ups you made me do so I'd pass physical. I love you, friend. Happy birthday."

Everyone else took up the cheer. Charlie blinked furiously as Gina hugged her tightly.

"And now, someone else has something he'd like to say," Gina said, disentangling herself from Charlie's embrace.

Gina stepped down, and Rhys stepped up. Charlie sniffed and used the excuse of pushing her hair behind her ear to wipe a tear from her cheek.

"How you doing there, tiger?" Rhys asked, a small smile on his lips.

"Let's just get this over with."

Everyone laughed.

"Suck it up, Charlie," Becky heckled from the rear of the patio. "Take it like a woman."

Rhys took her hand. "Not so long ago, someone asked me why I wasn't married yet. I'll leave it up to you to guess who'd ask such a forthright question. And no, it wasn't my mother."

Everyone laughed. Charlie gave Rhys a dark look.

"You asked some pretty pointed questions that night, too, if I remember."

Rhys squeezed her hand. "My answer to this very direct question was that I hadn't met anyone I wanted to spend the rest of my life with yet. I was completely wrong, of course. I had met her—she was sitting in front of me, doing her damnedest to make the best of a bad situation. It just took me a while to work it out."

For some reason, her stomach did a slow, nervous roll. As though it knew something that she didn't. Rhys didn't take his eyes from hers as he continued talking.

"Charlie, you are the best person I know. I love the way you never do anything by halves. I love the way you refuse to retreat. I love your quiet sense of humor. I love you. These past months with you have made everything else in my life suddenly make sense. I literally can't imagine my life without you in it. Better yet, I don't want to."

It took Charlie a moment to realize what was happening as Rhys stepped down to the patio and sank on to one knee. The hand holding hers was trembling as he looked up into her face.

"Charlie, will you marry me? Will you let me make you and The Bean happy for the rest of our lives?" Rhys's voice was husky with emotion and she could see the nervousness and hope behind his eyes.

Everyone was silent, barely daring to breathe as they waited for her response, but her mind was one big echo chamber, empty of thought.

She looked at Rhys and saw his handsome face and broad shoulders and felt the powerful pull of his personality. She loved him so much it scared her. The sound of his voice, his little gestures and habits, the way he laughed, his energy, his drive. His essential goodness. His integrity. The way he made her feel. The future he offered her—a life filled with laughter and challenge and love.

He was a dream. A fantasy. Too good to be true. Yet he was on his knee in front of her, and he'd asked her to marry him.

This was happening. To her.

The shuffling of feet sounded and a motorbike drove by on the street—and still Rhys held her gaze, waiting patiently. Allowing her to get to where she needed to be in her own time.

I want this so badly.

Her life had been full of compromise and disappointment. Everything she'd ever had she'd earned three times over. She didn't feel as though she'd earned Rhys and The Bean. They'd simply happened, a gift from the gods, and the cautious, wary part of her was afraid to trust that they were real.

It feels real. And I want it so badly.

She stared into Rhys's dark, unwavering eyes and the answer rose up inside her.

If you want it, reach out and take it. Be brave. Not just for The Bean, but for you and Rhys, too.

She opened her mouth. "Yes."

He smiled. It was only then that she could see that he'd been deeply unsure what her answer might be. And still, he'd knelt before her and laid himself on the line in front of their friends and family. On impulse, she stepped down to the patio, and before he could stand she joined him on her knees.

"I would very much like to be your wife," she said.

She reached out and cupped his jaw in her hand and drew him close for a kiss. A cheer went up and she heard a champagne cork pop, closely followed by another. Rhys smiled against her lips and she started to laugh. He wrapped his arms around her and she splayed her hands over his back and held him tight.

"I love you," she whispered.

He pulled back from her and brushed her cheekbone with his thumb. Then he plucked a velvet box from his pocket. She smiled, understanding why he'd been so intent on her reaction this morning when he'd given her the earrings.

"It should fit, but if it doesn't we can easily get it adjusted," he said as he pulled out a delicate filigree ring studded with what looked like hundreds of tiny white diamonds.

"Good God," she said, shocked by how beautiful it was.

He grinned and slid the ring on to the fourth finger of her left hand. It was a little loose, but she closed her hand to prevent it from sliding off.

"We'll get it fixed," he assured her.

"Rhys, it's absolutely stunning."

Everyone wanted to congratulate them then.

She was pulled to her feet and hugged by Holly, then Becky and Gina and Meg. The rest of Rhys's family got in on the act next, then her army buddies. Charlie felt dizzy from all the attention, and before long her face started to ache from smiling so much. Everyone was so excited, all talking at once. Rhys was on the other side of the patio being thumped on the back by his brothers. She kept searching him out, as though some part of her was afraid that she'd imagined the past ten minutes.

She glanced at her ring. It was so beautiful it took her breath away. Rhys had obviously put a lot of time and effort into finding it, and the thought of him searching for just the right ring for her made her chest ache with emotion.

Suddenly she felt a little breathless and on the verge of tears. This was all so lovely, but it was overwhelming, too. So much happiness. So much expectation.

Waiting for a break in the conversation, she excused herself and slipped into the house. The bathroom was located behind the living room and she shut the door and felt her shoulders drop a notch. She sat on the edge of the tub and clasped her hands in her lap.

She would give herself five minutes then she would go back out again. She wanted to stow away as many memories as she could. After all, she would remember this day for the rest of her life.

The day Rhys asked her to marry him—and the day she'd had the courage to say yes.

Sitting alone, the sound of the party a distant rise and fall in the background, she acknowledged that her answer would have been very different if he'd asked her the same question even a month ago. A month ago, she hadn't been ready to believe all this could be hers. She'd been so determined not to be caught short if something went wrong. So determined to keep one eye on the exit, in case he changed his mind or got sick of her or decided that she wasn't any of the things he seemed to believe about her.

Somehow, slowly but surely, she'd started to accept that what Rhys felt for her was real. That he wasn't going away. That this wasn't some cosmic screwup that would correct itself just when she'd allowed herself to believe.

Rhys loved her. A part of her still reeled in stunned surprise every time he articulated as much to her, but at some point she had decided to accept him at face value.

She'd decided to trust the warmth she saw in his eyes and the passion of his lovemaking and the reverence of his touch. She'd decided to choose happiness. To allow herself to believe that she was loved. That she was worth it. That she mattered.

She spread her hands over the mound of her belly, thinking about the future that she and Rhys and The Bean could build together. For a moment, she felt as though she could almost split in two with happiness. That there wasn't enough of her to contain it all, it was so big and deep and complete.

A tap sounded on the bathroom door. "Charlie?"

She smiled. "Come in."

Rhys slipped inside, shutting the door behind him. "Too much?" he asked as he perched beside her on the tub.

"It's lovely."

"But loud."

"It's perfect."

"So you're not angry with me for ambushing you?"

"No."

"I wanted to make a statement. I wanted you to know how loved you are. How proud I am of you."

"I know."

"Do you?" He reached out and traced first one eyebrow, then the other. "I don't know what I did without you, Charlie. I can't even remember what my life was like."

"I can. My life, I mean," she said. "I can remember looking at the world from the outside. Always from the outside. But you brought me inside."

He'd given her a family. He'd given her unconditional love. He'd soothed her fears and been patient with her anxieties and, even though she'd pushed him away, he'd hung in there.

Because she was worth it.

What a revolutionary concept. One he'd helped her believe in. She smiled.

Rhys cocked his head to the right. "What?"

"I was just thinking we should write to that condom company and thank them for their inferior product."

"You're right, we should."

"Dear Sir/Madam. I'd like to thank you for helping me make the most magnificent, amazing, beautiful mistake of my life—"

"Without your faulty latex, I might never have met the woman of my dreams. And I might never know what it's like to finally feel comfortable in my own skin."

"I think that's my line, not yours," she said.

"It's mine, too."

They both smiled.

"We can share it," she suggested.

"Along with everything else."

"Yes."

They kissed. The too-happy feeling filled her again, but this time she didn't feel overwhelmed. Rhys was with her. He had her. He wouldn't let her down. And she wouldn't let him down, either.

They were a team, he and her and The Bean. Finally, she understood that.

* * * * *

LARGER-PRINT BOOKS!
GET 2 FREE LARGER-PRINT NOVELS PLUS
2 FREE GIFTS!

Harlequin

Super Romance

Exciting, emotional, unexpected!

YES! Please send me 2 FREE LARGER-PRINT Harlequin® Superromance® novels and my 2 FREE gifts (gifts are worth about $10). After receiving them, if I don't wish to receive any more books, I can return the shipping statement marked "cancel." If I don't cancel, I will receive 6 brand-new novels every month and be billed just $5.44 per book in the U.S. or $5.99 per book in Canada. That's a saving of at least 16% off the cover price! It's quite a bargain! Shipping and handling is just 50¢ per book in the U.S. or 75¢ per book in Canada.* I understand that accepting the 2 free books and gifts places me under no obligation to buy anything. I can always return a shipment and cancel at any time. Even if I never buy another book, the two free books and gifts are mine to keep forever.

139/339 HDN FEFF

Name	(PLEASE PRINT)	
Address		Apt. #
City	State/Prov.	Zip/Postal Code

Signature (if under 18, a parent or guardian must sign)

Mail to the **Reader Service:**
IN U.S.A.: P.O. Box 1867, Buffalo, NY 14240-1867
IN CANADA: P.O. Box 609, Fort Erie, Ontario L2A 5X3

Not valid for current subscribers to Harlequin Superromance Larger-Print books.

**Are you a current subscriber to Harlequin Superromance books and want to receive the larger-print edition?
Call 1-800-873-8635 today or visit www.ReaderService.com.**

* Terms and prices subject to change without notice. Prices do not include applicable taxes. Sales tax applicable in N.Y. Canadian residents will be charged applicable taxes. Offer not valid in Quebec. This offer is limited to one order per household. All orders subject to credit approval. Credit or debit balances in a customer's account(s) may be offset by any other outstanding balance owed by or to the customer. Please allow 4 to 6 weeks for delivery. Offer available while quantities last.

Your Privacy—The Reader Service is committed to protecting your privacy. Our Privacy Policy is available online at www.ReaderService.com or upon request from the Reader Service.

We make a portion of our mailing list available to reputable third parties that offer products we believe may interest you. If you prefer that we not exchange your name with third parties, or if you wish to clarify or modify your communication preferences, please visit us at www.ReaderService.com/consumerschoice or write to us at Reader Service Preference Service, P.O. Box 9062, Buffalo, NY 14269. Include your complete name and address.

HSRLP11B

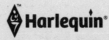